REINTEGRATION

BOOK 1 OF THE REINTEGRATION TRILOGY

by

Ashley Bogner

Copyright © 2017 Ashley Bogner

All rights reserved. No part of this book is to be reproduced, republished, transmitted, or photocopied in any format without the author's clear, written consent. Brief quotations may be used in reviews.

This book is a work of fiction. Any similarities between the characters, locations, names, and events and real-life happenings are unintentional and coincidental.

ISBN: 1973886278
ISBN-13: 978-1973886273

cover design © 2017: Magpie Designs, Ltd
photo credits: Pixabay
texture credit: Sascha Duensing

DEDICATION

To my fantastic parents, who supported this dream of mine in so many ways.

Thank you.

REINTEGRATION

1

Tomorrow, everything changes.

Tomorrow, the day of my Final Test. The day I will prove my worth to the Federation. Does every trainee dread the significance of the Final Test as much as they anticipate the excitement, or am I an exception? Thompson believes I'll do well, but I can't say I share in his high opinion of me.

Twenty-six hours. I have twenty-six more hours until the biggest moment of my life.

The doctors will notice my lack of rest over the last few days, assuming my tracking device keeps a record of sleep patterns like it does overall health. How can I sleep when all I can think of is the possibility that I might fail my Final Test? I have one day left to study and prepare. I'll take the test tomorrow and my life will change.

"Worrying isn't going to help you any, Katherine," I mutter to myself, but the words do little to lessen my anxiety.

I tap a button on the wall, stifling a yawn behind my other hand. The overhead lights hum to life. Tugging on the corner of my grayish-white comforter, I pull the thick blanket tight, then tuck the edges under the mattress. I push a second button on the wall, and the closet door slides open. Seven identical uniform shirts hang in the narrow space. I pull one of the shirts off of its hanger, running my hand over the material. The color is similar to that of the sky before the sun rises, no longer black but not yet blue. The pants are the same color, and I pull a pair out of the drawer.

My tablet, sitting on the built-in shelf over my bed, buzzes. Who would send me a message this early in the morning? I drape my clothes over the end of the bed, then grab the device. I read over the message displayed on the tablet's screen.

To the trainees of City 45: Since today is the sixtieth anniversary of the Federation, your training is cancelled for the morning. You will resume normal training assignments after lunch. Please report to the Center of Announcements and Ceremonies by 8:00 a.m. Your mentor has been notified of this change in your schedule.

The Federation's sixtieth anniversary? Today? Of course. Head Regulator Olson mentioned something about it yesterday.

After I change into my uniform, I fold my sleeping clothes and set them in one of the closet drawers. Another yawn escapes me. Maybe breakfast will help wake me up. I grab my identification card off the shelf, since I'll need it to order food in the cafeteria. I clip the card to the front of my bag, which is just large enough for a tablet to slip inside.

Will I need my jacket today? I glance out the window. The sun begins to creep over the edge of the Wall. Not a cloud in the sky, a good sign. The Wall, taller than any of the structures in the city, is our protection from the world beyond the Federation's borders.

A barrier between us and *them*.

Shaking my head, I pick my bag up off the tile floor and zip it closed. I grab my shoes and slip them on. With the day off from training—and if the activities at the Center of Announcements and Ceremonies don't take too long—I have more time to study for my Final Test. I exit my bedroom, adjusting the buttons on the sleeve of my shirt.

Sixtieth anniversary of the Federation. When was the last time we had a ceremony? The door closes behind me, and I step into the empty hallway. No one else is in the hallway, but I'm not alone. The security cameras attached to the ceiling see and record everything.

One of the cleaning workers exits the room across from mine, carrying a metal box filled with bedsheets. What is she doing? The cleaners aren't supposed to take our laundry for another few days. She slips her identification card into the pocket of her yellow-colored uniform. The bedroom door slides closed behind her.

"Oh, good morning." The cleaning worker looks my way and smiles. "Trainee Simmons passed his Final Test and has been relocated to the Citizens' Dormitory. I'm sure a new occupant will move into the room within a few days."

Citizen status. What every trainee longs for—the day they take on their full occupational responsibilities. If I pass my Final Test tomorrow, I too will be allowed to leave the Trainees' Dormitory and gain the independence that comes with adulthood.

If I pass.

"Katherine? Are you even listening to me?" My friend

Reintegration

Chelsea stops in the middle of the designated concrete walkway.

"Sorry. I guess I'm just tired today."

She shrugs her shoulders and resumes walking. "I was telling you about what my mentor said yesterday. Anyway, she said that if a citizen fails to show up for their routine check-ups, it goes on their record. It's not like a Violation or anything, but it still looks bad. I mean, how silly is that?"

"Well, according to Regulation 55—"

"You're the only person I know who's memorized every single law." Chelsea shakes her head.

"I haven't. The only reason I remember Regulation 55 is because I was up late studying."

Chelsea smirks, as if she's mocking my devotion to my occupation. Why hasn't she asked about my Final Test? Her own test is in a few weeks, so doesn't she understand how stressed I am? Maybe I don't want her to ask. How can I admit my fear of failing?

We arrive at the Center of Announcements and Ceremonies. I unclip my identification card from the front of my bag, while Chelsea glances in one of the large windows and messes with her bangs. I hold my card under the scanner by the building's door.

Chelsea grabs her own identification card. "Hopefully I'll see Spencer here."

"Spencer?" The scanner's light flashes green and the door slides open. I clip my card back on the front of my bag. "Is he the one who works in the Food Processing Center?"

"He's also my *boyfriend*. We started dating yesterday."

"Oh." I enter the building. Chelsea scans her card and follows me. A new boyfriend? "What happened to David or Daniel or whatever his name was?"

"We broke up. I was ready to, you know, move on."

"You two had been together for what, a few days?"

"Why would it need to be longer than that? Staying with one guy for too long is...dull."

And why do I always start these conversation, despite knowing how they're going to go? Chelsea has the shortest attention span I've ever seen. "I'm surprised you haven't gotten bored with me too," I mutter.

"What was that?" Chelsea cocks her head to one side.

"Nothing. Just talking to myself." We walk down the hallway, toward a door labeled *Auditorium*. I glance at the security cameras attached to the ceiling. Screens on the walls depict pictures of the former Council Members and their names.

"I haven't been here since I graduated from Primary School." I step into the auditorium, pushing through the crowd of trainees. We must be the last ones here. Everything about the auditorium looks the same—same stage, same rows of gray-colored chairs, same assortment of trainees wearing all different colors of uniforms. Then I was ten-years-old, fidgeting in my chair, eager for them to call my name and tell me what my occupation would be.

Now I'm older and dreading my Final Test.

"Katherine? I've got someone I need you to meet."

Chelsea's voice jerks me back to the noisy bustle of the auditorium. She saunters over, dragging some guy with her by the arm. Who is this? He wears a white uniform similar to Chelsea's, indicating that he too is training in the medical field. They must work together. He's tall, handsome, and dark-haired. There's no reason why I should meet him, unless...

No. She isn't doing this to me *again*, is she?

"Katherine, this is Harrison." Chelsea grins and pulls her companion toward me. The innocence on Chelsea's face denies the fact she has to know how much I hate this. I shake Harrison's hand and force a smile. Chelsea looks around the room, then turns back to me. "Spencer and I are hanging out this evening. You and Harrison could come and it could be a double date."

"Thanks for the offer, but I can't today. I'm busy." I avert my gaze, hoping neither of them will push the issue.

Chelsea stares at Harrison for several seconds, then grabs my arm and pulls me away. "Um, what's your problem?" Annoyance fills her eyes. "I'm trying to help you. This chronic singleness of yours is…pathetic. It's not normal. I spent all week trying to find a guy for you. I think you and Harrison might really hit it off, you know? He's cute, he's super smart, and there's no reason why you wouldn't like him. Just once I'd like to see you actually go on a date."

I look over her shoulder at where Harrison stands tapping the screen of his tablet. Is it fair of me to dismiss him so quickly? He could be nice. Maybe he'll be different from all the other boys I've known.

And maybe I'll stop lying to myself and stop looking for something that doesn't exist.

"Not today. Sorry."

My friend plants her hands on her hips. "Can't you just be normal for once? Can't you just let go, have a little fun every now and then? Don't you want to know what it's like to be in love, kiss a boy, think about something other than being a perfect little trainee? No rule says we can't do those things. Who knows? You might enjoy yourself. I always do."

"I need to prepare for my Final Test tomorrow." I finger the strap of my bag, turning away so she won't see how badly her words sting. This is the closest Chelsea's come to asking me why I always turn down the could-be boyfriends she likes to find for me. How can I tell her the truth? She'd never understand.

No one will ever understand.

"Your Final Test is tomorrow?" Chelsea frowns at the floor. Tomorrow will be the biggest day of my life and she *forgot* about it? How could she forget about her best friend's Final Test? Doesn't she care?

Sometimes, I think she's friends with me out of habit, not because she cares anymore.

"Yes, it's tomorrow."

"That's disappointing. I was hoping you could come with us." Chelsea walks back over to Harrison. "Katherine can't come."

"Maybe that's for the best. I'd be terrified that she'd give me a Violation or something." Harrison winks at me. My uniform always gives away my occupation of Regulator. I bite my tongue to keep myself from scolding his lack of seriousness about what receiving a Violations means. The official record of a breach of regulations goes into a citizen's file and can never be removed. Violations may be rare, but having more than three of them results in serious consequences.

And they're certainly no joke.

"It was nice to meet you, Harrison." I'm grateful when he walks away, leaving me alone with Chelsea again. If I could tell her the truth, and not worry that she'd laugh or roll her eyes or in some way ridicule me, I would. Because I do want to know what it's like to love someone, how it feels to kiss a boy. I've wanted that for a long time.

But relationships never last.

They aren't worth the heartbreak I've seen other people have.

An automated voice fills the perfectly square room. "Please take your seats."

"Time to see what this is all about." Chelsea sits in one of the mid-row chairs, so I sit next to her. The cool of the metal seeps through my clothing, making me shiver. The dozens of other teenagers all find their seats as well.

I shove my bag under the chair and a brown-uniformed trainee slides into the chair beside mine. A woman enters the auditorium. Everyone around me claps, so I do the same. The woman, wearing a tan uniform, strides across the room, her head held high. I straighten up in my seat. Only five people in the entire Federation wear uniforms of that color.

She's one of the Council Members.

Stepping up onto the carpeted stage, the woman approaches the microphone. The wall screen behind her displays a zoomed-in image of her face. After several seconds, the clapping dies down.

"Hello, trainees of City 45. I'm sure you're eager to know why you were asked to come here." Her pleasant, vibrant voice resonates throughout the room. She smiles, and her gaze locks on mine for a brief moment before she resumes speaking. "Well, I am Amelia Haynes, and I'm here to commemorate this wonderful occasion. Today marks the sixtieth anniversary of the Federation."

A Council Member. Here, in City 45. She looks different from the pictures I've seen of her. More like a real person and less like the images of the former Council Members I learned about in school. I turn to Chelsea, but she doesn't seem as excited as I am.

"War. Violence. Oppression. These things were the ways of the Past. Before the Federation, people were cold and brutal to each other, unwilling to peaceably resolve their differences. The world needed to change. The Federation brought this change and vowed to make sure the horrors of the Past would never resurface.

"Sixty years ago, we accomplished an incredible feat. We defeated the Intolerants, exiling them to the Outlands. For years, the Federation has continued to make strides in moving beyond the violence and narrow-mindedness of the Past. We have come far, but we can never forget the desperate measures we were forced to take to ensure that peace would last for generations to come."

The Council Member shifts her gaze from one trainee to the next. Her face glows beneath the bright glare of the artificial lighting. "Sixty years ago marked the beginning of the Federation; the beginning of a new society built upon the principles of peace and equality. Here we are now, still enjoying a peace that will last until the end of time."

Someone in the row behind me begins clapping, and soon we are all applauding Haynes's words. Our prestigious visitor takes a step back from the microphone, her smile of contentment frozen on her face.

"I don't believe it," Chelsea whispers, her words nearly deafened by the other trainees' clapping and cheering. She slouches in her chair, tossing her long red hair over one shoulder. "I have better things to do with my time then listen to a speech about stuff I already know. We've been learning this since Primary School."

Reintegration

And I've had to deal with Chelsea's impudence since Primary School. "Well, it is the sixtieth anniversary of the Federation."

Chelsea rolls her eyes. "You're no fun, you know? All you care about is rules, rules, rules. It's not my fault I would rather have some fun now. We get the morning off from training and this is what we have to do?"

I clench my jaw shut and stare straight ahead. This isn't the first time Chelsea has accused me of being too rigid when it comes to the Federation's laws, even the little ones. Shouldn't every citizen strive to observe all laws and regulations? They're important to the overall functioning of our society.

Not to mention breaking a rule can result in a Violation.

Haynes holds up a hand to silence the crowd. At least now I'm saved from thinking of a less-than-kind retort. Once the clamor dies down, she continues her speech. "I am proud of all of you. You, the trainees of the Federation, are the reason why our peace will last." She looks at me again. "You are the future."

While she's speaking, the door on the left side of the auditorium slides open with a faint hiss. A Regulator walks into the room, tablet tucked under his arm. With brisk, heavy footfalls, the Regulator walks up the steps onto the stage. Sweat darkens the collar of his navy blue uniform. Worry mars his face.

"I think that—" Haynes stops when the man reaches where she stands on stage.

What's going on? The Regulator gives Council Member Haynes his tablet. He points at the screen and speaks to her in a frantic whisper. I catch a few snippets of the conversation.

Something about a "serious issue" and "needs to be handled immediately." Haynes taps the back of the device with one finger.

    I turn to Chelsea to see if she knows what they're talking about. My friend, however, isn't paying attention to the Council Member and Regulator anymore. She waves and flashes a smile at the cute guy five chairs down. There's only one thing capable of catching Chelsea's attention. Boys. Chelsea's dated more of them in her short life than I could count. A strand of hair has fallen free from my ponytail, so I blow it out of my face and turn back to the two on stage.

    At least a minute passes before Haynes gives the Regulator his tablet back and walks out of the auditorium. No one moves until the door slides back in place. The panic-stricken man looks around the room, then steps up to the microphone. "Um, you are all dismissed."

    Without any explanation of Haynes's abrupt absence, he, too, leaves the room. I reach for my bag shoved under my chair. Like all trainees, I bring my few belongings with me everywhere. I unzip the top of the bag, withdrawing my own tablet and setting it on my lap.

    Chelsea jumps out of her seat. "Well, I'm glad that's over with."

    Most of the trainees file out of the auditorium, but Chelsea grabs her own bag and walks toward the boy she noticed earlier. They kiss so I divert my gaze back to my tablet. He must be Spencer. I've seen him around the city, but I haven't spoken to him much. I don't bother going over to talk to them. Next week she'll introduce me to someone new anyway.

    I tap the screen. No messages from Thompson. Does he know what all the fuss is about? I'll ask him later. With a sigh,

Reintegration

I put my tablet away.

Nothing interesting like this ever happens in City 45.

2

The Regulation Center looks identical to every other building in City 45; two stories tall, built of steel and glass so sunlight dances off every angle. The only variance between structures is the sign in front of each one bearing the name of the building. To me, however, the Regulation Center always seemed different from the rest of City 45's facilities. This is where I've come every day since turning thirteen. Everything I know about my career I learned in this building.

Holding my identification card under the scanner, I wait until the light flashes green and the building doors slide open. I clip my card back on the front of my bag.

"It's lunch time. Why are you here?" Regulator Vail approaches, tablet in hand. Vail's duty is to monitor everyone who enters and leaves the building. His tone is curt and abrupt, as always, but his demeanor is *off* like he doesn't want me to be here. Why does he care?

"I need to see Thompson. He's here, isn't he?"

"He's in one of the training rooms." Vail tucks his tablet

under his arm and returns to his post at the far side of the room. I don't envy him, his duty being to stand there until Regulator Weston replaces him. Regulating may be important, but most of the duties are dull. We prepare for things that can happen, but those things never seem to occur.

Regulator Vail has never been much of a talker. I walk down the long, narrow hallway, glancing in each of the glass doors. Surveillance Room. Storage Room. Training Room One. I pause for a second look, but no Thompson. I keep walking. Training Room Two. No sign of him yet.

I find Thompson in Training Room Three. Again, I scan my card. Thompson doesn't look up, even as I enter the small training room. He sits at the table in the center of the room, typing something on his tablet. Pausing for a second, he drums his fingers on the table's steel surface. The door closes with a click. At last he notices me.

"Why are you here, Katherine? Why aren't you at lunch with your friends, enjoying the hours off from training? The sixtieth anniversary of the Federation won't happen again." One side of Thompson's mouth quirks into his ironic half-smile. Even so, tiredness strains his voice.

"I wanted to talk to you. What are you doing?" I pull out the chair opposite the one he sits in. How many times have we been in one of these rooms, while he taught me the laws of the Federation and the duties of a Regulator? Tomorrow I won't need a mentor anymore. I'll be a real Regulator—not just a trainee—and ready to take on even more responsibilities.

"Well, I'm turning in my final reports on your training to the Council. What do you need to talk about?" Thompson leans back in his chair, setting his hands on either side of his tablet. His uniform is identical to mine, dark blue in color. Like on all Federation uniforms, his last name is stitched in white lettering across the shirt's left breast pocket and his seven-digit citizen number is on the right. The only difference? Thompson carries a stunner.

I do not.

All Regulators—except trainees—have the silver stun weapons. If I pass my Final Test tomorrow, I'll be given my first stunner.

"Something strange happened today. One of the Council Members came and gave a speech today. Mid-way through her speech, though, a Regulator arrived and told her something. She left soon after." Haynes was so calm and pleasant during her speech. What did the Regulator say to frighten her so much? I lower my bag to the floor, frowning at my distorted reflection in the table's surface. "Did something happen, Thompson?"

"I don't know." Thompson shakes his head, but he resumes typing on his tablet. "Don't worry about it. You need to stay focused for your Final Test tomorrow."

I sigh. "I've been trying to forget about it."

"There's no reason to be nervous. You'll do fine, Katherine. You're a smart girl." A hint of pride creeps into Thompson's voice, a tone he uses on rare occasions. I allow myself a faint smile. At least he believes I'll pass.

At least he cares.

My mentor clears his throat and avoids my gaze, something he always does after a show of emotion. Chelsea never talks about her mentor being so invested in her well-being. I'm his first trainee, so Thompson probably still needs to find the difference between *engaged* and *attached*. Maybe it's because most mentors have multiple trainees but Thompson only has me. Not many people are chosen to be Regulators, since it's not a much-needed occupation anymore.

"The Final Test is different, but considering how well you did on your previous tests, I expect you'll succeed." His random switches from personal compliments to monotone comments are nothing new to me. I shift my posture and the soles of my shoes squeak against the polished tile floor. A faint scent of chemicals lingers in the air. The cleaners must have come last night.

"Different? In what way?"

"You know I'm not permitted to give you details about the Final Test before it's given to you. But as long as you don't tell anyone, I think it'll be okay." Thompson pushes his tablet aside, his demeanor becoming almost childlike and unfitting of a man more than twice my age. He bends the rules, more than a Regulator or mentor should. I admire him for a lot of reasons—but not his occasional tendency to rebel. In most cases, I would remind him how his job is to set an example for me. At the moment, however, my desire to know more about the Final Test trumps my wanting to follow protocol.

"The Final Test doesn't involve questions and answers like the tests you've taken before. The Final Test isn't a measure of your skills, but rather a way to determine if you're ready to do your duties without a mentor's help." He leans forward. "You'll be assigned a career-related task to complete. The Council deems a student ready to advance based not only on if they complete the task, but also how they handle themselves in the situation."

"What was your Final Test?" I've never asked Thompson about his own test before. The discussion never seemed relevant. But with mine tomorrow…what can I expect? He already told me more than he should have.

He doesn't answer my question. A far-away look fills his eyes, like he's not here in the present moment. His entire demeanor changes, from calm and relaxed to stiff and abrasive. After several moments of awkward silence, Thompson finally speaks. "I don't think the nature of my Final Test will help you in any way with yours. The assignment given to me was a rare occurrence, something you won't have to deal with."

How do I respond? Regulators' duties were different when Thompson was my age, but the sharpness of his voice takes me back. Unusual silence falls between us again.

Until a shrill alarm cuts through the air.

I resist the urge to clamp my hands over my ears. Thompson bolts to his feet, grabbing the back of his chair to keep it from falling over. Each piercing wail cutting through the building makes me cringe. Two Regulators run past the training room door and toward the elevator at the end of the hallway.

"Stay here, Katherine," Thompson shouts, smacking the button on the wall and opening the door. Fear lines his face. I'm about to ask what the alarm is for, but he slips into the hallway without another word. Stay here and do what? This hasn't happened before.

Five long minutes pass before the alarm dies, giving way to silence. Well, what would be silence if my ears weren't ringing. Should I go find Thompson and make sure he's okay? Why did the alarm go off? Is someone hurt? A dozen different emergency situations flash through my thoughts, but none of them make sense. Why the alarm?

Soon, Thompson returns, his face pale. My mentor lingers in the doorway, breathing heavy. "You need to leave now, Katherine. Something's…come up. Please go."

"Well, what happened? What was the alarm for?" I stand but don't make any move to exit. Whatever occurred, it must have been bad for Thompson to be so shaken up about it.

My mentor reaches down and grabs my bag off the floor. Why won't he explain what's going on? He places a hand on my back and steers me toward the door. Does this have anything to do with what spooked Council Member Haynes so much? Once I'm in the hallway, Thompson shoves the bag into my hands.

"You can't kick me out with no explanation." I pull the bag's strap over my head, glaring at him.

"The Council Member told me not to tell anyone. I'm sorry, Katherine, but you're included in that. Haynes is contacting the Council as we speak to figure out what should be done. Please, go now. Come back tomorrow morning for your Final Test."

"Okay." It's hard to be angry with him when he's on the verge of panic. Haynes needs to consult the Council? The situation must be more important than I first thought. I turn to leave, then stop in the middle of the otherwise empty hallway. "Did someone receive a Violation?"

Could a Violation cause a frenzy like this? Thompson's never been this flustered and jumpy before.

"No, not a Violation. The situation is much worse," Thompson says, fingering the stunner clipped to his belt. Without any further explanation, my mentor half-walks, half-jogs down the corridor. I wait a moment longer, then head for the main entrance. I won't learn anything more today. My head spins from trying to sort out Thompson's last words.

What can be worse than a citizen receiving a Violation?

3

I arrive at the Regulation Center twenty minutes before my Final Test begins. Approaching the main entrance, I grab my identification card. The plastic rectangle quivers in my grasp, so I hold it tighter in an attempt to fight the way my hands shake. Today is the day. If I pass the test, I'll advance into adulthood. If I fail…

I can't fail.

As I hold my card under the scanner, my thoughts drift to yesterday's unusual events. I slept little last night, but not from agonizing over my Final Test. All I could think about was the genuine look of horror on my mentor's face. Even when I returned for training after lunch, he didn't seem like himself. Something happened—something important.

Thompson stands in the lobby of the building, arms folded across his chest. He looks up as I enter, his already-tense posture stiffening even more. Regulator Vail gives me nothing more than a bored glance as I walk through the lobby. *He* doesn't appear worried about anything.

"Council Member Haynes wants to speak with you, Katherine."

"Really? So is my Final Test cancelled?"

"No."

"What does she want to speak with me about?"

"Follow me." Thompson turns and heads down the hallway. I do as he tells me, but have to quicken my pace to match his long strides.

"Why would a *Council Member* want to talk with me on the day of my Final Test?" I'm a trainee; Haynes is one of the five leaders of our government. We've never met before. How can I be of any significance to her?

He stops in front of the elevator and pushes a button on the wall. He's taking me to the top floor. "Actually, your Final Test is what she wants to discuss with you."

What?

Before I can ask for clarification, the elevator doors open. Thompson steps into the elevator, ushering me inside as well. Haynes wants to talk to me. Panic grips me. Maybe I did something against regulations. Thompson reaches over and taps the control panel on the left side of the elevator doors. After he hits an upward-pointing arrow depicted on the screen, the doors close.

"Believe me, Katherine, I didn't want to put you in this position," Thompson says softly. "Haynes was set in her decision."

"What do you mean? Her decision of what?" If this has to do with my Final Test, Haynes must be giving me an assignment Thompson doesn't believe I'm ready for. "You don't think I'll succeed?"

His sudden change in attitude doesn't make sense. Up until now, Thompson said he believed I would pass. He seemed sincere then. Thompson doesn't move, not even when the elevator doors open. I shift my bag from one shoulder to the other, waiting for him to answer. I'm about to meet one of the Council Members to discuss my Final Test. Any confidence left in me dissipates. Either he thinks I'm ready or he doesn't.

"That's not what I meant, Katherine. I don't doubt your capabilities. She is involving you in something you shouldn't have to worry about." Shaking his head, Thompson steps off the elevator and disappears down the hallway. What does he mean? What does Haynes want me to do that's so problematic?

I wonder if this has anything to do with yesterday's mysterious events.

Nothing this exciting ever happens.

I follow after Thompson, passing by several rooms. Communication Center. Weapon Training Room. Storage. Thompson stands by an open door, waiting for me. He clips his identification card to his belt, since adults aren't required to carry bags with them like trainees are.

I read the screen on the card scanner—Conference Room. I enter. This is one of the larger rooms in the Regulation Center, furnished with a long table and five chairs. Sunlight streams in through the tall windows.

Council Member Haynes gets out of her chair, walking toward us. Exhaustion lines her face. Did she sleep at all last night, or was she awake trying to sort out whatever happened yesterday? Like Thompson, she's somewhere between thirty-five and forty years of age. Not a wrinkle to be found on her tan uniform. Perfectly-straight brownish-blond hair frames her face.

Reintegration

"You must be Trainee Holliday." Haynes smiles, shaking my hand. She may be tired, but she's more relaxed than Thompson. "I'm Amelia Haynes. Your mentor has turned in plenty of good reports about you, and that's partially why we're here today. I'm guessing you're wondering why I wanted to speak with you."

"I am." Will someone finally tell me what this is all about? Haynes and Thompson are being so cryptic. I just want to know what my Final Test will be.

"Come sit." She gestures at one of the chairs. I set my bag on the tabletop, sitting down in the chair. Haynes takes a seat across from me, folding her hands in her lap. "There has been a…situation."

So this is about her interrupted speech and the alarm. Thompson sits next to me, the chair legs scraping against the floor as he does so. Haynes winces. She fixes my mentor with the same expression a caretaker gives a difficult child. Have they argued about the nature of my Final Test?

Haynes places her tablet on the table. "As you know, we have worked very hard to protect our citizens from the Intolerants. We have removed them from our cities. We've erased all their propaganda. Despite the measures we've taken, they do exist in the Outlands."

I nod. I've learned about the group of rebels since Primary School. There's no need for her to remind me of the Intolerants' existence. I stare out the window, where the sun reflects off the grayish-silver surface of the Wall. The Intolerants resisted the formation of the Federation, which resulted in a war. During the battles, most of the Outlands were destroyed.

What are the Outlands like? A barren wasteland struggling

to support life? The remains of abandoned pre-Federation cities? Have the surviving Intolerants established towns of their own? They must have a government system. The Intolerants may be ruthless, but they can't have survived this long without some sense of order. I shake my head. I shouldn't be thinking about these things. The Intolerants, the people who live in the Outlands, are our enemies.

Looking back at Haynes, I wait for her to expand. And she does. "The issue is, one of City 45's Regulators captured an Intolerant yesterday morning."

"I'm sorry?" I bite back a nervous giggle. They captured an Intolerant? Within City 45? This must be a joke. I glance between Haynes and Thompson. "I don't understand. How…?"

"We don't know how he managed to get inside City 45. We're still investigating the matter." Haynes taps the table's surface with one finger. "The issue now is that an Intolerant was found inside the city."

Haynes pushes her tablet to my side of the table. The picture on the screen is from security camera footage. A man stands between two buildings, face turned away from the camera. He doesn't have a Federation uniform, a tablet, or a visible identification card. The clothes he wears are strange. A shiver runs through me. Who knows how long he was inside the city before the Regulator captured him.

"Has this happened before? An Intolerant being found inside the Federation?" I pick up Haynes's tablet and give it back to her.

"Not in over a decade. So this is a delicate matter that needs to be handled with the proper care." Thompson shoots Haynes a look, his face calm but his eyes expressing anger. If

Haynes notices my mentor's irritation, she makes no show of it.

"When will the Intolerant be executed?" I can't help but wonder if he knew what the consequences of his actions could be.

"Well," Haynes replies. "That is why you're here. This has to do with your Final Test."

Several seconds' worth of silence falls over the room as I try to make sense of everything Haynes told me. How can the capture of an Intolerant relate to my Final Test? I just now learned about the situation. I won't be of any help, considering I've never seen an Intolerant before now. I twirl a lock of hair around my finger. Whatever she wants me to do, Thompson doesn't approve. He said Haynes is involving me in something that doesn't concern me.

"What does my Final Test have to do with any of this?"

Haynes smiles again. Does she find my directness amusing in some way? "I'll explain in a moment. The Intolerants once posed a direct threat to the Federation, and execution was the safest way to deal with them. We couldn't allow them to roam free and pose a threat to our citizens, could we? In the past few months, however, the other Council Members and I have been discussing alternatives to execution.

"The war against the Intolerants is over. Their numbers are too few to pose any kind of real threat. It would be impossible for them to overthrow the Federation. What we are now up against is a few remnants. A few misguided people who do not realize all we've done to make the world a better place."

"Are you saying you want to allow the Intolerant to become a citizen?" The words sound crazier out loud than they do in my head.

"In a sense." Haynes pauses. "For several years now, we've talked about an idea. I've mentioned it in the Council before, but we've never acted on it. Mainly because we never had an opportunity. Now we do. Let me ask you something, Trainee Holliday. What—"

"Katherine." Chelsea and Thompson are the main people I talk to on a daily basis. The formality of using my rank and last name sounds…foreign.

Haynes isn't annoyed like I expect she'd be. "What is the main problem with the Intolerants?"

She keeps asking me questions any child could answer. "The Intolerants are radical in their beliefs. They think their ideas are the only correct ones. They refuse to accept the Tolerance Act."

"Why?"

"Why do they think that way?" Another simple question. I wish Thompson would provide further explanation as to what the purpose of this conversation is. He hasn't said anything for a while, and the tight-lipped expression on his face tells me my mentor's not in the mood to talk. I sigh. "They think that way because of what their society teaches them."

"Exactly. People are more prone to believe in something if it's the view they've been taught since childhood. In the case of the Intolerants, the children are taught their way is the only way. The primary reason the Intolerants behave as they do is because of their background. How would you fix that? How could you make it where an Intolerant could be a peaceful member of society?"

"You couldn't. You can't change the way someone was raised." The whole line of discussion is absurd.

Reintegration

"What if it was possible, Katherine?" Haynes leans forward, lowering her voice, excitement dancing in her eyes. "What if you could change someone's entire perspective about everything?"

I open my mouth to speak, but no words come out. What Haynes suggests is impossible. It has to be.

Haynes looks down at her tablet again. "One of our Experimental Medicine Specialists, Doctor Vincent Perry, is the one who proposed an idea to the Council a while ago. He's created a way to make what we're talking about a reality. Doctor Perry calls the idea Reintegration. The idea is we can erase a person's memory. We can start from scratch, see if an Intolerant can adapt to a more peaceful lifestyle."

Everything we know about the Intolerants...can it all change? Doctor Perry's search to fix the Intolerants could make our lives easier. No more execution. "You believe the best decision is to perform this Reintegration thing on the Intolerant?"

The question I don't ask, but want to, is how all of this relates to my Final Test.

"We aren't sure." Thompson draws a warning look from Haynes. Is the question of Reintegration's validity another thing they argued about? "Reintegration could work, and we would no longer have to use execution. There are drawbacks to Reintegration, however. It could fail, and we could end up creating more problems than we had to begin with. All it could prove is that the Intolerants can't be reasoned with."

"Your Final Test is today." Haynes ignores my mentor altogether. In other circumstances, their obvious distaste for one another would be comical. "In order to prove you are ready to become a Regulator, we are going to let you decide. This will be your Final Test."

"My Final Test is determining whether to go the route of Reintegration or execution?" I'm seventeen-years-old, a trainee. They can't expect me to make such a huge decision.

"Yes." Haynes nods, discounting any notion I have that maybe she's joking.

"But...Reintegration has never been attempted before?"

"No. It hasn't." Thompson leans back in his chair, like Reintegration's newness proves it's not worth the risk.

I frown. "So you don't know if it will work?"

"There is a chance it won't," Thompson says tersely. "A number of things could go poorly. The Intolerants are dangerous. If the procedure fails, he could escape and cause harm to our citizens and to our facilities. There is also the Intolerant to think about. He is just a boy, after all. The procedure could cause serious health or mental defects. Let's say—"

"The Council already discussed these things with Doctor Perry. He assured us the things you're suggesting are worst-case scenarios. Doctor Perry is a brilliant man and has spent a long amount of time developing the procedure. Yes, there is a slight chance Reintegration could fail. That chance, however, is very, very slim." Haynes continues tapping her finger on the table. A tic?

She eyes Thompson, not me, as she talks—almost as if she's trying to convince him of Reintegration's worth, more than she's trying to convince me. "You're suggesting execution then?"

"I don't see what all the fuss is about. One of the Intolerants shows up in the city. As far as we know, we apprehended him before he came into contact with any of our citizens." Thompson draws each word out, like he knows Haynes won't agree with what he's about to say. "We defeated the Intolerants years ago. They've exiled themselves to the Outlands. Sooner or later, they'll all die out. There's no need to worry ourselves over whether we execute the Intolerant or not. If you want my opinion, I say we send him back to the Outlands."

"Send him back?" The Council Member's cheeks pale. "That is not an option."

I haven't seen this side of my mentor before. Is logic or sympathy the motive behind his suggestion? Part of me thinks it's the latter. He's concerned about the Intolerant's well-being. Thompson wants to send the Intolerant to the Outlands, but not because it's the logical choice. He feels sorry for the man we captured.

"Execution and Reintegration are our only options," Haynes persists, turning her attention back to me. "Katherine? What do you think?"

Execution. The familiar, safe choice. Execution means ending a life for the good of the Federation. Can I be the one, however, to declare the Intolerant deserving of death? The thought of a Regulator injecting the lethal dose of poison into his body…my stomach churns.

Reintegration. New and untested. If Reintegration fails, many people could get hurt. If Reintegration succeeds, we'll have a more humane way to treat captured Intolerants—if more ever come to the Federation.

I need more time to think things over.

"If he's from the Outlands, why is he here?" I'll ask anything to learn more facts about the Intolerant.

"We don't know." Haynes shakes her head. "Why he's here doesn't matter. He's an Intolerant. I have no doubt he came here to cause harm to our citizens. The Intolerants have always used terrorism in their attempts to destroy us."

"How can you be sure of his motive?" The Intolerants may be violent and unpredictable, but terrorism can't be their reason for everything. "What if this one came for other, less radical reasons?"

"What other reasons?" For the first time, I detect irritation in Haynes's voice—irritation aimed at me. No logical reasons come to mind. Heat rises in my cheeks. The Council Member fixes me with her penetrating dark eyes. "No, Katherine, there can be no other reason. The Intolerant came on our sixtieth anniversary. Why, unless he was planning to ruin a day celebrating our triumph? I'm glad City 45's Regulators apprehended him so quickly, before he could carry out his plans."

An image pops into my mind of explosions and destroyed buildings. What if she's correct, and the Intolerant came to blow up a facility filled with unsuspecting citizens?

"I know this is a big decision, so how about this? We'll take a short break, and you can think about it. In a couple of hours, you can come back here and tell us your decision." Haynes stands.

I too, stand, and grab the strap of my bag. A few hours to think this over will be great. My head hurts from trying to mull over all this information. At least I can't fail my Final Test. All I have to do is choose between execution and Reintegration. The choice I make doesn't affect me, but rather the Federation as a whole. I need more information. I want to know why the Council chose me, but for now I'll settle on determining what should be done with the Intolerant.

I have an idea to learn more, but neither of them will agree to it.

"Could I be allowed to speak with him? The Intolerant, I

mean. Can I determine for myself what his intentions are in coming here?" I set my bag back on the table. Thompson jerks his gaze to me, eyes wide. Even if Haynes accepts my plan, he won't.

But he can't protect me forever.

"I don't think that's wise," Haynes says. "The Intolerants are dangerous. How would talking to him help in this decision?"

I need to know why the Intolerant came here. If I question him, maybe that will create the best opportunity for me to learn more about the mysterious insurgents who live in the Outlands and find out if this one is like the rest.

"I want to have as much as information as possible. This decision is one of the biggest I may ever make. I want to make sure I know exactly what's going on. I'll be careful. I promise."

"I don't—" Thompson starts to say, but Haynes cuts him off.

"If you think it will help, I see no reason to object."

I nod. A mix of excitement and terror surges through me. The Council Member believes I'm ready to help. I'll meet an Intolerant for the first time. Few have even seen the Intolerants in recent years. Are they as violent and crazy as I've been taught to believe?

Maybe they really could become a part of the Federation.

4

The Regulation Center's detention block is located on one of the lower levels. I follow Thompson down the hallway, passing by several empty cells. The detention block hasn't been used in years, but now two guards stand near the elevator entrance. Regulator O'Hara waits by the last cell, turning as we approach.

Thompson hasn't spoken to me for several minutes. Is he upset because I want to question the Intolerant myself? Does he wish Haynes wouldn't have brought me into this? He stops before the Regulator guarding the Intolerant's cell.

"My student would like to interrogate the Intolerant."

Regulator O'Hara frowns. "He tried escaping again this morning. I don't think letting a trainee handle an interrogation is a smart idea."

I can't believe the Intolerant attempted to escape, not once, but twice. The Regulator turns his head to look at the cell door, and a surprised gasp escapes me. A brownish-purple bruise covers part of his left cheek. I don't avert my gaze until he notices my stare. The last time I saw anything similar was when two of my schoolmates fought in Primary School. So the Intolerant is capable of violence. Haynes must be correct in her speculations. This Intolerant can, and will, inflict violence on the members of the Federation. What will I do if he tries to escape again? Thompson and the guard will be waiting outside the cell for me. If the Intolerant does attempt another escape, I won't be in too much danger.

O'Hara grunts and smacks the wall next to a flashing red button. "If anything happens, I'll be ready to trigger the alarm."

So the alarm yesterday went off because the Intolerant managed to escape. He didn't make it far, but the knowledge that he's even bold enough to try is unnerving. I straighten my posture. I won't show any sign of fear or uncertainty. This is my Final Test, and I will complete it. "Are you going to let me talk to him, or what?"

The guard raises his eyebrows. Thompson sighs. "Very well. Let her in."

"If you think it's a good idea." With an exaggerated shrug of the shoulders, the guard taps in a code on the door keypad.

Thompson's fingers brush against my arm. "Be careful, Katherine. I can help you if you want me to."

I've never seen Thompson be so open about his concern for what happens to me.

"No, thank you. I can handle it." I force as much confidence as I can into those words, then step into the cell. My heart pounds. I'll be stuck in close quarters with the enemy. A dangerous enemy who will hurt me if he gets the chance. I stand close to the doorway, leaving several feet of distance between me and him.

The Intolerant lays on the cot pushed against the far wall,

staring at the ceiling. The door closing behind me makes me jump. I shove my hands in my uniform pockets so he won't see how they shake. Three or four feet separates us. I mentally calculate how long it would take for him to cover the distance. A second or two?

Several moments pass before he sits up, swinging his legs over the side of the cot. The man—no, he's not quite a man. More of a boy. He can't be much older than I am. The Intolerant sweeps his gaze over me, like he's trying to determine if I'm an easy opponent. My heart pounds even harder.

"Will I be executed now?" His voice is strong but quiet.

"Your death has been postponed." I linger by the door. He's bigger than me, so if he decides to attack, I won't last long.

Maybe I should have asked Thompson for a stunner.

The Intolerant looks away, jaw clenched. He wears a button-up shirt with the sleeves rolled up past his elbows. Similar in style to a Federation uniform shirt, but made of a rough-looking material. The color is red, a color no one in the Federation wears. Pants, blue in color, the cuffs frayed and dirt-stained. Do the Intolerants wear clothing to designate their occupations?

When he looks back at me, fear lurks in his eyes. A look of worry, not terror. A sense of calmness hangs about him, even though he's our prisoner. "How long?"

"I don't know. I only know your death has been temporarily postponed." More or less true.

"But I'll still be executed?" Hope clings to every word. Does he think postponement means the Council is considering allowing him to live?

I hesitate to answer his question. If we execute him, we'll

take his life. If I choose Reintegration, we'll be erasing his past, taking away every aspect of who he is. He'll be alive and breathing, but he won't be who he is anymore. Either way he—whoever he is—will be gone.

"Yes."

"Oh." He frowns at the floor between his shoes. What is it about him? Why is he so calm, even when he knows he'll die soon?

"They told me you tried to escape." Maybe the longer I talk to him, the more I'll learn about why he came here to the Federation. He hasn't made any move to hurt me. I try to let myself relax. If I don't seem tense, maybe he'll open up a little.

"If you were captured and faced execution, wouldn't you try to escape? Besides, the living conditions aren't anything to brag about." He shrugs his shoulders. No one can blame him for being unhappy here. The cell has no windows, and the walls and floor are made of concrete. I would go insane in the small, confined space. The Intolerant crinkles his nose. "Food's garbage, too."

"But twice?"

"Worth a shot. The first time the thug outside just dragged me back here. Second time he smartened up." The Intolerant holds up his hands, bound by metal cuffs. He lowers his hands back down to his lap, a mischievous grin tugging at his lips. "Well, they say third time's a charm."

I frown. So far, he hasn't offered any helpful information.

"What's the number on your shirt for?" He cocks his head. A few locks of hair fall into his face, but he makes no move to brush them away. His hair is thick, blond, and curls a little at the ends—not to mention a tad bit longer than standard regulation would allow. Another reminder he's not from the

Federation.

I look down at the seven-digit number stitched on the front of one pocket. "It's my citizen number. If anything bad happens, they know how to identify me. You don't have numbers in the Outlands?"

What a dumb question. Of course the Intolerants don't use citizen numbers. They're Intolerants. Their way of life is very different from ours.

"Nope. We use names in the Outlands. May not be as accurate, but at least it's more personal." There it is, that smile of his. He has a nice smile, charming and kind of boyish at the same time. "I'm Matthew. Matthew Braddock."

"We use names, too. The numbers are for security reasons. But I'm Katherine Holliday." I shouldn't be giving him all this information. I need to remember the reason I wanted to talk to him in the first place. "Why are you here?"

Matthew might be calm and easy-going, but he's still one of them. The other Intolerants sent him here for a reason—an anti-Federation reason. He *did* come here on the Federation's sixtieth anniversary. Matthew Braddock is a violent criminal with ill intentions. There is no other logical explanation for his existence here.

"Why I'm here is my concern." His expression becomes neutral. Matthew has a secret about what's going on. He came here with a specific purpose, and now he won't be able to carry it out. What is his purpose? Is he here to perform an assassination or something equally horrible? "Doesn't matter now, does it? You're gonna kill me, after all."

"I could help you, if you tell me what you need." A lie. My goal was to learn his motives. If it takes a lie to learn the truth, so be it.

"You wouldn't. None of you would." Matthew leans back against the wall, twisting his hands as if he thinks he can pull them free of the cuffs. Whatever he came here to do, it's important to him.

Despite my resolve to not feel sorry for him, I can't help but pity him. Criminal or otherwise, he's young. Young and frightened. "You came here alone?"

Matthew nods, snorting a nervous laugh. "Stupid of me, huh?"

"How many of you are there? How many of you live in the Outlands?"

"Who knows?" Another shrug. He averts his gaze, indicating that he knows the answer but doesn't want to tell me. The one person who can tell us so much about the Outlands, and he won't say a word. The Intolerants taught him to be this way. Before they sent him here, they must have told him to avoid telling us anything, no matter what.

"I'd hate to have grown up in the Outlands. Here in the Federation, we're more civilized."

"My table manners aren't too bad. I promise." Matthew smiles, but it seems a little forced. I can't believe I said that out loud. "You may be 'civilized' here, but everything's dictated for you. The government tells you what you can and can't believe. No one fights over anything 'cause everyone's been brainwashed to think the same way. All because of the Tolerance Act. That's what you call it, right?"

"Yes. The Tolerance Act, but you're mistaken about other things. The reason for the creation of the Tolerance Act was making sure people can believe what they want without opposition." Is it possible for one to feel both irritation and sympathy toward a person at the same time? If anyone's been "brainwashed", it's him. The Intolerants have taught him to believe a twisted view of our society.

"So it's wrong for me to say the Tolerance Act is wrong? A bit ironic, don't you think?" Is he mocking me? "The truth is, the Federation isn't much different than the cell I'm in. The difference is you accept it and call it 'peace'. If you really think about it, you'll see I'm right."

I've never heard the words "right" and "wrong" used so many times in a conversation. The Tolerance Act forbids us from using those words. Saying someone is "wrong" and you're "right" is the same as condemning their beliefs.

"The Federation is safe. You can't say the same thing about the Outlands, can you?"

I glare at him, but he glares back, squaring his shoulders. "I'd rather have freedom than safety."

He's so stubborn, but his loyalty to the Intolerants has gotten him nowhere. The Intolerants don't believe in freedom. If they did, they wouldn't persecute others for having different views. Dozens of quotes from my school studies flash through my mind. The teachers told us about the importance of safety. The original Council built the Federation on the principles of safety, peace, and equality.

Before I can reply, the cell door opens and Thompson steps in the doorway. I look away from the confused boy who doesn't understand reality. He can't. The Intolerants engrained him with their thinking, twisted him to hate the Federation. Isn't that why he came here? They sent him here to act on hatred.

Thompson grabs my arm and pulls me out of the cell. The Regulator closes the door again and my mentor's grip relaxes on my arm. He can't make me leave. I wasn't done yet. Even with all the things we talked about, Matthew Braddock told me nothing helpful.

"What's going on?" I turn to Thompson. "I wasn't finished."

"You were in there long enough. There's no telling what he'll do. He tried to escape twice. I don't doubt he'll try again." I look over my shoulder at the closed cell door. "He didn't threaten me in any way."

"You wanted to give him a chance?"

I don't say anything in response. I don't have anything *to* say in response. We captured an Intolerant, a terrorist. When Haynes told me about him, I believed he came to harm the citizens of City 45. Now I've met him, and he's nothing like I expected. Matthew's not the bitter, violent Intolerant we're taught about as children. He had the opportunity to hurt me, to try one last escape, but he didn't.

What if he's different from the other Intolerants?

I enter the conference room. Haynes smiles, leaning back in her chair. "I hope you learned what you wanted to know."

"The conversation didn't go as planned. He wouldn't tell me why he came here." I sit in the same chair I occupied earlier. Thompson lingers in the doorway for a moment, then sits next to me. "Talking to him was interesting, I guess. Matthew Braddock seems—"

"He told you his name?" The Council Member sits up straight, her eyes widening.

"Yes." The second the word leaves my mouth, Haynes grabs her tablet and begins typing. Is she sending a message to the other Council Members? Matthew has to be someone important, if his name bothers Haynes so much. "Do you know who he is?"

"No, no I don't," Haynes stammers, blurting the words out a little too quickly. What is she hiding? Is she keeping secrets from us? After finishing typing, Haynes pushes her tablet aside. "He's nothing more than a simple rebel, one of the last members of a dying group."

Matthew is important. Otherwise, Haynes wouldn't have acted so surprised when I told her his name.

Haynes is the one who breaks the following silence. "Have you made a decision?"

I am so close to shedding my trainee status. After I tell her my decision, I'll be given my responsibilities as a Regulator. All I need to do is choose one. Execution. Reintegration. Once I say one of those words, I'll pass the test and put all this behind me. I dislike both options, but Matthew's fate doesn't affect me. In a few minutes I can walk out of this room and never have to think about Matthew or Reintegration ever again.

Execution. A fitting sentence for a rebel who came to commit an act of violence. Or did he? Despite all the evidence, all the signs that he came with ill intentions, something makes me question my conclusion. Every time I looked at him, I saw defiance, not hatred, in his eyes. What if he came here with different motives than we think? He didn't do anything harmful before the Regulators captured him.

Maybe he didn't have time to carry out his task.

Maybe he wasn't going to do it at all.

But he *is* an Intolerant. Violence is all he knows.

"Exe…" The rest of the word dies in my throat. Why can't I make my decision and be done with it? Execution is safe.

Proven. Logical. By executing the Intolerant, we ensure he won't pose a threat to anyone ever again. Execution is also final. If I choose execution, I subject him to a death sentence. He's not a faceless, nameless enemy anymore. Talking to him face-to-face changes everything. In choosing execution, I'll kill the confused, delusional, blond-haired boy who hates the Federation because of what they taught him to do. He's the enemy, but I'm not certain he's a terrorist. No matter what Matthew Braddock may be, there's one thing I cannot do.

I can't be the one to declare him deserving of death.

I take a deep breath.

"Reintegration."

5

I made my decision.

Final Test complete.

"Very well. Doctor Perry will perform the procedure this evening." Haynes stands and pushes in her chair. In our previous conversation, she seemed to believe Reintegration is the best choice. Why let me decide if she knows what's best?

"So Katherine's Final Test is finished," Thompson says. Of course my Final Test is finished. Haynes asked me to choose between Reintegration and execution—so I did. "I'm assuming the next step will be to inform the Council Katherine is ready for her responsibilities?"

Haynes shoots me an apologetic smile. "I'm afraid not, actually."

What is she saying "no" to? The completion of my Final Test or the next step? It can't be that my Final Test isn't over yet. I did exactly what Haynes told me. I performed the assignment to the best of my abilities.

"Generally, a trainee's Final Test takes no more than a few

hours. But your Final Test, Katherine, is more than choosing what should be done with the Intolerant. That was only the start. Your new assignment is to make sure the Intolerant properly adjusts to our society." Haynes says it like I should be happy to be given an assignment like this.

I am far from happy.

"What?" Now I have to make sure the Intolerant "properly adjusts"? What does that even mean?

"Over the next six weeks, your job will be to monitor the Intolerant's adjustment to Federation life. We can't declare the Intolerant a citizen unless we're certain Reintegration works. You'll report the Intolerant's progress to Doctor Perry and me. Any sign that Reintegration has failed, execution will be carried out."

Haynes obviously doesn't understand my confusion.

"I thought this was my Final Test. Making my decision, I mean." I jump out of my chair, not even trying to hide my vexation. She lied to me. The Council Member gave me an assignment, but now she's including another.

And it's not a small task.

"Katherine." Thompson lays a hand on my arm and pulls me back into my chair. I bite my tongue. With a sigh, Thompson turns back to Haynes. "I'm not real sure this is a good idea. If Reintegration fails, Katherine could end up getting hurt in the process."

"That is why she will be sending in weekly reports. We'll know in advance if Reintegration isn't working quite as anticipated. Katherine will be fine. I think she is more than capable of handling herself." I can't tell if her words are the result of confidence in my abilities or indifference about my well-being.

"This is a larger issue than understanding what a Violation

is or learning the duties of a Regulator. What we're dealing with now is a serious dilemma, one I don't think Katherine or any trainee would be prepared for." I appreciate Thompson is trying to help me, but arguing with her won't do any of us any good. Thompson will only irritate her if he pushes this further. I'm upset about this, too, but there's no way around it.

"If Katherine is going to become a Regulator, she needs experience. What better experience than this situation?"

"I have a question," I say, before Thompson can fire a reply. "If Reintegration fails, will I also have failed my Final Test?"

"Not at all." Haynes's tone softens. "The Reintegration procedure itself is out of your control. What we're testing you for is how you handle the situation."

If I do my best, I can't fail. "I understand."

"You will send in weekly reports to the Council. You'll inform us as to how the Intolerant is adjusting to life in the Federation. Any word he says or action he does that you feel may be a sign of failure, you let us know. We need to be able to remove him from the situation so he doesn't pose a threat to you. Reintegration is an important development, but your safety is more important."

"Of course." *Why are they doing this to me?*

"The procedure is scheduled for tomorrow morning. You, Katherine, will come with us to City 1. Please be at the train station within two hours so we can leave." Haynes tucks her tablet under her arm and strides for the door.

Final Test?!

I stare at the message from Chelsea and the craziness of

the last few days and my irritation over how Haynes changed my test on me floods back. At least I found a few moments to forget it all. Going to City 1 would be fun, if I didn't have to wait for Doctor Perry to perform his special memory-wiping procedure on Matthew.

I don't have much to say about it, except that it'll take me six weeks to complete it. Six weeks, no lie. I have to go to City 1 tonight.

I set the tablet aside and resume packing my clothes for the trip. Like everything in the Federation, my bedroom is immaculate, thanks to the cleaners who come by once a week. Orderly. Pristine. The walls are white, providing little contrast to the light gray tile floor. I grab my tablet's charging cord off the shelf above my bed. I shove it in my bag, then make sure my identification card is clipped to the front.

A few seconds later my tablet beeps. I glance at the clock on the shelf. The green numbers blink back at me. Thirty minutes until I need to be at the station. I pick up my tablet for a second time.

Why do you have to go to City 1 for your Final Test?

How do I respond to her message? No one told me I couldn't divulge the nature of my Final Test, but no one said I could, either. Am I allowed to tell Chelsea about Matthew Braddock and his complexity? About Reintegration and the possible repercussions? Most likely not. Thompson said this situation is a "delicate matter."

I can't tell you the specifics. Sorry. I'll talk to you when I get back.

I turn off my tablet and slip it in my bag. Chelsea will be mad at me for not telling her. But I can't betray the trust of Haynes and Thompson. Besides, if I explain things to her, someone will find out. One valuable thing I learned while training to be a Regulator is all messages sent and received from a tablet are monitored. The communication specialists monitor our messages for our safety.

"Why do they need to monitor us?" I once asked Thompson, during the only other time I've been to City 1. He brought me there to show me the Museum, a building dedicated to the history of the Federation and the Tolerance Act. The displays in the Museum serve to memorialize the founding of the original Council. I looked around the room, making a mental note of the location of all the security cameras.

"They monitor us to make certain no one breaks the Tolerance Act."

"What happens if you break the Tolerance Act?" I was thirteen at the time. Even as a child, I cared about the rules and regulations of the Federation.

"When a citizen breaks the Tolerance Act, they receive a Violation, which is a very serious matter," Thompson replied. "If someone finds out you've broken the Tolerance Act, you have to be interrogated. The Violation is permanently entered into your record."

"You said if. Do people ever get away with Violations?"

"Sometimes. It's rare, but there are times when people commit a Violation but are never caught for it." Thompson steered me toward a map of the Federation. The map showed the locations of all forty-eight of the Federation's cities and the vast expanse of land that makes up the Outlands.

"Have you ever committed a Violation?" I said as a joke. The Council wouldn't have made him a mentor unless he fit the mold of a perfect citizen. Because mentors are responsible for training the Federation's youth, they're held to a higher standard than the average citizen.

Thompson's answer piqued my curiosity more than anything in the Museum could have.

"Yes. Once." He stared at the map for a while, a far-away look in his eyes. I'll never forget the confident, almost rebellious smile that came to his face for a short moment. "And they never caught me for it."

Thompson never told me what he did or how he got away with it. I've never asked, because he'll never tell me. I've spent years training under Thompson, but I don't know a single thing about him. Regulation Mentor Phillip Thompson is something of an enigma to me. The day in the Museum is the only time he's ever given any indication about his life before training me.

There's no way to explain why I haven't turned him in, either. I should. If I'm going to be a Regulator, I need to be strong enough to give people the Violations they deserve.

But with my mentor...I can't do it.

"Where're we going?" Matthew sits across from me on the train, his wrists still bound by handcuffs. He no longer wears his Intolerant clothing but a gray-white colored prisoner's uniform.

I glance up from my tablet at him. According to the screen on the wall, we're not even a quarter of the way to City 1. Except for the Regulator standing by the door leading to the next train car, Matthew and I are alone. Haynes and Thompson are in a meeting of some sort in the other car. For the safety of the other citizens, no other passengers are allowed with Matthew and me.

No one told me what to say if Matthew asks about where we're going. He's attempted to start a few conversations with me, but none of them lasted long—my fault, not his. Once Matthew noted my obvious disinterest in talking to him, he tried chatting with the stone-faced Regulator. That little endeavor got him nowhere. I tap my tablet's screen to pause the game I'm playing. Maybe I should talk to him. Council Member Haynes *is* forcing me to follow him around everywhere for the next six weeks.

My new best friend is an Intolerant. Lucky me.

Matthew leans forward, resting his elbows on his knees. "Am I going to my execution now?"

Sort of. The execution of his memories, not his body. I wonder if I'm allowed to tell him the truth. In a few hours, Doctor Perry will begin the procedure that changes who Matthew Braddock is. If Reintegration works, Matthew won't remember a word of this conversation. Then again … Haynes might not like it if I explained the situation to him.

"Yes?"

An amused smile replaces his worried expression. "You're asking me?"

"Yes." I repeat, firmly this time. Why is he always mocking me?

The cute little smile vanishes. "I thought my execution was 'postponed' for a while. Guess they sped up the process, huh?" Despite his sudden seriousness, he remains calm. What is it about him? He's so so…different.

"Your execution is out of my control."

Matthew stares at the train's metal floor, lacing and unlacing his fingers. He swipes his hand across his nose, eyes glassy. I watch him, noticing for the first time how exhausted he looks. In a short amount of time, he was captured, imprisoned, and interrogated. Now he believes we're taking him to his execution. Several more seconds pass, but he doesn't make eye contact with me. How does he feel at the moment? Alone? Terrified? Angry?

"I'm sorry. I guess I'd be scared too, if I knew I was about to die." I soften my tone. My previous comment about having no control over his execution may have seemed...cold. Intolerant or not, Matthew has the same emotions we do. If I believed I was going to die, I would want someone to comfort me, too.

"I'm not afraid of dying." Matthew inclines his head a little bit. He's so close to crying, but manages to maintain his composure. I'd be a sobbing mess. "There's something better after this, anyway."

What in the world is he saying? Something better after what? He offers no explanation, and I don't ask for one. More evidence he's delusional? Another strange notion the Intolerants put in his head?

"I guess you wouldn't have come here if you thought this was how it would turn out."

"I knew it was a possibility. But I had to try."

"What's so important to you anyway?" Why did the Intolerants send him here? He didn't answer my questions earlier, but maybe now he'll open up. He does believe he's going to die today, after all.

"You don't have something you love so much you're willing to die for it?"

Where did that question come from? Whatever Matthew came here to do, he's willing to die for it. But for me...do I have anything I would give my life for? Protecting the Federation, or to save Thompson or Chelsea, maybe. I admire Matthew's self-sacrifice. He believes his cause is worth fighting for. I don't know if I feel the same about mine.

"Oh. Wow," Matthew says when I don't reply. "I can't imagine what it's like growing up here, just—"

"You don't know what you're talking about." I shake my head. I shouldn't be so angry with him. This is the way he's been raised. The Intolerants have taught him to hate us. He can't know any better.

"Oh, come on. You've grown up not having anyone who really cares about you and you have no freedom." I open my mouth to speak, but he raises his voice. "No, you don't. Everyone's so afraid to speak their mind because if they do they get punished for it. There are things they don't tell you. A lot of things they don't tell you. I know—"

"You're crazy," I hiss. My heart pounds in my chest, part of me wanting to know more, even though I shouldn't. The other part of me, the sensible side of me, wants him to shut up, to stop trying to convince me everything I know is a lie. Matthew Braddock irritates me in a way no one else ever has.

"I'm not. Why do you think we didn't join the Federation in the first place? Because we know it's wrong." He doesn't even flinch at his use of the word wrong. If he wasn't already an Intolerant, he would be given a Violation for breaking the Tolerance Act.

The Regulator by the door jumps a little, whipping his head around to look at Matthew. Breaking the Tolerance Act is the most serious crime in the Federation. If Matthew knows this, he doesn't show it. He believes what he's saying. He honestly believes the Federation is his enemy.

"If the Intolerants really cared about others' well-being,

they would have joined the Federation." I match his stubborn glare. Matthew needs to see his faulty logic. "If they really cared about you, they wouldn't have sent you here, by yourself. You're about to be executed, and none of your fellow conspirators are here to help you."

The second the words leave my mouth, I wish I could take them back. Matthew stiffens. He starts to say something, then stops and looks away. How dare he accuse me of not having anyone who cares when the people who raised him sent him into a dangerous situation.

Matthew doesn't say another word, but stares off into space. Conversation over. Any pleasant discussion we may have had I ruined with those two sentences. A horrible feeling washes over me. I don't apologize, but grab my tablet and resume my game. This is why Matthew needs to be Reintegrated. All we want is to help him. He doesn't know any better. He doesn't know what we can offer him here.

We can keep Matthew safe.

6

"Subject's vital signs are normal."

I look at the doctor and let out a breath of air I didn't realize I was holding in. Haynes told me the procedure was safe, that the hard part was to come. But science can fail us. It did in the Past, so it is possible something as new and untested as Reintegration could have some complications, maybe even kill the subject. This thought lingers in my mind. If the only other option is execution, aren't we helping Matthew by offering him a chance at a long, healthy life?

"Nothing out of the ordinary." Doctor Vincent Perry taps the screen of his tablet. He's young, maybe twenty-four or twenty-five-years-old. He has short dark hair and a close-trimmed beard. A slow, relieved smile comes to his face for a split second. "I would say Reintegration is a success so far."

I nod, approaching the medical bed where Matthew lies. Doctor Perry completed Reintegration last night, but Matthew is unconscious from sedatives, even though it's now midmorning. If Reintegration works, everything changes. The Federation has made substantial progress in finding a non-violent method for protecting our society from the Intolerants. This way we can help them, not eliminate them. They need to see all we want is to show them the peaceful world we've created.

I slept little last night. My restlessness was due partially to being in one of City 1's unfamiliar boarding rooms, and partially due to wondering about Matthew and Reintegration. Haynes informed me during breakfast today that Matthew survived the procedure. The medical center here is similar to the one in City 45—big, sterile, and packed with white-clothed scientists. The individual medical rooms, too, remind me of the ones in City 45's medical center.

The entire room is white. The floor. The walls. The sheets on the bed. Doctor Perry's uniform. I've been to a medical center many times, for routine check-ups, but never for major injuries.

"Do you think it will work? Do you think the transition will go as planned?" I grab Matthew's arm and turn it over. Earlier, Doctor Perry placed a bandage over part of Matthew's forearm, covering the place where they installed his tracking device. I roll up my sleeve and look at my own arm, at the thin scar that gives away where mine is. Every citizen is fitted with a tracking device after they're born.

Thompson once explained to me how the people originally hated the tracking devices. They felt it was an invasion of their privacy and argued that the government shouldn't be able to monitor all their whereabouts. Then the Council revealed to them the tracking devices serve a two-fold purpose, not only to inform officials where we go every day. The devices also monitor our health and alert the doctors when we are ill or in danger.

Like everything in the Federation, the tracking devices are designed to keep us safe.

"I don't know. He could wake up and remember his past. We won't know anything until he's awake." Perry shrugs his shoulders, casting a sidelong glance in Matthew's direction. He taps his foot on the polished tile floor, impatience seeming to radiate off him. No wonder he's eager for Matthew to wake up. Reintegration is his creation. Doctor Perry wants Reintegration to succeed more than anyone else. "If this is successful initially, you will need to turn in reports over the next several weeks. I don't know if this will work long-term."

"I understand." Haynes already told me this. A lot rests on my shoulders, Matthew's fate included. I can't let anything slip about Reintegration once he's awake. If I do, he'll suspect. He will know we lied to him. Even if we have created a long-term solution, if I inform him how we've altered his mind, this entire procedure will be for nothing.

"You're lucky to be alive." Doctor Perry shines a little flashlight into Matthew's eyes. Reintegration may not have killed Matthew, but there could be other side effects. I set my bag by the door. How long until Matthew can return to City 45?

Perry lowers the flashlight, shoving it in one of his pockets. With a pleased nod, he types something on his tablet. Matthew blinks a few times, glancing around the room. He sits on the edge of the medical bed, wearing a plain whitish-gray colored patient's uniform—so different from his Intolerant clothing. His gaze rests on me for a split second. Does he recognize me? After a few seconds, Matthew rolls up his sleeve, glancing at the bandage wrapped around his arm. "What happened?"

Maybe Matthew's disinterest is a sign that he doesn't remember me.

"You work in a factory. There was an explosion. You fell and hit your head," Perry explains. So the Council assigned Matthew to be a factory worker. I would have done the same. They don't know whether or not Reintegration will work, so they don't want to give Matthew access to confidential information. I wonder what his occupation was in the Outlands. His lean, muscular build tells me he's used to physical labor.

"I don't remember the accident. I don't remember much of anything." Matthew takes a deep, shaky breath, finally looking away from his bandaged arm. Frustration clings to every word he says, like he's a child who can't figure out how to solve a mathematical problem.

Doctor Perry walks to the other side of the room and opens a cabinet. "What do you remember?"

"I know my name. Matthew Braddock, correct?" He doesn't wait for an answer, but continues to list things off. "I'm seventeen-years-old, I think. You said I work in a factory, so that must be true."

His trust hits me like a slap. I should be happy, since Reintegration is going well so far. Instead nausea threatens to overcome me. We're lying to him. We stole his memories and are trying to convince him he belongs in the Federation. He's no longer Matthew Braddock, the Intolerant. Now he's whatever we tell him he is.

"I know her, don't I?" Matthew's eyes bore into mine, those eyes that are so innocent and believing.

The doctor glances over his shoulder at me, his hand still

in the cabinet. Matthew knows who I am. He remembers me. If he remembers I interrogated him...then Reintegration has already failed.

"How do you know her?" Perry pulls some things out of the cabinet.

"I don't know," Matthew says. "She just looks familiar to me. Did we work together?"

"No, but we knew each other briefly. You lived across the hall from me at our dormitory." I manage a smile. He needs to believe we're friends, not enemies. I can't say we're good friends, though. Matthew will expect me to know more about him than I do.

Maybe I'm a better liar than I first thought, because Matthew nods and looks back at the doctor again. My stomach is still in knots. Why do I feel this way? I'm performing my duty. That's all. I'm not being deceitful to cause harm. I'm trying to help. The only way I can help Matthew avoid execution is by convincing him he's one of us.

"How long until my memory comes back?" Matthew examines his arm again. The bandage has captured his attention more than anything else. Something about him is so...childlike. His curiosity and his naivety could be signs of Reintegration's success.

"To be perfectly honest with you, I don't know." Doctor Perry walks back over to Matthew, carrying a device that is smaller than a tablet. "You may never remember everything. I need to take a blood sample, okay? Roll up your sleeve for me."

Another compliant nod from Matthew. He does as he's told, exposing his non-bandaged arm. I've never seen any kind of medical procedure performed on anyone but myself. The only reason Haynes allowed me to be here is because she wants me to start observing Matthew as quickly as possible.

Doctor Perry has Matthew clench his hand into a fist so he knows from where to draw blood. Matthew does everything he's told without question. He winces when the doctor finally presses the device to his arm and pushes a button.

"How likely is it that I will remember things?" Matthew looks my way again, studying me.

"You remember your name and your age. A good sign. I'm just trying to prepare you, because I would be surprised if everything comes back." Perry looks at the device, then presses a piece of cotton over the spot on Matthew's arm. He steps outside the room, carrying the device. The door slides in place behind him and he leaves me alone with Matthew.

Doctor Perry explained Reintegration to me earlier today. It's basically a medicine coupled with brain surgery, "more advanced than the ones of the Past". The doctors changed Matthew's mind, erasing most of his memory, but kept a few things. His name. His age. His ability to perform simple tasks like speaking, walking, and eating. At this moment, it's crucial we're firm in what we tell him. I make a list in my mind of everything Perry and I told Matthew.

He works in a factory.

There was an explosion.

Matthew and I were acquaintances.

Before we can exchange any words, the doctor returns to the medical room empty handed. He grabs his tablet off the counter and types something. "Overall, you seem to be doing very well. There are just a few more things I need to do."

After setting his tablet down, Doctor Perry unwraps the bandage from Matthew's arm. Matthew stares at the one-inch long cut on the underside of his forearm as Perry disposes of the bandage in the trash container. Do the Intolerants use tracking devices? Most likely not, if Matthew didn't have one.

"Is this from the accident as well?" Matthew holds up his arm.

"Yes and no." Perry grabs a fresh bandage out of a drawer, then walks back over to Matthew. The cut is too straight, too neat to be an injury. "Your tracking device was damaged in the explosion. We had to replace it. Nothing serious."

"Was anyone else hurt in the accident?"

Unbelievable. Matthew suffers from memory loss and believes he survived a near-death event, but he stops to ask about the other workers? He can't remember anyone who could have been harmed. I don't know what to make of this boy who is so trusting, so compassionate, and so innocent.

"Some other workers sustained minor injuries, but like you, everyone else is going to be fine." Doctor Perry pulls off his white disposable gloves and throws them too in the garbage. Lying seems to be so natural to him.

I've done my best to stay out of the conversation. I'll mess this up if I say too much. In a moment of stupidity, I'll tell Matthew everything. If I end up being the reason Matthew learns the truth, will that mean I fail my Final Test? Matthew nods and looks at me again.

"Can I leave now?" Matthew glances from me to Doctor Perry, then back to me. "I feel fine."

"Not yet." Perry grabs his tablet. "It's only a precaution, just so we can run some final tests. You'll be released in the morning. Tomorrow Katherine will show you around the city."

"Katherine." Matthew repeats my name, drawing out each syllable. I introduced myself when I questioned him. If he remembers—somewhere, somehow—I look familiar to him, then my name may also be familiar. I shift from one foot to the other. Reintegration could fail all because Matthew remembers me. "Do you think if I go back to places I've been before, I'll remember things?"

Perry clears his throat. "Maybe."

"At least it's possible." Matthew grins, his initial confusion over. That smile is a momentary glimpse of the boy he was before we stripped his life away from him. I've never met anyone who is so characteristically happy about everything. Even now, after Reintegration, Matthew faces the world with an optimism unlike anyone else's.

"Of course." For the first time, Doctor Perry's encouragement sounds forced.

My tablet beeps, cutting through the silence that fell over the room. Matthew watches me pull my tablet out of my bag. The look of pure fascination on Matthew's face is almost comical. I try to interpret his curiosity. Either the procedure worked or the Intolerants don't have technology in the Outlands. I read over the message from Thompson.

I'm being sent back to City 45. You're to stay here in City 1 until tomorrow morning. Meet me at the train station within the hour so I can talk to you. I have something I need to give you.

"I'm afraid I have to go now," I say, slipping my tablet back in my bag. Thompson wants to give me something? Strange. But I won't complain about the interruption. I need to get out of here, away from Matthew and his perceptive stare. What if he knows something's up? What if he remembers me, and not as a casual friend?

How can I keep this charade going?

Without any further explanation, I tap the button by the door. Maybe by tomorrow Doctor Perry's tests can confirm

Reintegration may still succeed, even though Matthew remembers me. I exit the medical room and step into the hallway, not allowing myself to relax until the door closes behind me.

One day down.

Six more weeks to go.

"I was surprised you chose Reintegration."

I glance over at Thompson, who stares at his tablet. He doesn't look up, not even when I sit down next to him. We haven't had much time to talk without Haynes present. The train to City 45 will leave in a few minutes, according to the screen on the far wall. Only a handful of people wait in the station's sitting area. Few people travel to and from cities on a regular basis.

"It seemed worth a shot. I like a challenge." Do the words sound as hollow as they feel in my mouth? "You think I should have chosen execution?"

Thompson hesitates. "I don't know which option you should have chosen."

"Execution would have been safer." I sigh. As a child, my Primary School teachers taught me the importance of safety. We know execution works and that it is the best way to keep our citizens protected from the Intolerants. Reintegration is…different. No one knows how it will turn out. Reintegration is the opposite of safe.

"It would have, but you chose Reintegration." There is a question veiled behind Thompson's words. He knows I chose Reintegration. Now he needs to know why I made that choice.

The strange thing is, I'm not even certain myself.

"I felt sorry for him. The Intolerant, I mean. Wherever he

grew up, whatever his former life was like, he never knew the peace we have. I guess I just wanted to give him the opportunity to see the way we live." We speak in hushed voices, so the other citizens don't hear. A thought pops into my mind, one that makes a chill run through my body. "I chose Reintegration, so now I have to make sure it works. If I had chosen execution, would I have had to...?"

I can't bring myself to say the final words. My new duty is monitoring Matthew's adjustment to Federation life. It doesn't seem so implausible to assume that if I chose execution, I would have had to carry out my decision.

Thompson frowns. "You want to know if you would have had to kill him yourself."

I nod.

"Yes. It's what you would have had to do." Thompson continues staring at the tablet screen. A sense of fatigue hangs about him, something I never noticed prior to now. Gray lines his brown hair. Exhaustion fills his brown-green eyes. Is this a result of the stress of the past few days? Or is the burden of mentoring weighing down on him? Having a student must be demanding. At last he looks at me, setting his tablet in his lap. "You don't think you could, do you? Be the executioner?"

"I don't think I could have," I whisper. I couldn't kill someone, even if the procedure was humane and necessary. I couldn't be the one to inject the lethal dose of poison into someone's body. Realization creeps over me. I'm weak. I can't be a Regulator if I'm unable to complete the difficult tasks.

"There's a line from one of your lessons. I've never forgotten it. 'Sometimes we have to do things we wouldn't ordinarily do in order to preserve the Federation.' " Thompson watches a gray-clad factory worker who sits in the chair across from him. The worker pays no attention to us, but Thompson lowers his voice even further. "Would executing him have been safer? Perhaps."

An automated male voice echoes through the room. "The train to City 45 will depart in five minutes. Passengers may now begin boarding."

Thompson stands, as do all the other people in the sitting area. They disappear down the hallway, but my mentor lingers. I rise to my feet, clinging to the strap of my bag. For a moment, panic sets in.

This is the first time I'll be away from City 45 without a teacher. Most students yearn for their independence. The Federation encourages it, actually. By the time we're old enough to begin official training, we should be able to take on most of our responsibilities without help. Here I am, seventeen-years-old and in the middle of my Final Test, but I'm terrified because Thompson won't stay in City 1. Even though I won't be here much longer, I don't want to be alone.

"You, um, said you have something to give me?"

"Oh, yes." Thompson stuffs his hand into his pocket, then pulls something out. Light bounces off the silver surface. He holds it out to me, the movement casual. Like he gives me a stunner every day. I take it from him. This isn't the Regulation Center's, but *mine*.

It fits in the palm of my hand and I wrap my fingers around it so the button is in reach. I've held a stunner before on the few occasions where Thompson showed me how to use one. This is different. Thompson gave me a stunner of my own. "I don't understand. I haven't finished my Final Test yet. Are you allowed to give this to me?"

Knowing Thompson, the idea that he would give me a

Reintegration

stunner without approval isn't so far-fetched.

"Yes. I discussed some things with Haynes this morning. She's actually the one who decided to give you a weapon, since you'll be working so closely with an Intolerant. You need to be able to defend yourself. You remember what I showed you?"

I adjust my grip on the stunner so I'm holding it how he taught me. "Of course. I'll be fine. Don't you need to go now?"

"Be careful, Katherine. This stays between us, but I don't think you made any error in choosing Reintegration. Execution was the safe choice, but you know what?" Thompson's gaze shifts to the security camera in the corner of the room. He doesn't bother to lower his voice. He doesn't have to, since few of the Federation's cameras can pick up sound. "The funny thing is, sometimes I wonder if safety was really worth everything else we lost."

Without another word, my mentor tucks his tablet under his arm and walks away. I watch him as he strides out of the room, never once looking back. What did he mean by that? In the Past, people were brutal and violent toward one another. The creation of the Federation brought with it peace and safety, something the world desperately needed. We couldn't have possibly lost anything that wasn't worth the peace we now have.

Weapon clenched in my hand, I exit the station.

7

Matthew no longer bears the appearance of an unkempt Intolerant. He wears a dark gray factory worker's uniform, and they cut his hair to meet regulations. With his hair cut and combed and his Intolerant clothing gone, Matthew already looks like he belongs here.

Doctor Perry hands Matthew a bag, identical to mine. "Your tablet and identification card will be in there. I think that's all you should need. Katherine will take you back to City 45 and make sure you find your way around."

"Okay." Matthew unclips the identification card and sets the bag next to him on the bed. The doctor's tests must have confirmed Reintegration's success, otherwise he wouldn't release Matthew into the world so soon.

After putting the identification card away, Matthew shoots me an impatient look. I can't blame him for wanting to leave the medical facility. He seems antsy this morning, paying little attention to Perry but glancing periodically at the door.

"I guess we'd better go now."

Reintegration

Matthew slides off the medical bed and grins at me. I never realized how tall he is until now. All the previous times we've spoken, he was sitting. Matthew stands a little taller than Doctor Perry, which means he has at least six inches on me.

I keep my hand close to the stunner, an added weight I'm not used to. If Reintegration does fail and Matthew attacks me, the weapon is my only chance at fending him off. The Intolerants taught him how to fight. I know very little about combat. Even with his memory gone, Matthew Braddock is a dangerous criminal. Or is he? Matthew injured the Regulator when he tried to escape, but it wasn't a life threatening injury. If Matthew knows how to fight and Regulators don't, couldn't he have killed the man in the detention block? He never made any move to hurt me, not in the cell or on the train.

No matter what Haynes thinks, I'm not one-hundred-percent convinced Matthew is violent or spiteful. The question I've asked a dozen times creeps into my mind again.

What if Matthew didn't come here to harm anyone?

But what if he did, and if he learns who he really is, I become his next target?

"The tablets are used for work and education. There's also a few games you can play during free time. I do that when I can't sleep." Reaching over, I tap the screen of Matthew's tablet. Brand new. Not a smudge on the screen, except for one of my own fingerprints. "The tablets have maps of the cities. There's also a messaging system, which you use to contact friends. Sometimes the Council will need to send out an update on something, and it will show up here as well."

Matthew nods, watching as I tap on icons to open the different functions on the tablet. We have several hours to go until we reach City 45, so now is the perfect time to show him all this. Later I'll show him his apartment. No need to rush things. He doesn't know anything, so a slow pace might work best for him.

"I think they already programmed me in your messaging system, in case you have any questions when I'm not around…" Sure enough, I find my name in his contact list. Other than his future work supervisor, I'm the only one on his list.

Mine's not very long either.

The white-uniformed woman sitting across from us keeps giving Matthew and me curious glances. Every child learns how to use a tablet at an early age, so she's probably wondering why I'm showing Matthew how the tablet works.

"Does all this make sense so far?" I lower my voice some.

Matthew sighs and rakes his fingers through his hair, causing a few tufts to stick up in various directions. He looks different now that his hair doesn't curl around his ears in a windblown way. It's still long enough for him to mess it up, which makes me smile. "Yes. I guess so. It's a lot to take in."

"It'll be confusing at first, but in time it'll become habit." I pull my own tablet out of my bag. No messages. I haven't heard from Thompson since he left City 1 yesterday afternoon. His final words linger in the back of my mind. Thompson breaks rules sometimes, but never before has he said something suggesting dissatisfaction with the Federation.

The more I learn about my mentor, the stranger he becomes.

When I look back at Matthew, he pulls up a map of the

Federation on the tablet's screen. Red dots cover the map's surface, marking where the cities are located. The Federation's territory is white, but the Outlands are designated by dark patches covering at least half of the country.

"There's forty-eight cities. We're City 45, here," I say as I point at one dot in the western half of the map. I point at a dot near the eastern border. "This is City 1, where we came from."

"Hmm."

Does "hmm" count as a response? Matthew glances around the train now, at the people, the wall screen, and the security camera on the ceiling. All trains in the Federation run underground, so there are no windows. Matthew shakes his head. "None of this is familiar."

"It'll take time." The lie tastes sour in my mouth. Here I am, promising him he'll regain his memory, when I know he won't. I'm *hoping* he won't, for his sake and mine. He needs to live. I need to pass my Final Test. We both benefit from this, even if he never understands those benefits.

"Why was I at a hospital in City 1 if we live on the complete other side of the country?" He stares at the map again. Matthew runs his finger in a straight line between the two red dots without touching the tablet's screen. "It's a long distance."

"Um." Neither Perry nor Haynes told me what to say if he asks why he was at City 1. "I guess because they have better facilities there. Injuries are rare in the Federation. Most of what the medics are trained for is handling minor illnesses, not major life-threatening incidents. Doctor Perry is one of few trained for serious injuries."

Actually, Doctor Perry's job is creating and improving medicines, but Matthew doesn't know that.

"Seems stupid."

"I'm sorry?"

"Well, I mean, you should always be prepared for accidents. Just because something doesn't happen very often doesn't mean it never will. You'd think they would have at least one good doctor in each city in case a major injury does occur. Like in my case." Matthew taps the tablet screen, making the map disappear.

There are doctors in every city who handle serious injuries, for the same reason the Council keeps the Regulators. Some things are infrequent occurrences, but they do still happen. Like Matthew's capture. Matthew is the first Intolerant to sneak into the Federation in years. It'll be another few years before another one tries to attack the Federation. The Council trains the Regulators to prepare for instances like this, things that happen once every few years. Some doctors learn to heal life-threatening wounds because, however rare, people do get hurt sometimes. How can we stay safe if we're never prepared?

But I can't tell Matthew any of this.

"Here. Give me your identification card." Standing in front of Matthew's new bedroom door, I hold out my hand. Matthew fumbles with the clasp that attaches the card to his bag. Another trainee walks past us and disappears down the hallway before Matthew manages to unclip the card and give it to me. I hold the identification card under the card scanner, until the door slides open. Matthew follows me into the bedroom.

It's a mirror image of my own, containing all the same features and furniture just on the opposite side of the room. Matthew reaches for his card, but I pull it back. "Don't ever lose this. This is important. You can get in big trouble for losing your card. Don't think you can keep it a secret if you do, either. You need this to access your apartment, to eat, to work…as I said, this is important."

"Trouble, huh?" Matthew sets his bag on the floor. I bend down and clip the identification card to the front of the bag again.

I open the door to Matthew's closet. Someone already hung up seven gray uniform shirts. His sleeping clothes and pants are folded in the drawers. An extra pair of shoes sits on the floor. I push the button on the wall and the door closes. "Not as bad as a Violation, but it does go on your permanent record. Children don't receive the cards until they turn ten."

Matthew wanders around the room. "A Violation?"

"A citizen receives a Violation for breaking the Tolerance Act, which I'll teach you tomorrow." I hold up the slender gray cord plugged into the wall. "This is to charge your tablet. I generally have to charge mine every three days or so."

"Okay." Matthew sits on the edge of the bed, shifting his gaze from one corner of the room to the next.

I sit next to him. "I don't think you've been paying much attention to me."

"I was just thinking. Sorry." Matthew runs one hand over the bed comforter. "Nothing is familiar. I don't know anything about myself. All I have is my name and what you've told me. Before I left, Doctor Perry asked me things to see what I remembered. My favorite color. The names of my close friends. What foods I like. I didn't know what to say to any of his questions. How can a person not know those things?"

Frustration marks his words. An awkward silence falls over us for several seconds. The only truth he knows is his name. Everything else he knows is a lie. A lie we've invented. "I'm sorry this happened to you."

I mean those words. We stole his memory, and I can't explain to him that we did it for his own good. Matthew believes he's the victim of a freak accident. I want to tell him everything so he'll feel better about his situation. But I can't. He's part of the Federation now. What was his life like with the Intolerants? Matthew can't remember his former life, so he won't know we only want to help him.

Matthew looks over at me, shrugging his shoulders. I never noticed before, but his eyes are brown. A deep, chocolate-like color. "It's not your fault."

There's a small stain on the white baseboard. I focus on that instead of Matthew. He *did* lose his memory because of me. "What's it like?"

"What do you mean?"

"What's it like not remembering anything about yourself? I can't imagine what that's like. It must be complete agony, not remembering who your friends are or how to do anything…"

"Well, at least I have one friend now." One side of Matthew's mouth quirks into a smile. What can I say in response? Chelsea is the only friend I've ever had, and most boys I know aren't interested in being *just friends*. "But to answer your question, I can't explain it. I know little things, like my name, but most things are just…gone. It's like a dark hole and you know something's at the bottom but you don't know how to get there."

"Sounds miserable."

He yawns. This must all be so overwhelming. Matthew fell asleep half-way through the train ride to City 45. I didn't bother waking him up until we arrived.

"You should rest. I'll be by later so I can help you some more. You're going to be seeing me a lot over the next few weeks." And I'll be reporting everything to the Council—every word he says and every move he makes. I stand, smoothing out the comforter.

"Sounds like a plan." Matthew shoots me a tired, but sincere, smile as he too stands. I hit the button on the wall and the door slides open. My bedroom is across the hall, so I don't have far to walk.

Day two, almost complete.

I lost my identification card once.

One year into my Regulator training, I walked to my apartment without realizing I didn't have my card. I searched frantically, retracing my steps all the way back to the Regulation Center. No sign of my identification card anywhere. I panicked, knowing I faced punishment for losing one of my few possessions. What thirteen-year-old wouldn't panic?

My fear only increased when Thompson exited the Regulation Center. He saw me, searching the walkway and on the verge of tears. I hoped he wouldn't ask me what I was doing, considering I hadn't found my identification card yet.

"Looking for something?"

I couldn't lie to him. He knew I lost something, even if he didn't know the lost item was my card. The sun was starting to set. I wouldn't be able to find the card in the dark, which meant I had no way to get into my room. My only option was to tell Thompson the truth.

"I lost my identification card. I don't know where it is. So—" Before I ever finished explaining things, Thompson reached into his pocket and pulled something out. I stared at the plastic rectangle in his hand. My card. He held it out to me, his amused look never disappearing. I took the identification card from him, flipping it over and reading the name and citizen number to make sure it was really mine.

"You left this in the training room," Thompson said.

I clipped the card to my bag, making sure the clasp stayed in place. I shifted from foot to foot and avoided his gaze. For the first time in years, I broke a serious rule. "Well, you're going to report this, aren't you?"

"You have your card back now, don't you? You and I are the only ones who know about this, so it'll be our little secret, okay?" My mentor smiled mischievously, then walked away. He didn't scold me about losing my card or tell me why he didn't report the incident.

We never talked about it ever again.

8

"See, let me show you how this works." Holding my identification card under the scanner, I look over my shoulder to make sure Matthew pays attention to me. It doesn't take much to distract him, so I always have to double-check before telling him something important. The screen on the card scanner lights up, displaying three meals I can choose from for dinner. I select the first option. After a few seconds, the screen fades to black. I step aside. "See? Simple."

The cafeteria bustles with activity. At least two dozen trainees sit at the tables, talking and eating and laughing. My stomach growls, reminding me I haven't eaten since an early lunch.

Matthew finishes ordering his food, so I grab his arm and pull him to the other side of the cafeteria. A good-looking guy in a brown uniform hands me a covered plastic container, then hands Matthew one, too. The overwhelmed look never leaves Matthew's face as I lead him to an empty table.

"You do this every day?" Matthew slept for several hours

this afternoon, while I played tablet games in my own apartment.

"Of course. What other option is there?" I frown, sliding into one of the chairs. I pull the lid off the container. Steam rises from each of the compartments, making my mouth water. Grabbing the fork wedged between two compartments, I start eating. Why am I so hungry? I shove a forkful of broccoli in my mouth.

Matthew sits across from me. "People don't make their own food?"

"No" How do the Intolerants live? I wonder about this a lot now, even though I shouldn't. Do the Intolerants have technology like we do? Matthew caught on to the tablet's functions quickly, so maybe they do. What kind of laws do they have and do they enforce them? Do the Intolerants actually make their own food, as Matthew puts it?

"In the Past, people didn't make good dietary choices. When the Federation came into power, they decided food needed to be regulated. The Federation determines what kinds of foods are healthy for people to eat, and also determines portion sizes to make certain people can maintain good health." I stop to take a bite of grilled chicken. "When you scan your card, it helps the Federation keep track of what you're eating and how often."

"Oh." Matthew removes the lid from his container. He ordered the same thing as me? Not that it should surprise me. How can he know what he does and doesn't like? I'm his only role model. Matthew and I eat in silence for a while, until he sets his fork down. "Can I ask you something?"

Uh-oh. He wants to talk about something serious. "Sure."

"You said we knew each other. What was I like before...you know?" Matthew picks his fork up again and stabs absently at his food. How frustrating would it be if I lost my memory and knew nothing about myself?

Haynes didn't do a good job of preparing me for any of the questions Matthew asks. Unless, of course, this is part of my Final Test. What can I say in response, except for what I know from interrogating him? I finish chewing, then say, "Well, we didn't know each other well, but you were stubborn. Easy-going, too, though."

Opinionated. Delusional. Calm in the face of death. Complicated. Unlike anyone I've ever met. I could add these things, but I don't.

"Stubborn and easy-going? Those things don't necessarily mix."

"You managed to pull it off." And he did. How could Matthew be so set in his opinions and yet at the same time be so respectful and composed? He is—was—an Intolerant, but nothing like the renegades we learn about in our history lessons.

Why wasn't he like the other Intolerants?

Chelsea plops down in the seat next to mine. "How was City 1?"

"It was...fine." I shrug.

My friend pulls the lid off her soup container. "What's up with your Final Test?"

"Oh, um, I'm not sure."

"Mindy House told me when she took hers they let her know in a few hours. Why's yours taking so long?"

"It's complicated Regulator stuff. Classified information."

"All I've heard from you is how things are 'classified'. Like anything that exciting ever happens around here." Chelsea rolls her eyes. "Whatever, though. It's not—who's this?"

She looks up from her food and notices Matthew for the first time.

"He's a friend of mine." Despite my words, she just smirks. Does she really think Matthew's my *boyfriend* and I won't tell her about it? If Matthew wasn't within listening range and I knew I could tell someone about my Final Test, I would clear the issue up real fast.

"I'm Matthew." He reaches across the table to shake her hand.

"Chelsea Newman. I've been Katherine's best friend since we were in Primary School." She flashes him a smile, which he returns in a polite sort of way. When Matthew offers no other information about himself, but instead returns to his food, Chelsea tugs on my arm. "Can we talk?"

No.

We are not going to talk about Matthew's potential boyfriend material.

"One second." I offer Matthew an apologetic smile as Chelsea pulls me out of my chair and leads me to the hall.

"Oh my gosh, Katherine. No wonder you turned down Harrison. I would have, too, if I was dating a boy as *dreamy* as this one," Chelsea whispers, a sigh escaping her lips at the end of the last sentence.

"What? No, you've got this all mixed up. I'm not dating Matthew. We're just friends, okay? End of story. I turned down your friend Harrison for other reasons." How did this conversation start?

She plants her hands on her hips. The look she fixes me with is a cross between scolding and shocked. "Anyway, he's *not* your boyfriend? Hello, Katherine. Are you insane? How can you not be dating a guy like him?"

Heat rushes into my cheeks. "We met a couple of days ago."

"And your point is...? He's *attractive*." Chelsea accentuates each syllable, saying the word in a sing-song voice. "Where'd he come from? How did you meet him? Why aren't you dating him?"

"I have more important things to do than date a guy I met a few days ago."

"If you don't, someone else will. I guarantee it."

"I don't care, Chelsea. If he wants to date someone, he can. We're just friends."

If we're even that.

"What don't you like about him?"

The fact that he's a memory-wiped, potentially-dangerous Intolerant, for starters. "It has nothing to do with whether or not I like him. I just don't want to be more than friends with him."

Chelsea rolls her eyes in a *you-are-so-dumb* way. But she still doesn't ask. She never asks. She'll never know that I don't date because there's no point in getting attached to someone when it'll just end with a broken heart.

Something I don't want.

I step out onto the walkway, the crisp morning air biting through my uniform. A faint glimmer of pale light appears over the top of the Wall. Several citizens walk past me, heading toward wherever they work each day. Matthew stands outside the building and watches everything, even though the sun hasn't fully risen yet and the world is bathed in a pale gray light.

"Why is the city walled?" Matthew runs to catch up with me as I walk down the walkway. He looks up as a few birds flutter in the dense tree branches overhead. There are few animals in the cities except for birds and the occasional squirrel.

"A group of revolutionaries still exist in the Outlands. Walls were built around every city to keep them out. For safety reasons, no one is permitted to leave the city walls. The Outlands are too dangerous."

"Makes sense, I guess." Matthew's voice trails off. I glance over at him, noting the way he squints in the dim lighting to see the Wall. "But it makes you wonder what's on the outside."

"Sometimes I do." The words just…escape. Have I ever admitted my secret out loud? I bite my lip. We're supposed to be satisfied with the life the Federation provides, not want to see what lies beyond it. There are times, however, where I wonder about the Outlands—especially now that I'm around Matthew. Being around him makes me think about things I shouldn't.

"You've never thought about sneaking away to find out?" Something very close to rebellion flickers through Matthew's eyes. A chill runs through my entire body. Me? Try to sneak out of the city?

Never.

"Matthew, look." I stop and grab Matthew's arm. "You can't say things like that. The Federation has rules in order to protect us. We can't question them or try to break them."

"You just said—"

"I know I said I wonder about things, too, but it's something I'd never act on. I shouldn't even be wondering about it.

Questioning the Federation's laws is not something we're supposed to do. Do you understand what I'm saying?"

Matthew nods, but after some hesitation. The rebellious spark doesn't leave his eyes. My palms sweat, so I wipe them on my pants. Two days. I've observed Matthew for two days and already he wants to break the law. Do I report this now or wait until Haynes requests a report? Is this a sign Reintegration is failing?

I turn away and keep walking. Can Matthew see how nervous I am? Reintegration *can't* fail. Matthew will die. I'll fail my Final Test. We both need Reintegration to succeed. Matthew's comments may be the result of curiosity and nothing more—at least I hope so.

Matthew frowns at the walkway and falls in step next to me. "I'm sorry. I didn't mean to upset you."

"It's not me you need to apologize to, Matthew. There's no need to apologize at all, actually. I just don't want you to get hurt." And I mean it. I barely know Matthew, but there's something about him that's so *likable*. Maybe it's his innocence, or his optimism, or how considerate he can be. "You don't want to be given a Violation."

Matthew shrugs his shoulders. "Does make you wonder, though."

"Today I'll show you the Tolerance Act." I sit across from Matthew, setting my tablet on the table. Thompson told me I could use one of the training rooms while teaching Matthew the Tolerance Act. Showing Matthew the Federation's core law and explaining it to him may help him understand. "The Tolerance Act was put into place sixty years ago. People were violent, causing harm to others for having different beliefs than they did. The Tolerance Act ensured people could believe what they wanted without facing persecution from others."

I push my tablet, with the text of the Tolerance Act displayed on the screen, toward Matthew. Every child is required to memorize the law, so I know each word by heart.

In order to maintain safety for all citizens, the Federation has created a new law that shall be known as the "Tolerance Act". According to this new law, every citizen shall adhere to the following principles:

1) No citizen shall declare their own beliefs, actions, or lifestyles as being the only "right" way.

2) No citizen shall condemn another citizen's beliefs, actions, or lifestyles as being "wrong".

3) Every citizen shall understand that morality is subjective.

Breaking any one of these laws will result in a Violation, the highest offense a citizen of the Federation can commit. Three Violations results in execution.

Matthew scans the document, his expression changing to one of confusion. "That makes no sense."

"What do you mean, it doesn't make sense?" My words come out curt and short despite how hard I try to sound nonchalant. Every muscle in my body stiffens. Of course the Tolerance Act makes sense.

"Well, the whole idea is nothing can ever be right or wrong, which is stupid. Something's either right or it's not."

"You're welcome to think so, but that's the purpose of the Tolerance Act. The Tolerance Act was created to show what people want to believe depends on their own personal views. No one can dictate that for them, nor can they be made to feel inferior because of their beliefs." I shrug my shoulders as if this is all no big deal. Inside, however, I want to scream.

Matthew doesn't want to abide by the Tolerance Act. If I can't convince him this is the way things are supposed to be, Reintegration will have been for nothing.

"Yes, but this is saying there is no such thing as 'right' or 'wrong'. And that's not true. *Everything* is either right or wrong. It's a fact. How can everyone be right about the same thing?" Matthew leans back in his chair, arms folded across his chest.

Spoken like a true Intolerant. "Because no one can be certain their one belief is correct. So if you can't know you're right, how could you condemn someone else for believing differently? That's the point of this."

"I understand what the point of the law is. I'm saying it just isn't logical. In a mathematic problem, for example, there's only one right answer. The same goes for everything else—science, religion, morality—someone can believe what they want, but believing doesn't make it right."

Where is he getting all this from? We erased his memory. He shouldn't even have any opinions. "Okay, well, if only one thing can ever be correct, then who determines just what the correct thing is? You? Me? The government?"

"No. " Matthew scowls. "Not us."

I let out a sigh, the result of the exasperation building up inside me. "Who, then?"

"I don't know." Matthew runs both hands through his hair, like he's trying so hard but can't think of the answer. "It's one of those things I think I should know, but I can't remember what it is."

What can I say? *Is* Reintegration failing? I set my tablet on my lap and start typing a message to Thompson. I have to go back and respell quite a bit, because my hands shake so bad I can't hit the correct buttons. Thompson is the only person who won't advocate for Matthew's immediate execution. But I need to tell someone.

I don't finish because a new message pops up, one from Chelsea.

I need to talk to you as soon as possible! I'm waiting outside the Regulation Center.

What's going on? Chelsea should be working now. Why is she here? I stand, deleting my message to Thompson. Matthew can't see it. "My friend is waiting outside to tell me something. We can go see what she wants, then work on something else, okay?"

"Sure." Matthew, too, stands. Does he think I'm changing the subject and avoiding the previous conversation? I *am* grateful for the interruption, as it will give me time to think of a response.

I don't want to turn Matthew in and inform the Council Reintegration might be failing. My attempt at saving Matthew's life could fail. I don't want to do this, but I have to. My duty as a Regulator is to protect the citizens of the Federation from the Intolerants. If Matthew does regain his memory, he could pose a threat to both myself and other citizens.

What if Matthew hasn't remembered anything? Somehow, all this talk of right and wrong seems to be something he *knows*, not something he remembers. How come he can't remember anything about himself and his past, but he is so set in his belief the Tolerance Act goes against what he's been taught?

I'm being illogical. Aren't I? Even as I exit the little training room, my thoughts drift back to our discussion. If our upbringing determines our sense of morality, how can he be so certain of his views if we erased his past? Matthew contradicts what I was taught as a child. Is he a fluke, a rare case that defies all logic? Are all Intolerants like this? Is *everyone* like this, with something inside that can never be removed?

Chelsea waits outside the Regulation Center, pacing between two of the large, shady trees by the walkway. I walk over to her, Matthew following behind. He doesn't look overwhelmed—his main facial expression of the past few days—at the moment. Instead, Matthew walks as if in a trance, his thoughts clearly preoccupied. I clench my jaw. Once my conversation with Chelsea is over, I'm telling Thompson. I need someone to help me sort out Matthew's irritating adherence to his Intolerant views.

"Thank goodness, Katherine." Chelsea runs over and hugs me. She steps back, waving her hands in the air. "Something really, really big has happened. I have to tell you. It's about my Final Test. They're giving it to me early. Tomorrow, actually."

9

They're giving Chelsea her Final Test tomorrow? She isn't supposed to take it for another few months. My friend looks like she may have a breakdown at any second. Tears well up in her big blue eyes. "I don't understand. Why are they giving it to me early? They never give trainees their tests early."

"I don't know. Maybe it's an error."

"The Federation doesn't make errors, Katherine!" Chelsea's voice rises both in volume and pitch. Matthew watches her, head cocked, lips parted slightly. I haven't told him yet how the education system works, so no wonder he's confused by this line of discussion. He doesn't know what a Final Test is or how important it is to a trainee.

He can't understand the stress of not knowing what happens when one fails the test.

"I'm sure everything will work out," Matthew, always the optimist, says when I don't offer an immediate reply to Chelsea's statement. His words don't help Chelsea relax any. I would be terrified, too, if I was Chelsea. Like she said, the Federation doesn't make mistakes. There's a reason her Final Test was assigned early.

"This test is a big deal?" Matthew's asking a question, not making a statement. He has no clue what we're talking about, but he won't ask what a Final Test is. The result of pride, not wanting to admit he doesn't know something?

"Yes, it's definitely a big deal." If Matthew's lack of comprehension as to what a Final Test is surprises Chelsea, she doesn't show it. Instead she chews on one of her fingernails. "Are they giving it to me because they think I'll fail?"

"I doubt that's it. Maybe they just really need you to officially start your occupation." I've never heard of this happening, but I've never seen Chelsea this anxious, either.

"Bailey disappeared when she failed her Final Test, remember? She was relocated or something. I don't want to be relocated."

"I think Regulation 97 talks about relocation. Or maybe it's 98? I don't remember for certain. I can look it up." I reach for my tablet, but Chelsea shakes her head. "But I know relocation doesn't apply to Final Tests, but to situations where the Council deems that punishment necessary. It's very rare"

"How do you know? No one knows what happens when we fail our Tests, Katherine! Maybe the Council deems it necessary. You're still waiting to hear back on yours, aren't you? That's not normal either."

Chelsea is correct about one thing. None of what's been happening the last few days is normal.

Matthew is especially far from normal. What he told me a few minutes ago replays in my head. Everything about that conversation and his refusal to agree with the Tolerance Act is…odd. If Reintegration worked, why doesn't he see the Federation isn't the enemy he was raised to think it is? Why does he have to stand there with that confused look on his face, calmly listening to our conversation, instead of showing himself to be the spiteful Intolerant he is deep down?

Why can't I know for certain what he's thinking, so I can just turn him in and be done with this awful assignment?

I form an idea, one that may give me some indication of what his intentions are. "Matthew? I'm going to go talk to Thompson for a few moments about our conversation earlier. You know, what we were talking about before we came out here? I need to ask him something important."

"Okay." He gives me one of his little half-smiles.

I stare at him for a moment. I'm going to go tell Thompson about Matthew's regulation-breaking comments, and all he can say is "okay"? Like I just told him I left something inside and need to go grab it?

Either he's very deceptive or very oblivious.

"You guys wait here." I walk toward the Regulation Center, expecting Matthew to ask me why or object to my leaving. But he doesn't. Instead Chelsea starts chatting with him about something trivial, as if she already forgot her anxiety about her Final Test.

I go inside and approach Regulator Weston. "Is Thompson here?"

"No, he isn't."

"Why not? Where is he?" I glance out the window, where I can see Matthew and Chelsea perfectly. He hasn't moved. Neither has she. Her mood changed really fast. My stomach clenches. She has that flirty smile on her face, and she's standing so close to him their hands almost touch.

"Trainee Holliday?"

I turn back to Weston. "Hmm?"

"I said I don't know where Thompson is. You can ask Head Regulator Olson. She'll know."

"Oh, okay. That's fine. I'll just message him later. It's not important." I don't even know what I'd say at this point. That Matthew disagrees with the Tolerance Act but has given no other indication of Intolerance? Refusing to comply with the Tolerance Act is Violation-worthy. I know that. But why isn't he acting like an Intolerant? "Thank you."

I exit the building, clipping my card back to my bag. I stop in the middle of the walkway when I hear Chelsea say, "Cool. We should totally hang out sometime. Speaking of which, are you doing anything tonight?"

"I don't think so. No? Why?" Matthew frowns at the walkway. Is he so clueless he doesn't know what she's doing? Maybe he does. He *has* to know what she's trying to do. For some unknown reason, the thought of Chelsea and Matthew dating makes me want to vomit. But why wouldn't he like her? She's certainly prettier than I am; her appearance is, as always, the epitome of perfect. Never a hair out of place. Her makeup is flawless—not that she needs it.

"I'm not doing anything tonight either. We should hang out, you know? Have a little *fun*?" Chelsea giggles. Neither of them have noticed me. I clench my hands into fists, my nails digging into my palms. I have no idea what keeps me from slapping her.

Why do I care? Like I told her, I have more important things to do with my time than date. But I know who he is. She doesn't know how polite he is or how sweet he is. She hasn't seen how *different* he is. All she knows is he's young and handsome. In a few weeks, she'll find someone better and break his heart. I know Chelsea. She'll never stop to get to know him or to learn everything I have about him. How long did she and Spencer last, anyway?

Matthew blinks. "I don't—"

Whatever he was going to say, he doesn't finish. Chelsea doesn't let him. She leans closer to him, and starts to move like she's going to kiss him. Until Matthew takes a very exaggerated step back, his eyes wide. Chelsea gapes at him. I can't help but stare at Matthew, too. Have I ever seen a guy so blatantly turn her down? Have I ever even seen a guy turn her down at all?

"Katherine!" Matthew notices me, and the relief that passes over his face is easy to detect. He doesn't so much as give Chelsea another look as he walks away, but says to me, "Weren't we just about to go do something? Maybe lunch?"

"Oh, yes. Um, I'll see you later, Chelsea. I'm sure you'll do well on your test." I catch up with Matthew, who didn't bother waiting for me. I want to mention we're walking away from the cafeteria, not toward it, but keep silent. It isn't even lunch time. What happened back there? He refused her for some unknown reason, but a not-so-nice part of me is happy he did. Chelsea doesn't deserve him.

I look over my shoulder as Chelsea spins on her heel and walks off. Who was that more embarrassing for, Chelsea or Matthew? I glance up at Matthew. "You've never had a girl flirt with you before?"

"Well, if I have, I don't remember it." He snorts a laugh, then becomes serious again. "I don't know her. That didn't feel…right."

What?

"Matthew, listen to me. You can't use 'right' and 'wrong.'" I grab his arm, making him stop. Before he can object, I hold up a hand. "I guess if you believe it, fine. But if you say it out loud, they could give you a Violation. All I'm asking is for you to keep your beliefs to yourself."

"I guess so..."

"*Please.*"

"Okay." He sighs. "If you think it's best."

"It is for the best," I insist. Why am I warning him? After lunch, I'm going to go tell Thompson what happened and inform him Reintegration is most likely a failure. I want Reintegration to work, but if Matthew refuses to abide by the Tolerance Act, then nothing else can be done.

"Seriously, though. Is she always like that? Or is it because I'm just so ridiculously charming?" Matthew's unconvinced scowl turns into a teasing grin.

"No, she's always been a flirt. But, c'mon. It's how things work. Girls and boys meet, they flirt with each other, they date for a while, they move on." I swallow, trying to hide the bitterness creeping into my voice. The breeze picks up, the piercing kind that seeps through clothing.

I expect him to make some witty remark, but none comes. Instead, his eyes soften. "You don't."

A dozen retorts flash through my mind, different things I could say to refute his statement. The problem is, he's correct in assuming I don't date. I never have, and I don't plan on it anytime soon. Everyone in the Federation dates. It's a societal norm, one I don't follow.

I'm not breaking a law. There aren't any regulations requiring girls to have boyfriends. Still...I never talk about my avoidance of this normal teenage activity. No one would possibly understand.

Then again, has anyone ever noticed? Or cared to know why I don't date?

"Well, I've grown up observing how this works. Like Chelsea, for example. She dates a guy for a while, then they break up. She pretends it doesn't bother her, but I know it does. My thought is if it isn't going to last anyway, why bother? I've had my crushes, but I've never dated anyone because I don't want to go through the heart ache of a break-up."

There. I said it. The one thing I've never told anyone before I'm now telling to someone I've known for a couple of days. I kick at the walkway, not daring to look him in the eye. He's going to think I'm being silly and childish.

"I don't believe in love." Why am I still talking about this? The words keep tumbling out. "Well, it's not that I don't believe in love. It exists, of course. I just don't believe in wasting your time on something that won't last. Love is a silly, fleeting emotion that eventually dies."

Matthew doesn't laugh or roll his eyes like most people would. "That's not the way it's supposed to be."

"Oh? How is it supposed to be?" This is the way things *are*. A lot of things were different before the Federation. They're the ways of the Past. Besides, the Federation has made certain everything is practical.

"Love isn't an emotion. Love is an action. When you love someone, you're willing to do *anything* for that person. You'll give your life for them, be willing to put aside what you want to make sure they're happy. Love is supposed to be until you die, not until you find someone you like better. You love someone because you want to be with that person and that person only, for the rest of your life."

"I stop walking altogether. "How do you know that?"

"I don't know. All I know is what you're talking about, the way people are living, isn't *right*." Matthew shakes his head. I don't even bother to correct his use of vocabulary. What is it about him? Why do I feel like he actually listens to me, in a way no one else does?

"What you're saying is crazy, Matthew. Nobody ever agrees to love someone else for so long. I've seen people date for several months at the most. Then it just ends."

"Because people are selfish," Matthew says quietly. "People aren't willing to really *love* someone because loving someone involves dedicating themselves completely to the other person. It takes work. Love isn't always easy."

I keep walking, this time in the direction of the cafeteria. Ever since Primary School, teachers told me love is temporary, the way you feel around someone you like. Love comes and goes. The idea that love can last forever is completely foreign to me, but also wonderful.

Something tugs at my heart. I *want* to know love like that. I want to know what it's like to have something you can hold on to forever. The Federation gives us things, but what we have isn't really ours.

What if the Council lies to us about love?

I lie in bed, playing a game on my tablet. I keep losing, even on one of the easiest levels. My mind drifts to what Matthew told me earlier today. Someone, at last, agrees with me on the subject of love. Not only did Matthew agree with me, but he *listened* to me in the first place. Now I have so many questions.

Is Matthew correct about love being more than an emotion?

Has the Council lied to us about love? Or do the Council Members not know themselves?

Is Matthew starting to remember his past?

What will they do to him if Reintegration fails?

Today, teaching Matthew the Tolerance Act sparked more questions than anything else. What if everything Matthew believes, the things contrary to what the Federation teaches, isn't a memory? He still seems so clueless. What if he hasn't gotten his memory back? Is everything Matthew believes a part of who he *is*, not necessarily what he *remembers*?

If this is true, than everything I've ever been taught about the Tolerance Act is false. The core foundation of the Federation revolves around the idea of relative morality and that everything we deem *right* and *wrong* is a result of our upbringing. What if Matthew proves even if someone doesn't remember what they were taught, they still have a clear sense of their morality?

Is everything I know a lie?

I close the game and pull up the messaging system. Matthew disobeyed the Tolerance Act. He doesn't even want to follow the Tolerance Act. I need to tell someone about Reintegration's possible failure. After lunch, I couldn't bring myself to tell Thompson. Matthew's words about love kept popping into my head. Am I so weak I can't do what's necessary? Taking a deep breath, I tap Council Member Haynes's name in my contact list. She's the one who I'm supposed to send my reports to if things start to go badly.

Reintegration

And the situation with Matthew couldn't be worse.

Today I showed Matthew Braddock the Tolerance Act. He strongly disagrees with the principles outline in the Tolerance Act, saying he believes 'everything is either right or wrong'—those were his exact words. Matthew's refusal to follow the law may be a sign that Reintegration failed. What do you want me to do about this? I know if Reintegration failed, Matthew could pose a threat to the other citizens in City 45.

I shift my hand to tap the icon labeled "send", but I don't select it. Do I really believe Matthew is dangerous? The other Intolerants are, of course, but Matthew never seemed violent. Unless…what if Matthew isn't an outcast among the Intolerants like I've been thinking? Maybe all the Intolerants are like him. What if everything I've been taught about them, too, is inaccurate? Do all the Intolerants believe, like Matthew, that love is more than an emotion? Do they put more effort into making a relationship last? Where else could Matthew have come up with his opinion of love? He must have learned it from somewhere.

How much has the Council lied to us about?

Maybe I'm being overdramatic. Who am I to say the Council has been lying? It's been years since the Intolerants fled from the cities. The Council Members can't know for certain what the Intolerants are like. Or maybe Matthew is rare. The other Intolerants could really be the violent, unreasonable people we think they are.

Either way, it doesn't explain why Matthew is different. Nor does it help me know what I should do. Well, I know what I *should* do. My duty is to report Matthew to Haynes. But what do I *want* to do?

Every time I think of Matthew, of his sweet smile and the sincerity in his eyes, the less turning him in sounds like a good idea. If Reintegration fails, the Council will most likely order Matthew's execution. Will I have to watch as they kill him? Will I have to do it myself?

Despite Matthew's Intolerant upbringing, I don't want him to face punishment or be executed. He's my responsibility, but it's more than that. The longer I'm around him, the more I want to *know*. I want to know who he is, who he was. I want to know more about where he grew up, what he thinks, why he feels the way he does about certain things. This isn't because I'm curious about life in the Outlands. No, something deep inside of me wants to really know *Matthew*.

I've never felt this way about a person before. Never.

I stare at the screen of my tablet, tears welling up in my eyes. What should I do? My entire life, everything has been decided for me. Now I'm faced with the one choice I have to make alone. I'm torn between duty and desire. The problem is what I want, I can never have.

I want to know more about the world Matthew grew up in.

I want to know the kind of love Matthew told me about.

I want Matthew to stay here, safe and sound, but I also want him to stay who he is.

I want to know if everything I've ever been taught is a lie.

I *want* these things so badly my heart hurts. Are these selfish desires? A sob builds up in my throat. He doesn't even know it, but Matthew has made me aware of something missing, a hole inside me somewhere I don't know how to fill.

Loneliness drifts over me. I can't tell anyone about what's going on in my head. Thompson? He may be my mentor, but he's also a Regulator. He'll give me a Violation. No matter how many rules he bent for me in the past, this is an infraction even

Thompson couldn't overlook. Chelsea would never understand. And Matthew... Matthew will hate me the second he learns how I've deceived him. I look back at my tablet. Once I tell Haynes, Matthew's fate is sealed. Turning Matthew in means I pass my Final Test. Haynes said the Council will evaluate me based on how I handle myself, not whether or not Reintegration succeeds. But how can I turn Matthew in, when I myself have wondered if the Federation is as good as I always believed it to be?

Without any more hesitation, I delete what I wrote.

10

I committed my first real act of rebellion.

I'm considering not turning Matthew in—the closest thing to treason I've ever done. I should tell Haynes. She will be strong enough to carry out the difficult tasks I cannot. But what, exactly, does carrying out the difficult tasks entail? Executing the one person who seems to understand me?

Maybe I could tell Haynes and try to convince her to let Matthew live. No, I can't do that. Telling anyone about the situation with Matthew means there's a good chance he'll die. Two questions linger in mind.

Do I tell the Council Reintegration is failing and risk Matthew's execution?

Can I keep Reintegration's failure a secret and risk receiving a Violation?

"It's been a week and I still can't remember anything."

Reintegration

Every day, Matthew comments about how he hasn't regained his memory. Today marks day seven of my Final Test. Should I submit a report to the Council today? Haynes may find it strange if I don't tell her about Matthew's progress. Not telling anyone about the possibility of Reintegration's failure isn't as incriminating as lying on an official report. Isn't it?

I set my tablet on the training room table. "I'm sorry."

"I was just hoping I'd start remembering things soon." Matthew sighs. "Maybe it's just wishful thinking."

"Don't give up hope yet. It has only been one week." Do I sound as convincing as I usually do when I tell him he'll regain his memory? I want to tell Matthew everything. I'm tired of lying to him. Every time I tell Matthew he belongs here or that he'll remember things in time, my stomach churns. Matthew thinks I'm his friend. If he learns the truth, how I've been lying to him, he won't like me anymore. What hurts more than anything else is the thought of losing Matthew as a friend. I can trust him.

He shouldn't feel the same away around me, but he does, considering how open he is with me.

"Maybe—" Matthew starts to say, then straightens up in his chair. Thompson enters the training room. He hasn't interrupted any of our meetings before. My mentor stands in the doorway, arms folded across his chest.

"Katherine, I need to talk to you."

"Okay." I stand, grabbing my tablet. What's going on? Thompson frowns at Matthew, but Matthew doesn't seem to notice. "I'll be back as soon as I can. If I'm not back by lunchtime, you go on ahead without me."

Matthew nods, so I follow Thompson out of the small training room. Why does he look so serious? He waits until the door slides closed before speaking. "Council Member Haynes needs to speak with you. She says it's really important."

"She didn't say what about?"

Thompson shakes his head, but the answer is obvious. If she's contacting us, she wants to talk to me about Matthew. Why? To inquire about why I haven't turned in a report yet? Does she know Reintegration failed? I step onto the elevator, and Thompson taps the button for the second floor. I haven't seen much of my mentor in the last several days.

"Have they given you a new student yet?" Talking to him about normal things might help ease my growing anxiety. I don't want to tell Haynes anything. Besides, I left Matthew alone. The only times I ever leave Matthew alone is during sleep times. What does he do when he's by himself?

"No, not yet. I won't be assigned a new student until you pass your Final Test."

The elevator doors open, and Thompson steps onto the second floor. For some reason, knowing Thompson can still help me provides some relief. Thompson walks to the third door on the left and uses his identification card to open the door. The communication room. The room is windowless, a large screen fixed into the far wall. Haynes contacted us using the video contacting system.

"Hello, Katherine," she says after Thompson closes the door, her expression neither pleased nor dissatisfied. "How is your Final Test going?"

"Fine." I wince. Did I say that too abruptly? "I was going to send in my report tonight."

The Council Member adjusts the buttons on her left sleeve. "That's why I'm contacting you. I thought you could come by City 1 and give your report in person this afternoon.

This is your first week, after all."

"You want me to come all the way to City 1 to give a report?" What does she want from a face-to-face meeting?

"Actually, I would appreciate it if you would bring the Intolerant as well. Doctor Perry wants to make certain Reintegration is going well. You can tell the Intolerant he needs to come for a check-up so the doctor can check on his health after the *accident*." A harsh demand lies below her kind tone.

Why does she keep referring to Matthew as "the Intolerant", like he's a scientific experiment, not a person with thoughts and feelings we've corrupted? I guess, to her, Matthew is just an experiment. To me, however, Matthew has become more than my "Final Test".

"Of course. I'll catch the next train to City 1."

"Wonderful." Haynes smiles. "I'm looking forward to hearing your report. Oh, and Katherine, you are being careful, aren't you?"

"What do you mean?"

"The Intolerants are dangerous. This one will be no different. Please, *please*, tell either Regulation Mentor Thompson or myself if Reintegration seems to be failing. I don't want you getting hurt in all this. This Intolerant…if he starts to piece together what's going on, he may play along until he finds an opportunity to cause harm to you or someone else. Please be observant and don't be afraid to inform us if something goes amiss. Reintegrating the Intolerant is not worth risking harm coming to you."

Every muscle in my body tightens. Does she know what I've done? I force a smile. "I understand. I'll let someone know the second things seem to be going…" I catch myself before saying the word "wrong". What is the matter with me? "Before

Reintegration seems to be failing."

Haynes nods, offering no indication that she noticed the slip. "I'll see you in a few hours."

Thompson pushes a button on the wall control panel, and the screen fades to black. "Don't hesitate to tell anyone if you suspect the boy of even the slightest infraction. The last thing anyone wants is for you to get hurt in all this. He's an Intolerant. I don't know why, but he didn't seem as violent as I expected when you questioned him."

Thompson noticed how different Matthew is?

"If he realizes he's been lied to…" Thompson looks away, rubbing the back of his neck. "We're treading on a fine line with Reintegration. It's been untried, so we don't know what the possible side effects are. The procedure could, down the road, cause some serious mental defects. He may not be violent now, but since we've altered his way of thinking the boy could become *unpredictable*."

Thompson's words fill me with curiosity rather than fear. Thompson *has* seen what I have. He does understand Matthew is different. My mentor doesn't think Matthew would hurt me out of his own reasoning, but he is concerned that Matthew could be damaged by the Reintegration procedure.

"I'll tell you if anything happens." Why should Thompson worry about me? I swallow down the urge to tell him the truth. Of everyone I've lied to, he and Matthew deserve it the least. But I can't tell him. No matter what happens, I can't tell anyone about my problems with Matthew.

"Thank you." There it is, the sudden gruff tone he uses after noticing any anxiety over my well-being. Maybe he'll be better with his next student and won't let himself become so attached. It was months before my bland, enigmatic mentor gave any sign of really *caring*. Thompson fights it, of course, but his concern shows every now and then. How hard is it, training a student every day for four years when you know you aren't supposed to be too involved?

"Well, I'd better go tell Matthew so we can get to the train station. I'm not sure how long this will take so we'd better get going."

"I feel fine. I don't need to see the doctor."

Matthew slouches in his train seat. Despite my best attempts, I can't suppress my giggle. He looks so serious about something so trivial. I point at the bandage wrapped around his forearm. "The good news is you'll probably get the bandage off today."

Matthew turns his arm over, then rolls down his sleeve. "Yeah, true. It's really been driving me crazy. This is the tracking device? They use this to know where everyone is?"

"It's for safety reasons. The tracking device also monitors a citizen's health. Some even say the Federation uses them to read our minds." My amused giggle turns into a nervous laugh. All I've been able to think about for the past several hours is whether or not Haynes knows I've lied. The mind-reading idea is only a rumor, but I've thought about whether or not it's true.

"That's ridiculous." Matthew snorts a laugh. "You can't be serious."

"I'm not saying I believe it." Maybe I do. The Federation always seems to know everything about us. Why can't they know our thoughts? With the technology we've developed, it could be possible. "I'd appreciate it if you wouldn't make fun of me."

"I'm sorry. I wasn't making fun of you. The idea that one person could read another person's mind is just…preposterous." Matthew nods and smiles at a citizen who walks past. He's always polite, although never overly-friendly.

I turn on my tablet. Chelsea should have been given her Final Test by now. Why hasn't she told me about it? Any time anything even remotely exciting comes up in her life, she has to tell me all about it, with every sentence ending in an exclamation point. I send her a message.

Haven't heard from you in a while. How did your Final Test go?

Matthew glances over. "What are you doing?"

"Seeing how Chelsea's test went. I haven't gotten to explain it to you yet, but a Final Test is a big deal." Why hasn't she contacted me? Is she mad at me because I couldn't tell her about my Final Test? Or does she blame me for Matthew turning her down?

"Ah."

Matthew could at least try sounding interested. Maybe he isn't because this is Chelsea we're talking about. I'm not sure he's over the whole Chelsea-flirting-with-him-when-they-just-met thing.

I slip my tablet back in my bag. "I'll explain to you how this works. A child goes through general schooling until they turn ten, when they take the Occupational Skill Determination Test. That test helps the Federation decide what field of work the child will go into. Schooling becomes more specific. Like, when I took the test, the Federation decided Regulation was the best line of work for me.

"At age thirteen, the child takes the Occupation Placement Test. That test helps the Federation determine what the child's exact future job will be. The child begins training for their particular occupation. They're assigned a mentor who provides hands-on experience. Before they turn eighteen, they're given the Final Test. The Final Test shows if the child is ready to work on their own and take on full job responsibilities."

"How do they determine what skills correlate with what job?" Matthew's curiosity at least seems to be piqued.

"They look at the child's personality, what Primary School subjects he or she had the best grades in, and teacher reports. Does the child show signs of leadership, or are they better at following orders? Is the child good in large groups, or do they prefer to work alone?"

If Matthew had been born in the Federation, they would have given him a government or scientific position. From what I know about him, he's observant, calm, analytical, and determined. If I assigned him a career, I would make him a doctor. He doesn't have the no-nonsense sort of personality most government workers do. Then again, isn't Matthew's optimistic, teasing nature part of what makes him so enjoyable to be around?

"What if the child hates what job they're assigned? Can they switch?"

"No, they can't switch. The Federation places everyone exactly where they should be." I pause. "And for the most part, citizens enjoy their jobs. The Federation chooses a field where they best belong. People are happiest when given jobs they excel in and like feeling a sense of accomplishment and knowing they're doing their very best."

"Do you like being a Regulator?"

Do I like being a Regulator? I haven't thought about it much. "I'm good at it, I guess. It's an important job. I'm taught to prepare for things to come. People aren't given Violations very often and Intolerants almost never come around, but I'm training so I know what to do if those things do happen."

"You don't sound like you enjoy it."

When I look over at him, he fixes me with those big brown eyes of his, watching me like he genuinely *cares*. No one has ever bothered to notice when I do or don't enjoy something. As a citizen of the Federation, I must do what I've been told, no questions asked. My duty is to be a Regulator. I do what I have to, regardless of my personal wants. We all have to make sacrifices to ensure the safety of the Federation.

"So you've taken your Final Test?"

"I have. I'm just waiting to see what the outcome is." I look down at the train's floor. Why is lying to him so hard? I could tell him the truth this very second, so I won't have to endure the nausea in my stomach every time I feed him another lie. "*Well, Matthew, I've been given my Final Test, but I haven't finished it yet. Do you want to hear something crazy?* You're *my Final Test. You don't belong here. I'm not your friend and I never was*". No, I can't tell Matthew the truth.

I'd lose the one person in the Federation who understands me.

Panic seizes me as the automated voice blares over the speakers, telling the passengers we've arrived in City 1. Matthew stands, hoisting his bag over his shoulder. What am I going to tell Council Member Haynes? Talking to Matthew provided the perfect distraction, but what good is a distraction when you realize it only prolonged the inevitable?

11

"I have been most interested in hearing your report."

Council Member Haynes sits down across from me at her desk. She has her own office, much bigger than Head Regulator Olson's office in City 45. White and gray, no other colors whatsoever in the well-lit room. I rest my hands on the arms of my chair, the metal cold to the touch.

I left Matthew alone at the medical center. What was I thinking? I left clueless, unsuspecting Matthew *by himself* with Doctor Perry. I should have waited until his appointment ended to come see Haynes. How long will Doctor Perry's tests take? What is he even doing to Matthew? Haynes wasn't very clear when she told me Matthew needed to come to City 1. What is Doctor Perry talking to him about?

Will Matthew tell the doctor how he feels about the Tolerance Act? He won't be given a Violation. Because Matthew's already an Intolerant, if he breaks the law, the logical solution will be to execute him.

"Katherine?" Haynes prompts, jarring me back to the present moment.

"Oh, yes. I'm sorry." I fidget in the chair. Can she detect my nervousness? "There isn't much to report, I'm afraid."

"Not much to report?" Haynes raises her eyebrows. Then she laughs. "Surely you have more to say."

"Matthew Braddock has been adjusting well. I've shown him around the city, explained the Tolerance Act to him, and so far, he's responded well. Will he begin working tomorrow?"

Short and to the point.

"That was the plan, yes. But you're certain? Nothing he's said or done has led you to believe Reintegration will fail?" Why is she so pushy? "The last thing we want to do is start treating him like a citizen and allowing him more freedom if he doesn't deserve it."

I twirl a lock of hair around my finger, unable to shake the feeling that she knows I'm not giving her the truth. How she could know such a thing is beyond me. "I am certain. From what I have seen, Reintegration is a success. Matthew has shown no signs of being a threat to the Federation."

I lick my lips. My stomach churns with the same feeling I get whenever I lie to Matthew. Why? I'm lying to help him, not hurt him.

Lying about Reintegration's failure isn't a permanent solution. Sooner or later, someone else will have a conversation with Matthew and learn what I have. I've put myself in a horrible situation, but I have to try to save Matthew's life. I'm the only friend he has.

I'm the only one who won't turn him in.

Reintegration

It's strange to think of Matthew as my *friend*. Chelsea has been the only friend I've ever had. What Matthew and I have though...feels deeper. One week ago, would I have been willing to lie to a superior to save someone else from possible execution? I'm risking receiving a Violation, which should terrify me, but doesn't. All I've been able to think of is making sure Matthew stays safe.

"It's only been one week. Time will tell if Reintegration is a true success. I am happy to hear things are going well so far." Haynes smiles, but it seems a little forced. Is she *disappointed* that Reintegration is succeeding? Or is she disappointed in me because she knows I'm lying to her?

She glances down at her tablet on the desk. After turning it on, she starts typing a message to someone. From where I sit, I can't read what she's writing. A few seconds pass and Haynes looks up. "Tomorrow the Intolerant will begin working. You'll need to observe him there for a few days. What's important now is making sure he hasn't been lying to you. If there's any chance he's learned about Reintegration, he could be deceiving you."

"Matthew wouldn't lie to me." She doesn't know him like I do.

Haynes blinks, surprise flickering across her face. Panic seizes me. Why did I have to sound so defensive? A slow, amused grin tugs at the Council Member's lips. "So you've grown fond of the Intolerant?"

"Well, I...I just don't think it's fair to assume he intends to cause harm when there's no evidence of it," I say, calmer this time. "I've been observing him, and he shows no sign of animosity toward me or the Federation."

Haynes's tablet beeps. She taps one finger on the desk's

surface, then types out another message. "You need to be careful, Katherine. I can understand why you may feel the way you do. He's an attractive young man, so I should have suspected this could happen. Don't let a teenage crush distort your perspective."

How shallow does she think I am? "I promise you, I'm not letting a 'crush' blind me to Matthew's Intolerance. I understand he *could* pose a threat, but I don't think so. You haven't been around him the way I have. You haven't seen how he's been kind and considerate toward me and any other citizen he's come into contact with. I mean this as objectively as possible, but I don't think Matthew poses a threat to anyone."

Haynes sighs. "I'll trust your opinion on this matter. I just wanted to warn you."

"I appreciate the warning." And I really do. She doesn't want me to get hurt in all this.

Haynes pushes her tablet aside, leaning back in her chair. "Katherine, has your mentor ever told you about his Final Test?"

"No." Thompson's Final Test is one of those topics he and I don't discuss. He made things very clear when I asked him a week ago what his Final Test was.

"Your mentor's Final Test was years ago, before you were even born. I'd been on the Council for about three years. The Federation hadn't had to deal with Violations in a very long time."

How do Violations relate to Thompson's Final Test?

"One of the other trainees was a good friend of your mentor's. This friend received three Violations in a one-month period. As you know, a citizen receiving three Violations in their lifetime is rare, but in that short amount of time? Unheard of.

I was called in to help investigate the issue, and we learned this trainee had become affiliated with the..." Council Member Haynes stops, then clears her throat. "He had become affiliated with a small remnant of the Intolerants. The Intolerants had deceived him into hating the Federation.

"The Council was uncertain as to how these circumstances affected your mentor. We decided the only way to ensure that he, too, hadn't been corrupted by Intolerant propaganda was to see how he performed his Final Test. The other Council Members and I specifically chose the assignment to fit the situation." During her entire speech, Haynes watches me with a studying gaze. Where is she going with this? "The punishment, as you know, for three Violations is execution."

She doesn't say anything else. My mind struggles to process her words. Of course, it makes sense...Thompson refused to tell me what his Final Test was, only that the assignment was a "rare occurrence". But what Haynes wants me to believe can't be true.

"Are you telling me Thompson *executed* his own friend?" My attempt at keeping my voice steady makes my words come out in an angry whisper. I grip the arms of the chair, the only thing keeping me from jumping to my feet. This isn't true. She has my mentor's Final Test confused with someone else's. Thompson couldn't have executed his friend. He's the man who did something Violation-worthy but didn't turn himself in for it. He's the man who didn't report my lost card all those years ago, the man who didn't want Matthew killed.

He's the kind of person who dares to break the rules to help someone else.

"You sound surprised. You shouldn't be. If we allowed

every citizen who committed multiple acts of treason to go unpunished, the Intolerants would have won years ago. I told you about his Final Test to help you understand what being a Regulator entails. Regulators are the ones who carry out the orders that guarantee peace and safety. For this reason, Phillip Thompson is a brilliant Regulator. He did what had to be done for the preservation of the Federation, and I'm sure he would do it again if the need arose. Why do you think the Council chose to put him in the mentorship program?"

Haynes sounds so nonchalant, so passive. I wanted to know the truth. Now I wish I could go back and unlearn what Haynes told me. Thompson did what was necessary. His actions reflected a determination to protect the Federation. Don't we all strive to have the same attitude? Why, then, does the knowledge of what he did make me feel sick inside?

No matter what he did two decades ago, Thompson wouldn't do it again. Would he? His words from the train station linger in my mind. *Sometimes I wonder if safety was really worth everything else we lost*. Those aren't the words of a man who would do anything to preserve the Federation. Did his Final Test make Thompson believe there are more important things than safety?

Haynes doesn't know Thompson's perspective has changed. She doesn't know about his own Violation, whatever it was. She doesn't know what he told me at the station. Hope replaces my shock. Thompson fooled the Council for years and is still doing so.

If he can get away with it, so can I.

I glance at the clock on her desk. Forty-five minutes have passed since I left him at the medical center. "Well, I had better go see if Matthew's check-up is finished. The last thing I'd want is for him to suspect where I went."

"That's probably for the best. I'm glad we had this little chat." The plastic smile on her face makes my blood run cold. She knows I've lied to her. Does she know *why* I've lied to her? Does she know Reintegration is a failure? If she knows, though, wouldn't she have confronted me about it? "Just remember what I've told you, Katherine."

"I will." How could I forget anything she just told me? I stand and grab my bag off her spotless tile floor.

Without another word, I exit her office.

I sit down in the lobby of the medical center. Where is he? The lady at the front desk told me she didn't know when Matthew's appointment was over, but I could wait for him. Needing a distraction, I turn on my tablet. No reply from Chelsea. Why won't she tell me about her Final Test? She must be mad at me.

As the minutes pass by, my nervousness increases. What if Matthew told Doctor Perry he disagrees with the Tolerance Act? What if they're executing him this very second, and I can do nothing to help him? I'm a horrible liar. I always have been. Maybe Haynes told Doctor Perry she didn't believe me.

I look at my tablet screen. One hour. Matthew's been with Doctor Perry for an hour. My check-ups back in City 45 never took longer than fifteen minutes. I start playing a game, trying to calm my frantic nerves.

"Katherine?"

I glance up, then shove my tablet into my bag. Matthew stands not three feet away, alive and well and perfect and smiling. If I wasn't trying to appear casual, I would hug him. Instead I stand and gather up my things. The frantic pounding of my heart lessens, but only a little.

"Go ahead and wait for me outside. I'll be there in a second," I tell Matthew. Doctor Perry stands by the front desk, speaking with the lady who told me where to sit.

"Okay." With his typical, obedient nod, Matthew shoves his hands in his pockets and walks out of the medical center. I don't move until the door closes behind him. Even then, I wait a few more seconds before walking over to Doctor Perry. He glances over at me, ending mid-sentence.

"Can I help you, Trainee Holliday?" The doctor's words are pleasant. He walks away from the desk and toward the middle of the room. Even the polite young lady at the desk can't know about Reintegration?

I follow after him. "So everything looks fine? Reintegration is going well?"

"Oh, yes. As far as I can tell, the procedure is a success. Council Member Haynes contacted me a little while ago to ask that same question." Is Doctor Perry who Haynes messaged in our meeting, to confirm what I told her? "It's too early to make a definite analysis, but I'm satisfied so far. Even if things fail in time, we've made considerable strides in trying to merge the Intolerants into our society. He seems to be adjusting?"

"Yes. I think he'll fit in just fine in the Federation." Another lie. "Well, I'd better let you get back to your work."

I walk outside, the warm breeze a sudden change from the sterile smells of the medical center. Doctor Perry doesn't suspect Matthew of anything. Hopefully, he'll report to Haynes and she won't suspect me of foul play anymore. For being such an awful liar, I've done a lot of it lately.

Reintegration

Matthew stands on the walkway, sleeves rolled up, wind tousling his hair. The bandage around is arm is gone now. Why did the Intolerants choose him to come here? Why did they have to send the sweet, innocent boy who doesn't deserve any of this? As I walk over, Matthew grins. "I'm glad we're done. I decided I don't like hospitals."

Hospital. Few people, other than some of the older citizens, use the word in the Federation. Despite my previous panic, his words make me smile. In such a short amount of time, Matthew decided he doesn't like going to the medical center? Maybe he wouldn't make a good doctor, after all. This is why I'm a Regulator, not a teacher.

"Everything went okay?"

"Yeah. He said he wasn't surprised my memory hasn't returned yet. He said one week isn't long enough to tell if I'll start remembering things." Matthew kicks at a loose stone on the walkway, watching it skitter away. "Thanks for waiting for me."

"Oh, of course." Heat rushes into my cheeks. I didn't tell Matthew I would be meeting anyone today. He would only ask questions, and the fewer lies I have to tell, the better. How much longer can I keep up with all this? I've lied to everyone—Matthew, Thompson, Haynes, Perry. Soon, there won't be anyone I haven't lied to.

"Are you okay?" Matthew watches me with a baffled look on his face, cocking his head slightly. "You seem kind of upset."

The desire to tell him the truth grabs hold of me. He deserves to know we were never acquaintances and the reason I'm standing here with him is because he's my Final Test. He deserves to know how we've stolen his memories and how we've tried to strip away everything that makes him who he is.

The Federation isn't where he belongs. He belongs in the Outlands somewhere, with his own friends and rules and interests.

What is this feeling, this emotion I have no words to describe? It sits in my stomach and churns like when food doesn't settle properly. It makes me want to cry and scream at the same time. This feeling makes me despise myself.

But I don't have a word for it.

The truth is there. All I have to do is tell him. What I'll say to him sits in my mind. Those words, however, never make it to my mouth. I'm selfish. I want Matthew to stay here with me, instead of letting him return to where he belongs. Once I explain things to him, he'll hate me. Regardless of everything I've done so far to help him, I'm still the one who did this to him.

What will I do when someone finds out about Matthew?

What will I do when Matthew finds out about *me*?

"I'm fine." My eyes burn from welled-up tears. I turn away and continue walking down the walkway. He can't see me cry. I can't let him know how weak and self-absorbed I am. "We need to hurry if we're going to catch the next train."

Matthew falls in step next to me. I don't dare look at him, but I imagine the worry etched into his face and the confusion in his eyes. He doesn't deserve this. As much as I want him to stay here with me, another part of me wants him to be able to go back to the Outlands. He's an Intolerant, and that's what he'll always be. We can try to steal everything from him, even his thoughts, but he'll always be *Matthew*.

He'll always be the sweet, innocent boy who knows what he believes and won't let anyone change it for him.

He'll always be the one who defies everything I've been told, the one who makes me wonder if there's something more than what the Federation has to offer.

12

I have to know the truth.

If what Haynes told me about my mentor *is* the truth, then I have one of the pieces that fits into the puzzle of Thompson's life. I left Matthew back at the apartments, promising him I'd meet him for dinner. I need time to be alone before confronting Thompson about his Final Test.

Matthew and I didn't talk much on the train ride home. My abruptness after his appointment dampened his cheery mood. I shouldn't have been so curt with him. It's not his fault he was Reintegrated and has no clue about his place of birth or identity. It's not Matthew's fault I'm a selfish, weak coward who claims to be his friend but who can't bear to do something as simple as telling him what he is.

I walk down the hallway of the Regulation Center. Where is Thompson? He's not in any of the training rooms, where I usually find him. Did he leave for the day already? He doesn't have any major responsibilities while he's between students. With a sigh, I approach the always-annoyed Regulator Vail. If anyone knows where Thompson is, it's him.

"Hello. Do you know where Thompson is?"

Vail gives me nothing more than a bored glance, although it's more than he gave me when I first entered the building a few moments ago. "Where's your Intolerant friend, Trainee Holliday?"

"I don't think that's relevant. You didn't exactly answer my question. Where's Thompson? Did he leave already?"

Vail taps the screen of his tablet. "Ah, well, he's contacting the Council at the current moment."

Why does Thompson need to contact the Council? "Thank you." I continue walking toward the elevator.

I arrive on the top floor and step into the empty hallway. Thompson's contacting the Council. Why? Doesn't Head Regulator Olson handle communication with the other cities? My heart skips a beat. He's contacting the Council about me. What other explanation is there? Thompson knows I lied to him about Reintegration. He's going to tell Haynes. Maybe Thompson isn't as reckless as I think.

The door to the communication room slides open. I slip around the corner, not wanting to be seen. When I risk a glance into the hallway, Thompson exits the communication room and strides for the elevator. Conversation over? His back is to me as he pushes the button on the wall for the main floor. What did he tell the Council? If he told them about me, then Matthew's fate is sealed. If not…

Why else would he need to contact someone?

I need to know what he said. If Thompson gave away my secret, then I need to know what to do about Matthew. My mentor disappears into the elevator. Using my identification card, I enter the communication room. The door closes behind me with a *hiss* and a *click*. Adrenaline rushes through me.

I grope my hand along the wall until I find the button for the lights. I look over the room, taking in the wall screen, the control panel on the wall, and a table. Do they record all the conversations? If so, can the recordings be accessed? I tap the control panel screen, half-expecting an alarm to go off. None does, so I scroll through the list of options. I tap an icon labeled "recent transmissions".

Sure enough, the screen displays the ten most recent communications sent between cities, providing the date. I select the first and most recent item, a communication involving Amelia Haynes. So Thompson did contact her. A feeling of betrayal washes over me. Thompson, who I thought I could trust, turned me in to the Council. How does he know the truth? I need to know where I slipped up.

With shaking hands, I tap one of the icon. An audio recording of their conversation plays through a speaker on the lower left-hand corner of the panel. Thompson's voice. Haynes's voice. I skip through the pleasantries. How much time do I have before someone else enters the communication room and finds me here? I stop the recording about thirty seconds into it.

"*...although I was going to contact you in the morning about some things. I would like to say I'm concerned about your student.*"

Haynes doesn't sound pleased.

"*Concerned?*"

Thompson doesn't sounds happy, either.

"*Yes. I have to say, I was not....satisfied with the report Katherine gave this afternoon. I couldn't shake the feeling she was hiding something from me. I believe your student is withholding important information about Reintegration."*

Stupid, stupid, stupid. I was too defensive earlier.

"Katherine? Lie to you? That's ridiculous. You told me you chose Katherine for this because you believed she was the most promising trainee in the Federation."

Key word being *was*.

"I did believe that, but the report she gave today was not what I expected. She was firm in that Reintegration is a success, and I was inclined to believe her. The more I thought about it, however, the more I realized she had been very short and defensive in her answers to my questions. I don't know what's going on, but Katherine is not being honest."

Haynes does suspect me of hiding information. What will she do? The only hope I have at this point of saving Matthew is that the Council Member can't prove anything. This is all speculation. She *thinks* I'm lying about the Reintegration results.

The lack of proof is the only thing keeping Matthew from execution and me from receiving a Violation.

"Why would Katherine lie to you about this? In lying, she would fail her Final Test and most likely be given a Violation. Katherine's a smart girl. She would know lying would only hurt her, and I see no benefit she could possibly gain from it."

Wait—Thompson defended me? Why else would he contact her, if not to tell her of some infraction on my part?

"I'm not sure."

Frustration underlies every syllable of Haynes's words. Earlier she suggested I had a crush on Matthew, but maybe she decided that wasn't good enough. She honestly doesn't know why I'm helping Matthew.

Neither do I. Helping Matthew defies all logic and reason.

Reintegration

It goes against everything I've been taught. I've never felt this way around anyone else, like I'd give up everything I have to help them.

"*If you want, I can speak with her.*"

"*No, I'd rather not alert her to the fact she's under suspicion. Time will tell what is going on. Doctor Perry told me he believes Reintegration is working as planned. Katherine's behavior is what's giving me second thoughts.*"

"*I don't understand. Doctor Perry is convinced Reintegration is a success. Katherine told you Reintegration is a success. I've been around the boy on a few occasions myself, and nothing has given me reason to suspect otherwise. I don't understand why you're accusing my student of betraying the Federation! If you should be concerned about anything, it's how Katherine could be affected if this doesn't go as planned.*"

I've never heard Thompson sound this angry. He was upset because Haynes accused me of treason? He's worried about my safety, not whether or not I betrayed the Federation? Heat rushes into my cheeks. There it is, the feeling I get whenever I lie to Matthew. I thought Thompson turned me in, but instead he's arguing with Haynes over my innocence.

"*I'm always struck by the excessive care you show toward your student. You're her teacher, not her protector. Katherine is almost an adult. It's time we started treating her as such. If she has betrayed the Federation, she will have to face the consequences.*"

"*I feel a certain amount of responsibility for Katherine. My main priority for the past several years has been to prepare her to be a productive member of society. If she gets hurt in the process, I'd feel like I've failed my duty as her mentor.*"

"*I can't say I understand, but if that is how you feel, I suppose I can't argue. Now. What was it you contacted me about?*"

"*Not to question the honesty of my student. I do wish to inquire about yours, though."*

"*My honesty? You must be joking.*"

Haynes laughs, as if to accentuate her point.

"*I'm not. Earlier today, I found files indicating Reintegration was tried before, about three years ago. And the procedure failed. Within two weeks, the subject regained memory and had to be executed. I'm not certain why you never felt the need to disclose this information.*"

Reintegration was attempted before and failed? The word *executed* stays in my mind. I've always known Matthew will be executed if the procedure failed, but hearing someone else confirm it yet again is…painful. Several questions flicker through my mind.

What were the circumstances?

Why did it fail?

Who was it performed on?

"*I don't see what the big concern is.*"

Was Haynes nervous? Her voice rose in pitch at the end of that sentence.

"*The concern is that Reintegration failed once before, but you still wanted to put Katherine in a situation where she could be harmed. If I had known—*"

"*If you had known about it, you would what? Not allow her to assume this as her Final Test? Convince her execution was the better route? Katherine's participation in this was not for you to decide, but the Council. As for the choice she was presented with, it was hers alone to make.*"

He contacted her about the first case of Reintegration? I tighten my grip on the strap of my bag. How could I have honestly thought Thompson held any ill intentions toward me? My mentor tried to save me from being brought into this mess in the first place. He wouldn't report me over losing my identification card. He gave me a stun weapon before I deserved one.

"*You never bothered to tell either Katherine or myself the previous results. You didn't provide her with all the information.*"

The tone Thompson uses reminds me of when he debated with Haynes over whether or not involving me in this was a good idea.

Defiance.

"*I didn't hide the files from you either, Regulation Mentor Thompson. They were always available to you, you just never bothered to look. As for Reintegration's previous failure, Doctor Perry has spent three years striving to perfect the formula.*"

"*What other files are available to me I haven't had the opportunity to look at yet? What other important information am I unaware of because no one ever bothered to tell me it existed?*"

"*Regulation Mentor Thompson, if you continue this line of discussion I'll have no choice but to give you a Violation.*"

Every muscle in my body goes tense. She wouldn't give him a Violation for asking questions about this, especially since they are legitimate concerns, would she?

Somehow, everything I know about the Council Member tells me she would.

"*I've said all I need to say.*"

How is Thompson brave enough to push the limits, but careful enough to know when not to cross over the line? I've always been more careful than brave. I never push the limits, no matter how much I want to. I once believed that nothing is worth defying the Federation for. Now I'm breaking every law in the Federation, and I can't even explain why.

I shut off the recording. Thompson risked receiving a Violation, all to make sure I would be safe. He may be my mentor, but in a strange way, he's also my friend. I push the button by the door that turns off the lights, then push the one above it. The door opens. No one caught me doing this.

"Katherine? Regulator Vail told me—what are you doing?"

I stiffen. The hallway is empty, except for Thompson, who stands a few feet away, a dumbfounded look on his face. I can't feign innocence, not when he witnessed me leaving the communication room, somewhere I never go by myself.

The door closes behind me. I can lie, like I have for the past week. Isn't there some excuse I can find? A few seconds pass. No, I've lied to Thompson long enough. He's done nothing but help me, and all I've done is deceive him. My mentor deserves to know the truth. "I heard you contacted the Council Member. I listened to the conversation. I thought you had…"

I let my voice trail off. If Thompson didn't turn me in, how much does he know about Matthew and Reintegration?

"You thought I *what?*"

"I thought you turned me in." I duck my head, unable to meet his gaze. What I said affects him, though. He rubs his temples, sighing. When I do make eye-contact with him at last, I want to go back and undo the last ten minutes of my life. He looks hurt. Wounded. I've caused him pain, and I want to take it back. "I assumed you knew about Reintegration."

Thompson folds his arms across his chest. "I suspected."

"But you didn't tell her."

"Why would I tell her?" The hurt doesn't leave Thompson's eyes. In a way, he reminds me of a Primary School child who's been accused of and punished for something he didn't do.

I shift from foot to foot. "Because Reintegration failed and I didn't tell you. That warrants a Violation, doesn't it? I broke the rules. You're a Regulator, so you should report it. Why didn't you tell her?"

"Because I know you, Katherine. You aren't like the Council Members or other Regulators. I know that when you look at the boy, you see more than an outcast who has no place in our society. You don't see an experiment. I know you look at that boy, and you see something more than I think any of the rest of us are capable of seeing." Thompson shakes his head. "I think I know why you chose Reintegration. You genuinely wanted to help him, and you didn't want to be the one to declare him deserving of execution. You chose Reintegration because you chose the option you believed benefitted *him*, not the Federation."

There isn't a trace of condemnation in my mentor's voice. He doesn't think choosing Matthew over the Federation is a bad thing? I bite my lip to keep from crying. "I've failed my duty as a Regulator and a citizen. I knew execution would be safer, but I—"

"Safety isn't everything, Katherine. There are more important things." Thompson places his hands on my shoulders. "You're strong. Are you risking receiving a Violation because you don't want Matthew Braddock to die? Yes. And it's one of the bravest things I've seen done in a long time. If you'd chosen execution, I don't think you would be happy with yourself."

For once, he compliments me without covering it up with a bland, disinterested comment. Why can't he yell at me, instead of praising me and acting like he's proud of me? I've hurt the one person I can trust. He deserves a better student than me. "Thank you for defending me, and I-I'm sorry."

"Well, I suppose I would have done the same thing." Thompson lets his arms fall back to his sides. "Regulator Vail told me you needed to talk with me about something?"

After all this, how can I ask him about his Final Test? Is what Haynes said even true? If it isn't, then I'll hurt Thompson further. "Oh, I was going to tell you about something Haynes mentioned earlier. It doesn't matter, though."

"Really? You came all this way, but it doesn't matter?" As always, Thompson can see through me in a way no one else can. "Oh, of course. Because she told you." When I don't say anything, he adds, "Did you listen to the entire conversation?"

How much more was there? "No. I shut it off after Haynes said she'd give you a Violation."

"Yes, well, she explained to me how she told you about my Final Test." Now Thompson looks embarrassed. "She also said you didn't take the news very well. I don't blame you. Yes, my Final Test involved executing someone I knew well. I didn't even know what he did, but that was my assignment. And I carried it out. You're stronger than I am, Katherine. You're stronger than most people. You're the only one of us strong enough to do the hard thing."

What Haynes told me is true. Thompson was an executioner. "So you no longer believe safety is the most important thing because you had to do something you didn't want to do."

"That, and some other things." Thompson falls quiet. Lost in his thoughts? I wait, but he doesn't expand. Why does he have to be so mysterious about everything?

But I've pushed him enough already.

"What should I do? I can't lie forever. Someone's going to find out about Matthew." I keep my voice low, even though we're the only ones in the hallway. "If Reintegration already failed once, Haynes will be especially skeptical of me."

Thompson glances around, like he, too, expects another Regulator to show up and overhear us. "Well, the only thing you can do is find a way to get him back to the Outlands. If he learns the truth of what's going on, it'll be difficult for both of you to keep the secret. Even if you could, he'd still be unhappy here."

I nod. Matthew doesn't belong here and he never will. I can delude myself all I want into thinking he'll eventually grow to be content in the Federation, but part of him will always know he doesn't belong here. My tablet beeps, so I pull it out of my bag. I read over the abrupt message from Matthew.

Where are you?

If I stay here any longer, he'll be suspicious. What excuse can I give him for being at the Regulation Center so long? I slip my tablet back in my bag, not bothering to send him a reply. "I need to go now. I really am sorry."

Thompson shrugs his shoulders.

I walk toward the elevator, not ready to see Matthew again. How can I look at him without remembering every lie I've told him? He's so trusting, and I've ruined his trust by deceiving him from the day we met. He knows so little, and what he does know is pure falsehood.

I can't sleep.

Dinner with Matthew was uncomfortable, to say the least. The whole time I ate, I kept thinking back to what Thompson told me. Matthew will never be happy here, despite how much I *want* him to be. He may not remember, but Matthew is an

Intolerant. The Federation can never be his home.

Which means I have to figure out how to get him to his real home.

But where is Matthew's home? I've never set foot outside the Federation, and Matthew has no memory, as far as I know, of his pre-Reintegration life. I can't send him to the Outlands and hope he ends up where he needs to be. Do I wait and see if he regains his memory soon? No, the longer I wait, the more I risk someone learning Reintegration failed. Besides, what if Matthew never regains his memory or it takes years for him to do so?

Is there a way to give him his memory back sooner?

All that matters now is making sure no one learns about Matthew. The best way to keep this a secret is if Matthew *knows* he needs to keep a secret. And I've kept so many things from him. It's time to make the hard choice.

I have to tell Matthew the truth.

13

"Are you okay? You've been acting funny lately."

I glance at Matthew. Maybe Thompson isn't the only one who can see through me. Then again—Matthew has no clue I've lied to him. He always seems genuinely interested in how I'm doing. He cares about me. Why can't I be selfless, like him?

"If something's bothering you..." Matthew tears a corner off his piece of toast, the same thing he orders every morning. Soon the nutrition experts will notice his lack of variety when it comes to dietary choices. "Have I said something to hurt you?"

"What? Of course not. You haven't done anything at all." It's me. I'm the problem in all of this. I stir my oatmeal around in my bowl, but I haven't eat much of it. Food has no appeal. What will Matthew do when I tell him who he is? How will he react when he learns how awful I am? Will he still smile at me like he usually does?

Of course he won't.

"Are you sick?" He persists, shoving the last of his food in his mouth. Today he starts work, but he doesn't seem at all daunted by the added responsibility.

I sigh, pushing my bowl aside, unable to eat any more. "Can I talk to you outside for a second? I have something really important I need to tell you. I've put it off long enough."

"Sure." Matthew stands, grabbing my untouched bowl and his empty plate. He walks toward the bin for the dirty dishes, navigating through the busy cafeteria. Why do I have to do this? Why couldn't he have stayed in the Outlands, where he belongs? He deserves to know the truth, yes, but I can't bear knowing my short friendship with Matthew will end.

I rise to my feet and walk outside, my head hammering from the din of the cafeteria. Or is it from thinking so hard about what I'm going to say? I stand on the empty walkway. Most people are still eating breakfast inside. There won't be a better opportunity to tell Matthew everything, when no one can overhear.

Matthew exits the cafeteria building and stands near me. I start to say something, but the words die in my throat.

I can't do this.

I can't tell him.

As if unnerved by my lack of dialogue, Matthew rubs the scar on his arm, something he does now that the bandage is gone. He won't be prepared for what I'm going to tell him. He hasn't suspected a thing, at least not that I'm the biggest phony he'll ever meet. How can he understand the ways I manipulated him?

He doesn't know what a horrible excuse for a friend I am.

"You're going to hate me," I whisper, hugging myself.

Why is it so cold all of a sudden? The sky is gray overhead, an abrupt change from the sun and warmth of the past few days. Matthew will never speak to me again. He won't tell me about love. He won't ask me questions because he'll know everything I told him prior to now has been a lie.

When I chose to Reintegrate Matthew, I never thought I would actually be friends with him. I thought he'd be like I was told he would be. My intention was to spend six weeks helping him adjust and then be done with him. Instead he's kind and curious and handsome and I find myself wanting to be around him *more*.

"Don't be silly. I would never hate you."

"You don't know what I've done." I turn away, fighting to steady my voice. Can he tell I'm shaking? Does he know I'm going to cry at any second? I'm about to lose the one person I've grown to care about in a way I don't even understand. "You couldn't possibly comprehend what I've done to you."

"What you've done *to me*?" Matthew snorts a cute little laugh. "You haven't done anything."

Why is he making this so much harder than it already is? The longer I procrastinate, the less likely I am to do what needs to be done. I take a deep breath. "Matthew, you aren't from the Federation."

I spit the words out as fast I can, and they come out in a jumbled blur.

There. I said it.

Tears burn my eyes as I wait for Matthew to be angry with me. What will he do? Matthew blinks, then one side of his mouth quirks into a smile. "I think it's a little too early in the morning for jokes, Katherine."

He thinks I'm making this up? Matthew should know by

now I'm not one to pull pranks. Then again—this whole situation is close to absurd. Why would Matthew believe he's a captured Intolerant whose memory the Federation took away? Why would he believe he's a freak science experiment? I wouldn't believe it either.

If he doesn't believe me anyway…I can force a smile, laugh, and reassure his idea that I'm making a joke. My trusting friend would be no more than a little annoyed with me. Annoyance is better than hatred.

No.

Lying again will ruin my chance of saving his life. I can't continue to be so selfish. I'm caught in the trap I created for myself. The only person to blame for this…is me. I have to find a way to convince him he really is an Intolerant. "There was no explosion where you hurt yourself. You didn't get amnesia because you hit your head falling. We took your memory from you. My job has been to lie to you to make certain you believed you were from the Federation."

Matthew's expression goes from amused to blank, like my words haven't sunk in yet. He stares straight ahead and doesn't move, not even when a communication worker brushes past him. Does he believe me now?

"You aren't a citizen here. You're an Intolerant, from the Outlands. For some reason you came here and were captured. The Council wanted to try an experiment and see if one of your people could be merged into the Federation. They called it Reintegration. We're all taught what a person believes is based on their background, so the plan was to erase your memory and see if we could convince you that you were one of us. My job was to make sure Reintegration worked. That was my Final Test. My work would be evaluated at the end of six weeks and

I'd receive my full Regulator duties." I don't stop for a breath, not until everything is out.

"So if what you're saying is true, I don't know anything about myself but the things I do know are a lie?" This is the closest thing to anger I've ever heard in Matthew's voice. He rakes his fingers through his hair in a typical Matthew-gesture. A look of shock, betrayal, confusion and hurt passes over his face. I focus on a small chip in the walkway. If I look him in the eye, I'll see the pain there, too.

A pain I caused.

"I'm so, *so* sorry, Matthew. I honestly thought I was helping you. They told me I could either choose Reintegration or execution. I'd met you and decided I couldn't kill you. All I wanted was to give you a chance to be safe, here in the Federation." Tears slip down my cheeks. The ache inside is unbearable, but I deserve it. "I have no excuses to offer. All I've done is lie to you because I didn't want you to learn you were my Final Test. The reason I'm telling you now is because I've grown to like you and I think of you as a friend...as my *best* friend." Even more so than Chelsea. "I need you to know the truth because I can't lie to you anymore. I can't."

Matthew doesn't say anything, which only prolongs my agony. He stares off into space, an almost dazed look in his eyes. Does he understand? "So, what now? I don't belong here because I'm a criminal. I can't go home because I don't know where home is. The one person I thought I knew just told me she's lied to me the entire time we've known each other."

His words are hollow and lifeless. How else should he feel? I told him he's a scientific experiment, a captured rebel who doesn't belong here. This is my fault, so I need to fix it—even if Matthew doesn't want my help.

"I-I need you to listen to me for a second. I know I've hurt you and you deserve to be angry with me. But you need to hear me out. If anyone finds out Reintegration's failed and you know the truth, they're going to execute you. Then you'll certainly never get home. If you listen to me, I can try to buy us some time so I can maybe figure some more things out."

Silence from Matthew.

"I can go talk to Thompson. Maybe he can tell me how to help you. What if he knows more about where you're from? You don't start working for another hour, so I can go over there real quick and talk to him. If I can figure out where you're from, you can get back to your friends or whatever and they can help you remember things."

He's angry with me, as he should be. Matthew swallows, hard. I overloaded him with information, but there was no easy way to explain the situation to Matthew. He and I can't be friends after this. I lied to him, and now I'm paying the price for it. After I lied to Thompson, a man I've known for years, I came close to ruining our relationship. My entire friendship with Matthew is founded upon deception. Now that the truth is out...things can never go back to how they were between us.

Another period of long, cruel silence.

"So, let me get this straight," Matthew says. "I'm an...Intolerant, and I was captured. The Federation decided to completely wipe my memory to make me one of you. They told you to watch me and make sure this little plan of theirs worked properly?"

"Yes. It was either this or execution." The breeze picks up, and I shiver.

"I'm just an experiment, then? I'm your 'Final Test'?"

"Matthew, please." I lay a hand on his arm, but he flinches. "I didn't *want* to do this to you. If I didn't choose between execution and Reintegration, I would have failed my test. I don't know what that means. I didn't want to choose either one, because either way we were destroying you. But I did, because I'm selfish and I didn't want to risk failure. Yes, I did this to you.

"I need you to understand, though, you aren't just my 'Final Test'. I do care about you. I really do. The reason I'm telling this to you now is because I want to help you get home. I understand you're angry with me. I've hurt you and lied to you, but starting now, I'll do anything to help you get back to where you need to be. I promise."

Maybe my words aren't sinking in. Maybe Matthew has closed himself off to me entirely, believing everything I tell him to be a lie. The longer I stand there, the more seconds feel like minutes. Why won't he speak to me? Why won't he tell me he despises me and be done with it?

"I told you. You hate me for this. I understand."

"I don't hate you, Katherine." Matthew shakes his head. "I-I'm overwhelmed. I'm confused. You're obviously sorry, and I do believe you were just trying to help me. I just…don't know what to think right now."

He doesn't hate me?

"I guess, in a sense, I've known something wasn't right with all this. I don't know what, but things never seemed right. I think it was when you showed me the Tolerance Act. That's what told me this was all wrong, I think."

Realization hits me.

Reintegration hasn't failed. Matthew remembers nothing

of his past and knew nothing of the truth before now. He disagrees with the Tolerance Act because he *knows* it goes against whatever he believes.

Reintegration never could work.

The purpose of the Tolerance Act is to show humanity's ethics are based upon how they were raised. With Reintegration, the Council could have *proved* that. If we erased Matthew's memory and he succumbed to our way of thinking, the Tolerance Act would have been proven correct. Instead Matthew remains certain of what he believes and what his sense of morality is, and not because Reintegration failed. Something inside of him told him when things didn't align. What is that "something"? In one week, the basis of the Tolerance Act was dismantled.

If morality is *not* relative, then why couldn't one certain belief be right or wrong?

What is it inside of Matthew that tells him when something is right or wrong?

Do we *all* have whatever it is?

What if we do? Maybe the feelings I got whenever I lied to Matthew were normal, the way I felt sick. Maybe that's what Matthew's been talking about, something I don't know how to describe because no one's ever told me it exists. What if we all are capable of discerning right from wrong, but we stifle the ability because the Federation tells us it shouldn't exist?

"I'll be back. I can go ask Thompson some questions. He might know more about where you're from." If Thompson doesn't know where Matthew's from, maybe he can find a file like the one he found about the first Reintegration attempt. "I wasn't told very many details about your past."

"Can you trust him?"

Reintegration

"Yes. He's the one person we can trust. I'm sure of it. He believes freedom is more important than safety. He wanted to help you initially. Thompson told Council Member Haynes he felt you should be sent back to the Outlands because the fight with the Intolerants was over."

"Do you want me to come with you?"

"No. I'll be fine. We don't want to raise suspicion."

Matthew sighs. "Okay."

"You wait here. I'll be back in time to get you to work." I walk away. I have to find a way to get Matthew home. There are other people he belongs with, a group of insurgents who live in a world entirely different from my own. I'll get him back there, if I have to die to do so. It's the least I can do to make up for my actions.

I'm tired of being safe.

I want to be free.

"Hey," Matthew calls after me, walking over so we're standing side by side. "Thank you for telling me. I know you can get in trouble for this, so I'm grateful."

"Of course. I've never done anything that felt more...*right*." For the first time in my life, I used a word forbidden by our society. The word feels strange in my mouth, but in a good way.

I'm not the model citizen anymore. I've broken more rules in the past week than I ever have in the entire seventeen years of my life. My crimes include lying to my superiors, breaking our society's manifesto, and helping an enemy escape the Federation's walls. Each deserves a Violation.

I don't care anymore.

14

Is going to Thompson for help too much?

He knows of my treasonous acts but didn't turn me in. I repaid his loyalty by hurting him yesterday. Am I justified in demanding any more of him? Thompson might be the only person able to help me. My allies consist of Matthew and Thompson. One doesn't even comprehend what's going on, and the other is risking everything for keeping my secret. Maybe I shouldn't drag Thompson any further into my plan. If I fall, he'll fall with me.

Even if I don't ask Thompson for help, I can at least tell him of how I finally told Matthew the truth.

A light drizzle of rain falls from the sky. I left my jacket in my apartment, so the tiny droplets soak through the thin material of my uniform shirt. My hair must be a damp mess. A rumble of thunder rolls through the sky. I quicken my pace until I arrive at the Regulation Center.

Reintegration

I stop in the middle of the walkway, shoving a lock of stringy wet hair out of my face. What's going on? The rain pelts harder against my body, but the wave of chills sweeping over me is the least of my concerns.

Two Regulators stand by the front door, beneath the overhang and out of the rain. There's no mistaking big, bulky Regulator Vail. I jog toward the building, blinking water out of my eyes. The other man is Regulator Weston, Vail's replacement. Why are they standing in front of the door, as if standing guard? The only place Regulators ever need to guard is the detention block, not the entire Regulation Center.

"Is Thompson here?" I slip under the overhang, reaching for my card. Where did this rain come from so fast?

The two Regulators exchange glances. Vail holds up a hand. "You aren't permitted to be here at the moment, Trainee Holliday. No one's allowed to enter or leave the premise until they're finished."

"Until *who's* finished with *what?*" I'm cold, I'm wet, and I've had a rough morning. Why can't they let me inside so I can talk to my mentor? I need to have Matthew at work by the end of the hour, so the sooner I can get back, the better. Neither man offers any explanation, so I hold up my identification card. "I'll be real quick, I promise."

Regulator Weston points his stunner at me. I've never had a weapon aimed at me outside of training. I lower my hand to my side, tightening my grip on the card. What regulation mandates the presence of guards who threaten to stun people?

"Can I please talk to Thompson?" Can't they see I'm standing outside in my sopping wet clothes? I can't return to the cafeteria. Not when something important is going on and no one will tell me anything. "I'm in the middle of my Final

Test, and I have a question for him."

Regulator Vail pulls his tablet from under his arm and begins typing something on it. A message? The thinner and younger Regulator Weston keeps the stunner pointed at my stomach. This is standard procedure for *something*, but I can't think of the circumstances where these measures apply.

After about a minute, Vail's tablet beeps. He stares at the screen, bewilderment replacing his typical, bored expression. "Very well. You've been given clearance. Please proceed to Head Regulator Olson's office."

"Thanks." I bite back sarcasm. Slipping between the two men, I hold my identification card under the scanner. All I need is a few minutes to speak with Thompson. A sense of dread clings to me as I step inside. What's going on? The lobby area is empty, except for me—probably a result of the guards limiting who they allow inside. Maybe it's just me, but I seemed to be an exception. As I walk down the hallway, I look into training rooms and offices. Empty.

The soles of my wet shoes squeak against the tile floor as I walk. What is going on today? This hasn't been done while I've been a trainee here, not even when they arrested Matthew. I stop in the middle of the hallway, two doors down from the Head Regulator's office. Guarding the front door. Limiting access. There's only one situation warranting these actions.

When a Regulator does something Violation-worthy.

They know I lied! What else? Someone realized I lied about Reintegration. Vail and Weston let me in so I can be given a Violation for my crimes. They'll arrest me and kill Matthew. I unzip my bag, reaching for my tablet. Matthew needs to know they may be coming for him next.

"Katherine?" Council Member Haynes's steps out of

Head Regulator Olson's office, her voice too sweet and too casual. She's here in person? Why is she here? Water drips off my clothes into little puddles on the floor. I make no move to follow the Council Member into Olson's office, so she walks toward me. "Oh, my. You must be soaked."

I *must be* soaked? I *am* soaked. Not an inch of my uniform stayed dry. Once I get back to my apartment, I'm changing into dry clothes. Assuming I'm allowed to return to my apartment any time soon. "I came to see Thompson."

"That's what Regulator Vail told me." Haynes grabs my arm and pulls me down the hallway. I don't fight. Why should I? There's no where I can go. I failed. Matthew's going to die, and it's all my fault. They may give me one Violation, but Matthew…they won't give him any more chances.

"You deliberately lied to us. You abused the power you were given and have betrayed us all."

I freeze, inches away from Olson's office. The Head Regulator sounds angry, talking to someone inside the room. About betrayal? What if…what if I'm not the one they're giving a Violation? If so, they would have arrested me back at my apartment. I gave no indication I was coming in today. The Head Regulator is giving someone else a Violation.

My heart pounds even harder. There's only one other person they could be accusing of treason.

"If you were in my position, you would have done the same." Thompson's calm, steady voice hits me like a slap. So he is the one they're charging with a Violation. Haynes changed her mind about punishing him for speaking out. Why? All he did was ask a few questions.

"No, I would have *not*," Olson snaps. "I understand we

have created these rules to preserve the Federation. You knowingly broke those rules, and must now face the consequences. I hope you will learn from this and won't make the same mistake again."

"I see no reason why I should be sorry for my actions."

Silence follows.

Haynes enters the office, pulling me with her. If Thompson had any chance of avoiding a Violation, he ruined it with that comment. It's one thing to say something suggesting treason, but it's another thing when the next day you still hold to what you said. Head Regulator Heidi Olson sits at her desk, gaping at my mentor. She doesn't even look up when Haynes and I enter.

Thompson sits on the opposite side of the desk, weaponless and flanked by two additional Regulators, but he shows no sign of humiliation. He looks proud of himself, actually. Maybe even smug. I can't speak, not even when he catches my gaze and manages a smile.

Why couldn't he have acted contrite and avoided what they're doing to him?

"I have nothing else to say to him." Olson stands, grabbing her tablet and identification card off her desk. Her words are short and clipped. The result of being flustered by Thompson's obvious lack of remorse?

The Head Regulator slips from behind her desk and exits the office. I ball my hands into fists. This isn't fair. Indignation surges through me. How dare they punish Thompson for something so minor, so insignificant when I've overlooked so many rules in my attempt to save Matthew.

Haynes nods at the two remaining Regulators. "I would

like to speak with Katherine alone. You may take him downstairs. I'll resume things later, so we can begin the relocation process."

Relocation? They're taking Thompson away?

"Due to the nature of his Violation, your mentor will no longer be allowed contact with you," Haynes tells me in a low, quiet voice. Thompson's confident smile vanishes. She didn't tell him already?

Where Olson was bewildered, Haynes is indifferent. The Council Member steps to the side of the room. The two Regulators, without saying anything, grab my mentor by his arms and haul him out of the chair. One pushes Thompson against the wall, while the other reaches for the cuffs attached to his belt. They're *arresting* Thompson, the one person I've grown to respect more than anyone else. The only person, except for Matthew, who's always seen me as more than a statistic, more than what my tests say I am.

They're taking him away from me.

Forever.

"You can't do this!" A mix of hysteria and anger breaks through my numbness. I shrug the Council Member's hand off my shoulder and lunge forward. He's not dead, but once they take him, he might as well be, if I can never see him again. I reach for one of the Regulators, clawing at his arm. Thompson did so much to help me. The least I can do is fight for him.

With one hand, the Regulator shoves me aside, into the corner of the Head Regulator's desk. Dull pain throbs through my lower back and my eyes start watering. The two young Regulators clamp the cuffs over Thompson's wrists.

"It's okay. Just stay there." Thompson doesn't struggle. The men pull him away from the wall and drag him into the hallway. My rebellious, reckless mentor does nothing as they take him, some place where I'll never be allowed to talk to him again.

My whole body shivers, and not from standing in my cold, wet clothing. This isn't happening. The door slides closed, cutting me off from Thompson. The one person who kept my secret I'll now be forbidden to see. The person who trained me and taught me everything I know.

Gone from my life forever.

"Well, I'm sorry you had to see that." Haynes sits in Olson's chair, folding her hands in her lap. "But your mentor committed a crime, one that cannot be overlooked. This is the first Violation you've ever had to witness. I'm sorry it had to be under these circumstances."

Her eyes are like ice, defying the words she just spoke. She's lying. She *wanted* me to be here for this. Why else would she authorize the Regulators outside to let me in? Haynes realized I'm helping Matthew, and she wants me to know she doesn't take Violations lightly.

If it weren't for me, would she have even bothered giving Thompson a Violation? He argued with her on some things, but stepped back when threatened with a Violation. If she didn't suspect me of treason, maybe Thompson wouldn't be in this mess.

The thought doesn't make me feel good inside.

"What did he do? Why can't I see him anymore?" I bite my tongue before I spit out any more angry questions. Why is she taking away one of the few people I care about? Why is she punishing him instead of me? Relocation is *not* standard procedure. Even when a citizen receives a Violation, they aren't forced to move.

She blinks once, then twice. "Well, the nature of the Violation is not the issue. The reason behind his relocation is that he's your mentor. The last thing we need is for his *irresponsibility* to rub off on you."

I cross my arms over my chest, refusing to sit. Something here is off. I'm familiar with all the Federation's laws. Mentor or not, Thompson shouldn't be relocated. "I don't think this is fair. You gave him a Violation for something minor. He wanted more facts and also wanted me to be protected."

"It doesn't matter what you..." Her voice trails off. "How do you know what he told me?"

How could I have been so stupid?

"I overheard a small portion of the communication you had with him. I didn't tell him I'd overheard." It's not like I can tell Haynes about my little spying job. A pathetic excuse, but nothing else comes to mind. "But I think this is a little ridiculous. Giving a man a Violation for a minor offense?"

"Your mentor's infractions go farther than the conversation we had, Katherine. There are things you can't understand. Thompson has committed a *serious* crime against the Federation. It isn't your place to question why we gave him a Violation."

My anger abates, replaced by a numb, empty feeling. There's nothing I can do to help Thompson, even though I'm the reason they gave him a Violation in the first place. If I come clean of my own acts of treason, won't I only make things worse for my mentor? Haynes would then know Thompson found out about my activities but didn't report them.

"What was it you needed to talk to him about?"

"Oh, I..." I never assumed I needed an excuse for coming here. What can I tell her? "Oh, well, I was just curious what I should tell Matthew's work supervisor about all this. He obviously will know Matthew never worked in City 45 before and that there was no accident."

Haynes shrugs her shoulders. "This is all part of your Final Test, Katherine. I'm sure you'll think of something."

"Oh, okay," I reply. She's so cold toward me. Haynes must more than suspect me now. Why? What makes her so certain I am committing treason, other than my terrible lying abilities? All this…arresting Thompson, wanting me to watch, forcing me to do everything alone…

She's waiting for me to make a mistake.

"How are things going with the Intolerant, Katherine?" She taps one finger on the top of Head Regulator Olson's desk.

"Very well, thank you." Another lie; another awful, nausea-like feeling.

Silence.

"I suppose I've kept you long enough. The Intolerant will need to begin his work shift soon. I'm sorry your morning had to begin like this, but however rare, things like this do happen. Giving Thompson a Violation is for the better of the Federation."

A week before now, I would have said something like *I understand* or *the Council knows best*. But I don't today, because I've begun to see the Council doesn't always know everything or do things correctly. I've learned things in the past week I would never have been taught if it wasn't for Matthew. There are things the Federation doesn't teach us, things I'm certain we're supposed to know about.

I don't say anything at all. I can't bring myself to tell her I support Thompson's arrest, even if doing so would maintain my façade. Without another word to Haynes, I exit the office.

I run inside the dormitory building, out of the pouring rain. Another trainee stares as I walk past in my sopping clothes. A dreary day to match a dreary moment in my life. Telling Matthew the truth went smoother than expected, but learning about Thompson's Violation and relocation....

"Are you okay?"

Matthew leans against the wall by the cafeteria room door, hands shoved in his pockets. Is he asking because I'm drenched or because he can see I'm upset? No malice or bitterness on his face, just a look of pure interest in how I'm doing. He should despise me for what I've done, but he doesn't.

"I went to the Regulation Center, but when I got there, they arrested Thompson. They're giving him a Violation and relocating him, which means they're sending him to another city and I won't be able to see him ever again." My eyes burn. Reality sinks in, a deep emptiness in my stomach. I saw Thompson for the last time this morning. "I didn't learn anything about you. I wanted to find the information you need, but with Thompson gone, there's no one else to ask."

Who would have thought losing Thompson was so hard? Maybe it's because I'm the cause of this. I let him down, like I let Matthew down. I didn't get to tell him good-bye. Everything happened so fast, in a blur.

I didn't get to tell him how sorry I am.

"I'm sorry, Katherine. I know he means a lot to you. Don't worry about trying to learn anything else about me. An opportunity will come up." Matthew can't mask the disappointment in his voice, but I appreciate he's trying to make me feel better.

"I really am sorry."

"I-I can't talk anymore. I need to go change so I can get you to work. I'll be back in a few minutes." Clenching my jaw, I run for the elevator. I need to be alone. Matthew, to my relief, doesn't follow me.

By the time I reach my apartment, the tears slip freely down my cheeks. Why do I feel so miserable? They haven't executed him. They're sending him to another city, but at least he's still alive. Thompson's gone, though. If Haynes's goal was to hurt me, she succeeded. If she wanted to overwhelm me with feelings of loneliness, confusion, and frustration—she got what she wanted.

After yanking off my shoes, I throw them across the room, where they hit the floor with a dull *thud*. I didn't ask for any of this. If I knew Reintegrating Matthew meant I would be under suspicion and would result in the loss of one of the few people who matters to me….

Why me? Why did they choose me for this awful assignment? I wanted a normal Final Test, not this life-altering event with ramifications I never expected. The Council wants me to do things and make decisions my training never could have prepared me for. Why does every choice I make affect everyone around me?

I rummage through my closet and grab a dry uniform. Haynes knows what I've done, even if she doesn't know how. Why can't she give me a Violation and be done with it? Why hurt me through the one person who's always been there for me, who always cared even if he had a strange way of showing it? Thompson did nothing other than try to help me. I'm the one they should be taking away, not him.

This is all my fault.

I enter the bathroom, setting my dry clothes on the counter. The girl in the mirror stares back at me with red, tear-glazed eyes. Grabbing the towel off the wall hook, I dry my face. Why I bother is a mystery, because a fresh wave of hot tears flows down my cheeks. My whole body shakes and a hiccupped sob escapes me before I can swallow it down. I grab the edge of the countertop in a desperate attempt of steadying my quivering hands. Three words reverberate through my mind. I don't have a term for the stomach-churning feeling constantly plaguing me, but at least I know now what it means.

All.

My.

Fault.

15

"I'm sorry for the delay. It's my fault, I promise."

It's my fault.

Everything is my fault.

I pull off my jacket and drape it over the back of the chair before sitting. Matthew's new work supervisor, an older man, fixes me with a skeptical look. The frown on his face deepens. Rain splatters against the office's sole window. I smooth out the front of my dry uniform shirt. Can the man tell I spent the whole morning crying, grieving the loss of Thompson?

He must not, for the supervisor doesn't soften his glare any. "Hopefully tomorrow you can make sure he arrives on time. I know factory work might not seem as important as Regulating, but we do just as much to keep the Federation functioning. There is a lot that we do."

Sheesh. What's the matter with this guy? "I understand every occupation in the Federation is crucial to the overall productivity of the cities. I will do my best to make sure Matthew is on time tomorrow."

"I would appreciate that. However, I'm not understanding why he's here." The supervisor—whose last name is Dodge, according to the name stitched on his uniform—reaches for his tablet. "My records indicate he has been absent due to recent injury, but I have no previous documentation that he ever worked here to begin with."

Matthew and I discussed what to say during the walk here. We finally came up with something easy for both of us to remember. "He originally worked in City 46, but there was an equipment error that damaged the facility and injured several workers. The Federation relocated him here since the factory in City 46 was virtually destroyed."

"Huh."

"You'll need to show him what to do, because as I'm sure your records explain, he lost his memory in the accident. I've also been assigned to help him adjust, so I'll need to stay here for the day." Will the news that I have to stay sit well with him? So far, he doesn't seem to like me very much. "This is all part of my Final Test."

"Huh." The supervisor looks at something else on his tablet, then shrugs and stands. His office is smaller than the offices at the Regulation Center. "I guess I'll have to show him around."

I step outside into the hallway where Matthew waits. Without a word, Dodge walks down the hallway in long strides. Matthew watches him leave, then shoots me a look I interpret to mean *what's his problem?* I shrug my shoulders and follow after the supervisor. Matthew falls in step next to me. He hasn't behaved any different around me since I told him the truth this morning.

On the walk to the factory building, I explained in further detail what happened with Thompson. Matthew listened and never once acted annoyed by my display of emotions. He even assured me what they did to Thompson wasn't my fault. It was my fault, but at least Matthew tried to help me. Nothing can change that I'm the cause of Thompson's Violation. My eyes well up with tears again.

Chelsea isn't speaking to me, for unknown reasons.

Thompson's gone.

Matthew is the only person I have left.

If anyone was to be my best friend in all of this, I'm glad it's Matthew. He understands me in a way no one ever has before. I won't let them take him away, too. I won't let them execute him as a violent terrorist. He's the furthest thing from a terrorist. Instead he's sweet and polite.

And he listens to everything I tell him.

Dodge pushes open a door at the end of the hallway. I'm met with the sounds of large machinery—a dull droning noise that would drive me insane. "Had to move some things around to fit you in. Anyway, this is where we create the tablets for City 45."

I've never been inside a factory before. The room is long and rectangular, a wide conveyor belt running down the middle. Workers stand on either side, attaching pieces before sending the unfinished product to the next person. Dodge looks at something on his tablet, muttering to himself. I don't envy Matthew. Endless noise, a supervisor with no ounce of positivity in his body whatsoever…maybe I should be more grateful for my assignment as Regulator. Thompson was always encouraging. My head already pounds from the whir of machinery.

Not to mention it's hot in here.

I roll up my sleeves, noting Matthew doesn't do the same. He watches everything, a look of curiosity on his face. What *did* he do in the Outlands? Several seconds pass before Dodge speaks.

"Okay, then. You're supposed to be at Station 15, over here." He continues walking to the opposite side of the room. Not one for chit-chat, is he? At one point as we walk, he barks at two workers to "stop yapping and get back to work".

This is a very different setting than the one I trained in.

Dodge stops near the end of the room, ushering Matthew between two other workers. I stand off to the side. What am I supposed to do? The supervisor holds up two pieces and shows Matthew how to put them together, then hands them to the next person. "That's all you have to do. Simple. But don't lollygag or else you slow this whole thing up. We're already starting later than usual. In three hours you get a break for lunch. Got it?"

"Yes, sir," Matthew says.

"Good." Without another word, Dodge walks away.

I jog over to him. What does he expect me to do, stand here doing nothing for several hours? "I need to stay here. What should I do?"

He sighs, walking toward a door marked "storage". He scans his card and enters the room. Dodge emerges a few seconds later, pushing a chair my way. "Here you go."

Better than standing.

"Thanks," I say, but he doesn't reply as he walks away. How does someone become so unhappy all the time? I turn back to Matthew, who shoots me a grin over his shoulder. How does someone become so optimistic all the time? I return the smile, pushing the chair against the wall. Sitting down, I turn on my tablet.

A message from Haynes displays on the screen. I read over her message. What? No. She can't be doing this to me. I read the message a second time, making sure I understood properly.

At the end of the week, please come to City 1 to give your second report. I would like to have all of your reports given in person until the six-week period has ended. This might be inconvenient for you, but there are things we may need to discuss.

Why is she…of course. Haynes can't properly assess my words through a message. The only way she can tell I'm lying is if we have a discussion face to face. Is that the point of all this? She knows I've committed treason but she has no proof? I have to give her five more in-person reports. In those five meetings, she's going to pressure me for the truth.

I'm going to snap one of these days.

"I have to go to City 1 at the end of the week and give my report." I don't even fight to keep the irritation out of my voice as Matthew and I exit the factory building so we can eat lunch. I hope Haynes will message me again, saying she can't meet me in person.

"I don't have to go, do I?" Matthew frowns. "There's no need for me to see the doctor?"

"Not that she told me about." Part of me wants Matthew to go, too. If Doctor Perry ran some more tests on him and confirmed how Reintegration is a success, then maybe Haynes will leave me alone.

Unless, of course, his tests prove Reintegration's failed.

A relieved smile passes over Matthew's face. "Oh, good."

"At least Doctor Perry is nice," I comment, more to myself than to Matthew. Perry's nice, unlike Haynes, whose sweetness is only on the surface. There's more to her than I can understand. Something tells me she's hiding things from me, like I've hidden things from her.

"Well, I've always felt like he treated me...strangely. Almost like he was afraid of me." Matthew pauses. "I guess I know why, now. Can't really blame him either. If I'm considered a criminal here…"

We haven't spoken about Matthew's real identity much. Neither of us knows. As of now, we know a few things, but nothing seems to add up to a piece of information we can use.

Matthew is an Intolerant.

Matthew's from the Outlands.

His full name is Matthew Braddock.

He's around seventeen-years-old.

Haynes knows who—or what—Matthew is.

I've never heard his name before in my life, yet the Council Member panicked when she learned who Matthew was. Is this another secret no one has told me, like how Reintegration was attempted before? Thompson didn't know what was so important about Matthew.

Council Member Haynes knows.

What have they done with Thompson? Where did they send him? He was the only one I could talk to without worrying of being suspected of treason. My mentor has been gone no more than a few hours, but it might as well be weeks.

I miss him, more than I ever thought I would.

"I sometimes feel like Doctor Perry sees me as…less than human, or like I have a contagious disease he's afraid of getting." Matthew shivers. I pull up the hood of my jacket. The rain is nothing more than a light drizzle now, almost a mist. "Is that how we're seen by everyone here?"

I stop walking, and Matthew does too.

"We're taught that the Intolerants are violent, erratic, spiteful…from the time we're old enough to speak they teach us the Intolerants want nothing but to bring us harm. 'If there was such a thing, the Intolerants would be evil', one teacher told me when I was younger. So, yes, if people knew you were an Intolerant they would be afraid of you. But they don't know you like I do. You're sweet and polite and caring. Not exactly the picture of an insane terrorist." I manage a half-smile, hoping to ease the worry lining his face.

"What if you're wrong about me, Katherine?" Matthew whispers. I glance over my shoulder, but no else is around to hear Matthew's use of forbidden words.

"What do you mean? Of course I'm not wrong. I've known you for weeks." I lay a hand on his arm. "Where is this coming from?"

"I don't know anything about myself. I don't know who I am or where I belong or if I even really belong anywhere. Because you don't know either. What if we—I—am what they say? What if I'm not the hero in all this, because I came here to do something terrible?" He meets my gaze, those big brown eyes filled with a pain I want to fix. How can he talk this way?

"You didn't come here to hurt anyone, Matthew. Before they erased your memory, I asked you why you came, and you told me it was because of something you loved. I think you meant *someone*. I think in the Outlands, you have people you

Reintegration

care about, and you came here to help them somehow. You didn't tell me because you wanted to keep whoever these people are safe."

A thought flickers into my mind, one I've tried to push away for some time. I lower my hand back to my side. What if there's a girl Matthew loves in the Outlands, with the kind of love he explained to me? Maybe there's a girl who loves him back with that sort of love, who grew up understanding what love is.

Maybe she deserves him, is the kind of person he can really trust, unlike me. Matthew deserves to love someone who's never lied to him in the ways I have. Maybe this other girl understands and belongs in a world I will never understand or belong in. Something stirs inside me, the same feeling I had when Chelsea flirted with him.

Jealousy.

I shouldn't be jealous. We haven't known each other very long, but I do enjoy being around him—maybe a little too much. When it comes time to let him go back where he belongs, will I be able to? Will I let the side of me that cares about his well-being override the selfish side of me?

I can't have a crush on Matthew. I can't.

Maybe I'm just upset because Thompson's gone. I haven't really had a guy for a friend before, so that's all.

I'm an awful liar, even when I'm lying to myself.

"I just don't know." Matthew shakes his head. "I don't know anything."

"I don't know why you came, but it wasn't to hurt anyone. Please believe me, Matthew. Even Thompson saw there was something about you that was different. You aren't the Intolerant we've been taught about."

Matthew continues walking, expression thoughtful. I follow, stepping over a puddle. "Sometimes," he says. "I think I remember things, just blurred images, really. I know it's there, somewhere, but I just can't grasp it."

"You never told me that. You're making progress." I playfully nudge his arm.

There it is, the adorable smile that makes his eyes dance. How could he possibly think he came here with ill intentions? Is it something he remembers? Maybe he remembers something violent the other Intolerants did and thinks he participated.

Why *did* Matthew come here in the first place?

I've come up with a myriad of reasons, but the first is the only one making sense. Matthew came here to help someone. Who? What did he come here to find? There are so many questions, but we won't know the answers until Matthew remembers something substantial.

How long will that take, though? One week in, and Matthew *thinks* he might be remembering things. Nothing concrete, nothing to help me know how to get him home. I don't have much more time. Five more weeks, and that's it. At the end of my six-week Final Test period they'll have more rigorous testing to prove the procedure worked on Matthew. Something will give them pause, especially if Matthew is regaining his memory.

I wasn't trained for medicine. How does all of this work? Is the Reintegration formula wearing off, and they can detect the amount of it inside him? Do they draw blood or something to test it?

For the first time in my life, I wish I had been trained in the science field so I would know what to expect.

Even if they couldn't detect scientifically that there's anything wrong with Matthew, I can't keep up my charade forever. If I have to see Haynes every week, how long until I make a slip? Once someone suspects Reintegration is a failure, I won't have any more time to figure out how Matthew is going to return to the Outlands and how to get him back to something familiar.

But where do I acquire this information?

If I pester Haynes about it, she'll know something's up. Thompson, who may or may not know something more about Matthew, is gone. The only person I could ask without worrying about receiving a Violation has disappeared from my life, and it's my own fault.

There's no one else I can go to, is there? I have to hope Matthew remembers enough before time runs out for him. Before the end of my Final Test, before they ship him to City 1, before they run tests on him, before...

How could I have overlooked this? In the small realm of people who knows the truth about Reintegration, I've forgotten one of the biggest assets. The one person I can ask questions around, who won't automatically accuse me of treason. The one person who won't suspect me of a hidden agenda.

Doctor Perry.

I have a plan. A pathetic, ill-formed plan, but a plan nonetheless. In case my plan fails, however, I need a back-up plan. But what? Time is running out, for both Matthew and myself. I have to succeed at learning where Matthew belongs.

As I walk to the Regulation Center to give myself time to think, I catch sight of the last person I expect to see. Chelsea walks down the walkway, past the medical center where she always trains. She's several yards ahead of me, so she doesn't notice me. I run over to her, grabbing her arm. "Hi."

Chelsea stops and turns. Her eyes widen for a second, then she averts her gaze and mumbles a half-hearted greeting.

"How are you? You never responded to my message." Why has she ignored me for the past few days? This is so unlike her. Something big must have happened for her to be this mad at me. "Were you given your Final Test?"

"Yes."

"Yes? That's it? How did you do?"

"I passed it." She should be elated, not standing here shuffling her feet like she doesn't feel well. Beneath her perfectly-applied makeup, she looks exhausted. She's always so perky and talkative. What's going on?

"That's great, isn't it?"

"Look, Katherine, I have things I need to do today. You're not the only one with an important occupation."

Why is she acting this way? Her words seem forced and flat, like someone told her what to say. It's not that Chelsea has never accused me of being overly-dedicated to my work, but this is the first time she's accused me of being arrogant about it. "I'm sorry. Have I said something? I just wanted to know how your test went."

She stares at the ground, a look of pure misery on her face. Chelsea glances over her shoulder, then back at me, lowering her voice. "They've changed my occupation. I'm not training for a medical career anymore. That's all I can tell you, okay? They told me I can't tell anyone about it. Not even you. I shouldn't even have told you this much, but I'm not mad at you. I promise. I don't know how long I can go without telling anyone, so I might as well tell you. *Please.* Don't ask me any more about it. I don't want to be given a Violation."

"They switched your occupation?" I blurt out. "I've never heard of them doing that before."

"I know, but they say it's really important and I have potential for it. They're going to train me for a while, and if I do well, I'll have a permanent occupation switch. If I fail, I'll go back to medical training." Chelsea frowns. "I'm surprised they didn't choose you, since you're a Regulator and all."

They're giving Chelsea a Regulator-like position? That's not a small switch. If they want Chelsea to be a Regulator, she'll have to undergo a lot of training. "I'm sorry. Thanks for telling me, though."

"I wish I could tell you all of it, but I've said too much already." She looks at her tablet. "I really need to go now."

"Okay. I'll hopefully see you around."

"Hopefully." She smiles, but it doesn't eliminate the lingering look of stress on her face. She walks away, and I watch her leave. Shaking my head, I continue on my way to the Regulation Center. Why has the Federation assigned Chelsea a new occupation? Children are trained in specific areas so when they become teenagers they're ready for a certain occupation. Making a career switch this late in a trainee's life doesn't make sense.

Something is going on. Reintegration, Thompson's relocation, Chelsea's new career…none of these things are normal. The Council is preparing for something, something none of us can imagine.

I need answers.

16

I haven't told Matthew my plan yet.

He'll just worry and try to convince me not to go. But I have to. I have to make up for what I did to him. He says he understands I didn't know any better. Maybe so, but I still want to do everything I can to fix this. He deserves to go home, where he belongs.

"Good luck going to City 1 today. From what you've told me about this Haynes woman, she sounds tough." Matthew pushes his empty plate aside, leaning forward and lowering his voice. "Be careful, okay?"

"I always am." I slip my hand in my pocket, fingering the small object I found at the Regulation Center. There's a chance I'll need it during my meeting with Haynes. My plan is the opposite of careful. I need information, lots of it, but no one will tell me anything. I'll have to investigate on my own to make sense of this mess.

Reintegration

I shove the last bite of food in my mouth. Grabbing my tablet, I glance at the time. In a few minutes, Matthew will need to go to his morning shift. I'll need to go to City 1 and get this report out of the way.

"You sure you'll be fine without me being there? I have to deal with Haynes, but you've got your cranky supervisor."

"At least I don't have to convince him I'm not a traitor." An amused grin tugs at one side of Matthew's mouth. "I can't get a Violation for being a poor worker, can I?"

"No." I laugh, but Matthew isn't a poor worker. I've watched how he works and how he interacts with the others at the factory. He gets things done in a timely manner, even volunteers sometimes for things he isn't required to do. Matthew is always polite and respectful, even to Dodge, who never gives any acknowledgement that Matthew's done well.

"I have something to tell you." Matthew lowers his voice even further as a trainee walks by. "I really think I am remembering things."

"What do you remember?" Does he remember anything about his past? Anything I can use in figuring out how to help him escape City 45?

"Hard to say." What's that supposed to mean? "It's usually things like voices, faces, objects, but it's all still fuzzy. I don't know anything for certain yet, but it's a start, right? I'll take whatever I can get."

How can I not be happy for him when he has a contented smile on his face? He doesn't care, does he, whether or not he knows enough about his past to leave the Federation? Matthew is just pleased to have something that's his now.

"Well, let me know when you learn something concrete, okay? The more facts we have available to us, the sooner we might be able to find something we can really use." I try my best to keep the disappointment out of my voice. At this rate, it could take months to learn where Matthew's really from.

We don't have months.

I need to learn more on my own. Someone has to know more about where Matthew belongs. The Outlands cover half of the country—he could be from anywhere. I can't help him escape the city walls and hope he finds where he needs to be. I need to give him something he can use to find the people he cares about.

What am *I* going to do when Matthew returns to the Outlands? I could make something up, tell Haynes or whoever inquires about his disappearance I had nothing to do with it. If I lie will enough, I'll be safe. They can't give me a Violation unless they know what I've done.

But I don't want to lie. Part of me wants Haynes to know I've learned to think for myself. I was presented with a choice—and I made it, on my own, with no help from the Federation. I *chose* to help Matthew because I want him to be free. I want to be free, too. If defying the Federation is how I achieve freedom, so be it.

I also want the other people in the Federation to learn what I have about love, about morality, about the Intolerants. Why shouldn't the others be allowed to know there is more than what the Federation gives us?

When Matthew is out of the city walls, I will come clean.

Matthew picks up his plate and my bowl and carries them over to the dish bin. He does that every morning, a gesture I find to be so sweet. What I want, more than anything, is to go *with* Matthew to the Outlands. I want to know what the world outside the Federation is like.

I can't, though, because I'll never belong there.

I enter the medical center. It's not too late to turn back. Doctor Perry won't be as eager as Haynes to prove me worthy of a Violation, but I can't trust him either. I have to guard my words. He's not suspicious like Haynes, but he's far from stupid. The last thing I need at the moment is to make a slip and have him report it to Haynes.

Doctor Perry is the only one who can tell me more about Reintegration.

I approach the young woman seated at the desk in the medical center lobby, taking a deep breath. Once I do this, I can't return to my normal life. But didn't I leave my normal life behind the second I lied to Council Member Haynes?

The woman looks up from her tablet. "Hello. Can I help you?"

"Hi. Yes, you can. Is Doctor Vincent Perry here? I need to speak with him about some things. It's important." I hand her my identification card.

"Katherine Holliday?" The woman reads the name on my card, then types a message on her tablet. A few seconds later, she receives a reply. "Yes, he is. He's downstairs working on something. If you follow me, I'll show you where he is."

She slips around her desk and gives me my card back. I do as I am told, following her down the long, well-lit hallway. Out of curiosity, I glance through the glass windows on many of the doors. The first floor contains several medical rooms like the one Matthew stayed in before Doctor Perry released him. We pass by a door labeled "Medicine Testing". Is this where Doctor Perry does most of his work?

"The Intolerants no longer pose a threat to the Federation, so the Council wants our doctors to invest more time and resources in making the Federation the very first illness free society. Doctor Perry has made many important contributions to accomplishing this task," the lady says upon noticing my interest in the room. I continue following her toward the elevator.

"Most simple, contagious diseases have been eradicated. We give our children extensive vaccines to make sure they stay safe from illness so they can be productive members of society. Workers no longer have to take time away from their duties to recuperate." The lady steps onto the elevator, pushing the button for one of the underground levels. "Genetic diseases are more difficult to abolish. Sometimes we have to help the evolutionary process along. Doctor Perry works on finding cures for the diseases after a citizen has one and some of our other doctors focus on preventing the diseases in the first place."

"Interesting."

Illnesses are rare, but they do occur. A couple years ago, a boy I knew unexpectedly disappeared. His name was Brian Coleman, and he was a few years older than me. The day after his disappearance, we were informed that Brian Coleman had contracted a fatal illness and died. I found his death strange, since he never struck me as someone with a sickness of any kind.

But it does prove the importance of work like Doctor Perry's.

The woman exits the elevator once it reaches the second to lowest level. I follow her down the hallway. She stops about halfway to the end of the hall, rapping on one of the doors. "Doctor Perry? The girl I told you about needs to talk to you.

She says it's important."

A few seconds later, Doctor Perry opens the door, eyes widening when he sees me. "Thank you, Julie. I'll talk to her."

Perry steps out of the doorway, letting me in, then closes it after the woman heads back toward the elevator. The doctor frowns. "What are you doing here? Is it the Intolerant?"

This is a storage area of some sort. Vials of liquid and pill bottles line the shelves. I shake my head. "No, everything's fine. Matthew has adjusted well so far. I just wanted to learn more about Reintegration itself."

"About Reintegration?" Doctor Perry walks toward the counter on the far wall. He grabs a vial, holding it up in the light. When I don't expand on why I needed to speak with him, he asks, "What do you need to know?"

I need to make this seem as inconspicuous as possible. Should I start with the important questions, or something simple and hope he tells me things on his own? I sit down in a chair shoved in the corner of the room, setting my bag on the floor. "Why try Reintegration at all? What's the point of offering the Intolerants a second chance? They've chosen the way of violence and oppression."

Perry glances over his shoulder at me, surprise passing over his face. This is a question I've wondered about frequently, even if it isn't the most important on my list. I have only theories as to why the Council attempted Reintegration, but nothing concrete.

"Well." Doctor Perry sets the vial back down on the counter, reaching for a small electronic device. "I can't say why the Council wants to do it, but I myself was eager to try it."

"Why?"

Perry taps something on the device's screen. It beeps, and

he sets the vial on the shelf. "Inventory." He smiles in a bored kind of way, then clears his throat. "To answer your question, Reintegration is the beginning of a much larger puzzle. I'm a scientist, not a government official, but I understand what Reintegration could mean for our society if it succeeds. I don't care about merging the Intolerants into the Federation, like everyone else does. Your mentor was correct when he said the fight is over. Why bring it back up again?"

I wince at the mention of Thompson. Another reminder he's gone.

"No, what I'm interested in is Reintegration itself. Reintegration's success will prove we've accomplished the most humane way to deal with those who pose a threat. No more executions." Perry grabs another vial and taps the device's screen. "If a citizen commits a Violation, we simply start over."

"The Federation could guarantee loyalty?" I don't add that the Federation is trying to strip away any freedom we might still have.

"Precisely."

"But Matthew….?" How can I ask this next question? "The Council doesn't care about trying to make Matthew a part of the Federation?"

"Oh, no, I believe that's what the Council wants. The boy, for example, is obviously intelligent and healthy. He has the potential to become a productive member of society. For me, however, I just want to know Reintegration works. If the Intolerant is properly Reintegrated, that's great. If not…" Perry falls quiet for a second. "The Council has decided if Reintegration fails again, the effort must be abandoned. They argue there's no need to waste more time and research on it when there may be more important issues to work on."

He sounds disappointed.

"Then what? What happens to Matthew?"

The truth is obvious, however. Matthew will face execution. "The Council has decided medicinal research takes a higher priority than Reintegration. The Federation's goal is to create a perfectly safe society—safe from violence, safe from technological mishaps, safe from illness." Why isn't he telling me how Matthew will be killed? Where is Doctor Perry going with this? "The last one is proving to be the most difficult. New medicines have to be created for new illnesses, existing medicines have to be improved, because not every case is identical. Unfortunately, we can't start giving everyone untested drugs if there could be unexpected side effects. That would only create more problems, so we'd need another solution."

What is he saying? Then it finally sinks in. He doesn't want Matthew to be executed. He wants Matthew to be his *test subject* for trying new medicines that could prove harmful. If he doesn't want citizens to develop problems, why is Matthew any different? Intolerant or not, Matthew is a person who—

I swallow down anger.

It's because of Matthew's Intolerant status.

Matthew's words about Perry seeing him as "less than human" become clear. I didn't believe him then. I do now. Matthew wasn't born in the Federation, so he's seen as holding a lesser position than the citizens do. An image flashes through my mind of Matthew being strapped down to an operating table, having dangerous formulas injected into his body…

I want to cry and vomit at the same time.

"T-the Council has approved of this?" I stammer.

Doctor Perry must notice the tremor in my voice, for he

gives me a baffled look. "The Council has yet to agree. They're going to vote on it if Reintegration ends up failing. It's a perfectly logical solution, Katherine. We gain nothing by executing the Intolerant."

Is the plan logical? Maybe.

Is it right? No.

Thompson's words on the train weeks ago...when he told me we lost something in our quest for peace, I understand them now. By believing there is no such thing as right or wrong, we've made ourselves numb. We reason everything by logic, with no questions asked regarding the ethics of it. In this case, no one considers how Matthew is a *person* with thoughts and feelings and who wants nothing more than to go home.

Matthew doesn't belong to the Federation, so now he's below it.

In a strange way, though, Doctor Perry doesn't want this for selfish reasons. He wants to do what we're taught since birth—preserve the Federation. By subjecting Matthew to being an experiment the rest of his life, the doctor can find ways to save a lot of citizens. Maybe Perry will find a way to cure several diseases, thus resulting in a safer, healthier society.

Can a person's motives be so right but their methods so wrong at the same time?

"I think Council Member Haynes wants something different," Perry continues, jarring me back to the present moment. "Apparently, she changed her mind about executing him, for political reasons. She sees the one we captured as perhaps our last chance to finding the rest of the Intolerants."

So she wants to glean information out of Matthew, the same information I need to get him home.

"How, if you erased his memory?"

Reintegration

"This is if Reintegration fails, Katherine. We'll know Reintegration is a failure if he starts regaining memory. There is, however, the possibility he won't remember *everything*, so we have a plan for that."

I sit up straight in my chair. They have something to give Matthew his memory back? A faint glimmer of hope replaces my worry. I want to grab my tablet and send him a message, but if I did, someone could read it and learn of my treason. "What is this plan, exactly?"

Doctor Perry continues his inventory, pulling items off the shelf and then returning them to their spots after he enters data on the electronic device. "Haynes came to me shortly after the procedure had been completed. She explained to me the alternative to execution she was going to propose to the Council. Like I already said, she wants to learn how to find the rest of the Intolerants. The problem is, she needed that to be possible so she asked me to create a way to undo Reintegration, if needed."

"And you did?"

"Yes and no. I've created something that *may* override Reintegration and *may* give the Intolerant his memory back. No guarantee it'll work, though. Untested." Perry shoves the device in his uniform pocket. "I think it's a pointless idea. The Intolerants are going to die out soon enough, anyway, between their limited numbers and the harsh environment of the Outlands."

What does Haynes want to do? Perry's correct in what he says. Learning where they are to capture them all doesn't make sense. As much as I hate to admit it, Matthew belongs to a dwindling people. What is Haynes trying to hide?

"How does this work? What you've created to undo Reintegration?"

"It's a simple medicine. That's the plan at least. It might not work, it could take a long amount of time, it may produce side effects. I don't know." Doctor Perry sets the last vial on the shelf. Is he finishing up? "I suppose it doesn't matter. If it doesn't work, we can at least say we tried."

It doesn't matter? Indignation surges through me. It doesn't matter that Matthew could be harmed for nothing? It doesn't matter Matthew will be a prisoner of the Federation for who knows how long? I have to bite my tongue to keep from saying something that will jeopardize my plan to save Matthew.

Perry enters in a code to a locked cabinet. *742.* The numbers display on the screen for a few seconds before it fades to black. The cabinet door slides open and Doctor Perry reaches in and grabs a bottle that's smaller than the others. He screws the bottle's lid off. Opening another unlocked cabinet, he pulls out a small plastic bag and pours two blue pills inside before putting the bag in his pocket. Perry smiles tiredly, replacing the lid and setting the bottle back in the cabinet. "I have to do a few more tests before deeming it ready for use."

He enters the code in again. The door slides closed and clicks as it locks. Doctor Perry just inadvertently showed me the medicine to give Matthew his memory back. How do I steal one of the pills? I stand, leaving my bag on the floor. Doctor Perry exits the room and I follow him. He closes the door and starts walking down the hallway.

"Oh, wait," I say. "I left my things in there."

The doctor seems a little annoyed as he walks back over and unclips his own identification card from the front of his uniform. He waves it under the scanner and the door slides open. "Go ahead. Let yourself out when you're done."

"I will."

Doctor Perry heads for the elevator. That went smoother than I expected. I step into the room, letting the door close behind me. I walk toward the locked cabinet, my fingers shaking as I press the buttons for the code. *742*. I half-expect some sort of alarm to go off, but none does. The cabinet opens.

Inside is an assortment of vials and bottles. What are the others for? I reach for the bottle that looks like the one Perry took. I won't take all of the pills, so hopefully no one will notice I've stolen some. After setting the bottle on the counter, I open the second cabinet Perry did and grab a plastic bag. I remove the bottle's lid and peer inside. There's ten little blue pills. I slip two of them into the bag, zip it closed, and shove the bag into my pocket. I mimic everything Doctor Perry did, screwing the lid back on and setting it in the same spot on the shelf. I key in the code again for the cabinet. Once I'm sure it's locked, I grab my bag off the floor and exit the room.

I don't dare to reach inside my pocket until I'm outside the medical center and walking toward the City 1 building. These two pills could get me into a lot of trouble if anyone finds out I have them. This is my one chance to make sure Matthew gets his memory back before it's too late. I shove the bag back into my pocket.

I slip my hand in my other pocket, making sure the other object is still there. I need a back-up plan in case Matthew doesn't agree to using the pills or if he does and it fails. Perry told me nothing about where Matthew is from. Does he even know?

Haynes *may* know, but if she needs Matthew to find the Intolerants, chances are she knows nothing. Unless, of course, she knows where the Intolerants are but doesn't know their strengths and weaknesses. Is that what she needs Matthew for? Haynes understands more about the Intolerants than anyone else, but she won't tell me anything.

I have a plan.

17

"I'm here to see Council Member Haynes."

The man at the front desk glances up at me. I hand him my identification card, like I did with the young woman at the medical center.

"She's in the middle of a Council meeting, I'm afraid." The man looks at his tablet. "I see you're on her appointment list for this afternoon. You're welcome to wait here until she's finished."

He hands me my card back, then types out a message on his tablet. Is he telling the Council Member I'm here? I thank him and sit down in one of the chairs. When will Haynes finish her meeting with the rest of the Council? What do they discuss in those meetings, anyway?

My plan is a risky one, and not necessarily well-thought out. I know what I need to do, but not how I'm going to do it. He looks at his tablet every minute or so. His job must be to alert the Council Members and other officials when they are needed for appointments. I watch as he stands up and walks toward the restroom—leaving his tablet at the desk.

That's what I need to set my plan into motion.

Standing, I leave my tablet on the chair and approach the man's desk. I look around the room, but no one else is in the lobby. I turn on his tablet. Sure enough, the screen is filled with messages labeled "send to" followed by an individual's name. I tap an icon at the top of the screen, which allows me to add a new one to the list.

Send to: Council Member Amelia Haynes
Appointment: Meeting with Council Member Josiah Whitley.
Time: 1:45, afternoon.

I read over what I've wrote, making sure everything mimics the desk clerk's normal style then tap "submit". I scheduled the fictional appointment to take place during my report—so Haynes will leave her office.

The man from the desk returns just as I sit in my seat. I watch him, not daring to take a breath. Will he notice something is amiss? He doesn't. I bite my lip to smother my relieved smile.

About two minutes later, Haynes enters the lobby. I stand, slipping my tablet into my bag as she approaches.

"I apologize for the delay. We've been in the middle of an important discussion we can't seem to agree on." Haynes smiles, a forced, tight-lipped smile. Does this important discussion have to do with Matthew's fate? "Well, let's head to my office for your report."

"I hope Reintegration is still going as planned?"

Reintegration

The more I'm around her, the colder Haynes's disposition is toward me. She taps one finger on the top of her desk, something she does whenever she's annoyed with me. I haven't even answered any of her questions yet, and already she's irritated.

"Yes, it is. Matthew started working this week, and he seems to be doing well."

"Good." This time she doesn't press me to give her more details. Maybe she's learned I can be just as stubborn as she is. "I also hope you are coping well with the relocation of your mentor?"

How should I respond? I haven't seen Thompson in a week, and any reference to him makes the loneliness return. "No, I am not coping well. Thompson has taught me things since I graduated Primary School. I've grown to trust him and respect him. Losing him has been like losing a friend."

"This is the only problem with the mentorship program, Katherine. It becomes too easy for trainees to grow attached to their teachers. In four weeks you'll be considered an adult and full citizen of the Federation. You need to learn to be independent."

"Is that why you've relocated him? To help me be independent?"

"Partially." Haynes doesn't expand on what the other part of the reason is. I won't push my boundaries. She shrugs. "Becoming independent is part of growing up, Katherine. In time, you'll see separation from your mentor is the only way you'll really grow up."

Haynes speaks to me like I'm a small child complaining about the start of Primary School. I'm seventeen. I shouldn't be too dependent. But does that mean I can't ever come to anyone else for help—least of all my mentor?

"Has he been assigned a new position?"

"The details of your mentor's relocation are not for you to know." Haynes purses her lips in a tight line. Why won't she tell me anything about what happened to Thompson? Why is she secretive about his relocation? She's hiding something. "I am curious—"

Her tablet beeps.

Haynes glances at the lit-up screen, reading the message displayed there. Confusion fills her eyes. The Council Member stands and heads for the door. "I apologize, I have something I must attend to. I'll be back in a moment."

She slips out the door. She left her tablet on the desk. I rise to my feet, glancing at the clock on the wall. I don't have much time to do this. Council Member Whitley's office is on a different floor, so that will buy me some time—but not much.

I grab Haynes's tablet. Reaching into my pocket, I withdraw the small object . It's an information storage device, used to transfer files from one tablet to another. I turn on her tablet, then tap on an icon labeled "files". I'm tempted to read them all now, but I don't have time to do so. I could search for files containing specific keywords. Do I have time? Do I even know what I need to find? I select all files on the tablet.

I plug the device into the side of the tablet. A box pops up on the screen, asking me if I want to copy all the files onto the device. I tap "yes", and a new message replaces the last, telling me to wait a few moments while the files are being copied. I glance over my shoulder at the door. If Haynes comes back while I'm doing this…

Within about thirty seconds, a new box pops up, saying "process complete". I unplug the device and shove it in my pocket, then push Haynes's tablet back where it was on the desk. I sit, letting out a relieved sigh. I wasn't caught. All I need now is to make it through the rest of my report.

Haynes steps back into the room. "I'm very sorry. There was a communication error of some sort. I'll have to look into it more later. For now, you and I can finish discussing your report."

"Errors do happen." I manage a smile, but every muscle in my body tightens. Will she find out what I've done? My gaze shifts to the security camera attached to the ceiling and my heart pounds faster. Every second of my crime was observed. If someone paid attention to what I did, my plan could be over before I even started it.

She sits back down. "As I was saying before I left, I'm curious as to how the Intolerant is doing *socially*. How has he interacted with other citizens? Is he making friends outside of you? Is he dating anyone?"

"No, no, he isn't dating anyone as of now." Why is she asking this?

"You look very nice today, Katherine."

I don't say "thank you", because the comment sounds more like an accusation than a compliment. Even so, I can't resist the heat that rushes over my face. I *did* spend more time on my hair and make-up today. If I'm spending a lot of time with a particular person, maybe I want to vary my appearance. And *maybe* that person is a somewhat cute boy. "He's been friendly with the other workers at the factory, but I don't think anything has gone beyond acquaintanceship."

"I see. He hasn't grown attached to anyone?" I shake my head *no*. Haynes raises her eyebrows. "That doesn't bother you at all?"

"I'm not following you on this."

"If he's been distant with the other citizens, couldn't that mean he's *choosing* not to become attached to anyone? Maybe he's remembering things and knows why he came here in the first place, and so he's planning out an act of terrorism as we speak?" Haynes never drops her gaze. Does she hope I'll admit Reintegration isn't going as planned? She knows I've lied. All she needs now is one second where I'm not paying attention.

"I told you last time I was here. I don't believe he came here for any violent reasons. Maybe he just isn't very social, or maybe he doesn't feel comfortable when I'm hanging over his shoulder all the time."

Haynes nods, a spark of inspiration flickering through her eyes. Oh, great. What did I say? She turns on her tablet, looking at something on the screen. "Hmm…that is an idea, Katherine. Starting tomorrow, the Intolerant is to begin his duties on his own. You are not to accompany him to work anymore. I think this is for the best."

What?

"Just like you needed independence from your mentor, the Intolerant might need independence from you. When your Final Test has ended, it wouldn't do us any good if he didn't know how to function on his own, would it?" She laughs, as if she's made a joke of some sort. Of course. If we aren't together, we have less time to collaborate on what we will and won't say. She wants to trap me—or Matthew.

I can handle not going with him to work every day. We don't talk much there anyway. At least I'll still see him in the mornings and evenings. If I can figure out where he belongs, he won't be here much longer. Haynes's motives are what bothers me about the situation.

"What should I be doing in the meantime?"

Reintegration

"Exactly what you did before your Final Test began."

How can I, if what I did before this was learn from Thompson? My mentor is gone, so I can't do any more training. I don't say this out loud, not wanting *her* to give me something to do. I shrug, like this is no big deal. "Okay."

Her tablet beeps, and she looks at it again. "I see you visited Doctor Perry today. He says you were very curious as to what would happen if Reintegration failed."

"Oh, well, he mentioned it first." The statement is true. Doctor Perry *was* the one to bring up Reintegration's possible failure before I did. "After he started talking about it, my curiosity was piqued."

"I'm glad to see you're showing interest in the future, Katherine. After all, you are the Federation's future." Haynes stands. Is my report over? "We'll meet again next week for your third report."

I nod, standing also. She dropped the conversation too quickly. Why? Why isn't she pressing me for the reason behind my visit to Doctor Perry? Why isn't she concerned that I was so interested in what would happen if Reintegration failed? I have more questions now, but this meeting did provide one solid fact.

Council Member Haynes is hiding something.

By the time I arrive back at City 45, it's nearly dinnertime.

I look over my shoulder every few seconds, expecting a Regulator to arrest me. I have committed at least a dozen Violations in the last two weeks. Haynes must be sure about some of them, but she's letting me go.

Why?

My mind refuses to focus on any of the other questions to which I need answers. Haynes hasn't punished me, even though she's certain I'm lying to her. She doesn't need me to confess. I've committed enough suspicious actions for her to give me a Violation. But she isn't. She's letting me continue on with my charade.

Why do I feel like she's always been one step ahead of me?

I enter the cafeteria, scanning the people in the room. No Matthew. He should have ended work about half-an-hour ago. Sighing, I step into the elevator and press the button for the second floor. Maybe he's in his room. Not like there's anywhere else he can go.

I slip my hand in my pocket, checking for the umpteenth time that the medicine I stole is still there. I have a way to give Matthew his memory back. Maybe. There could be side effects like Doctor Perry said. Giving the medicine to Matthew could harm him more than help him. Should I give it to him yet?

I have all of Haynes' files now. One of them must contain information about Matthew's past. Won't searching the files be a safer route than giving Matthew a never-before used injection? Matthew is regaining his memory anyway. If I can help him find where he needs to go, he'll be safe.

Won't he?

Life was so much simpler when the Federation told me what to do. I followed the rules and listened to my superiors. I trusted they knew what was best for me. Now, every decision I make has to be on my own. I want Matthew to escape, but I also want to keep him safe. Every choice I make now affects Matthew. I helped the Federation steal his life from him. Now I have to help him get it back.

What I'm doing is right. Why is doing the right thing so

hard?

I step off the elevator onto the second floor. The hallway is empty, as it usually is at this time. Some people are still at work while others are currently eating dinner. I grab my identification card. No one can find what I have in my pockets—a stolen medicine and a device filled with stolen files.

Shutting the door behind me, I slip into the safety of my bedroom. I pull both the plastic bag and the device out of my pocket and set them on the small table. Where can I hide them? Tomorrow the cleaners will come and change my bedding and take my clothing to be washed. What else do they do on cleaning days? Paranoia sets in. Are they also required to search our apartments for items like what I have? I've learned the Federation has as many secrets as I do. What else don't they tell us about?

If I fail to get Matthew out of the Federation, the Council will do one of two things to him. They'll either interrogate him to find the others or use him as a science experiment. Then again...they could execute him, too. What if after Matthew tells them where the other Intolerants are, they decide he's useless and kill him? Or what if the doctors won't need him very long and kill him as soon as they find whatever cure they need? No matter what, Matthew's life will be destroyed if I can't get him home in time.

As for me, the Council will give me so many Violations. Lying to a superior. Breaking the Tolerance Act. Assisting a criminal. Stealing important documents from a superior. If they catch me, I'll be declared an Intolerant.

I don't care what they do to me anymore.

Where do I keep the items for now? I'll take them with me until tomorrow. After the cleaners finish with whatever it is they do, I can hide the medicine and the device in my room. Once I'm finished with the items, I'll destroy them.

At that point, Matthew will be gone, in a place where the Federation can't hurt him.

18

"What did you want to tell me about?"

Matthew glances at me as we walk down the walkway—the one place I can tell him everything without fear of someone overhearing. The Wall looms before us, one more barrier between Matthew and freedom. One more thing Matthew needs to remember. He got in here somehow. Will he remember how to get back out?

"I might have found a way to give you your memory back sooner. I know you're starting to remember things, but we don't know how long it will take for you to remember enough. Haynes is on to me, Matthew. She knows I'm lying to her, but she's not punishing me. I don't know what she's doing, but she *knows*." I shudder, despite the sunshine overhead. Haynes has a plan. Maybe she's hoping to catch me while I'm in the middle of breaking the law and have concrete evidence against me. "I doubt we even have four weeks anymore to get you out of here."

How does she know what I've been up to?

Matthew stops walking. "You have a way to fix me?"

I wince. Why did I act like I have the perfect solution? "I...maybe. Matthew, you need to listen to me, okay? I *might* have found something to help you. Might."

Reaching into my pocket, I withdraw the plastic bag with the pills inside and hand it to him. "No one knows if it works. It could end up hurting you rather than helping you. It's one option, though. There's something else—"

"Where did you get this?" Matthew stares at the pills, then at me, a look of disbelief passing over his face.

"Well, I stole it from Doctor Perry. But Matthew—"

"You did what?" Matthew's eyes widen. He gives me the plastic bag back. I shove it into my pocket. "Why were you even there? I thought you were meeting with the Council Member today."

"I did, but look, we need to get you home. We don't have much more time. I don't even know how much time we have!" My frustration builds. All the odds are *not* in our favor at the moment. "I had to do something. Doctor Perry doesn't even know I took it, and he won't find out if I can get you out of the city as soon as possible."

Matthew stares at the grass next to the walkway. This is why I didn't tell him before I went to City 1. "You didn't need to do that. If anyone finds out you stole the stuff from him, you'll get a Violation, right?"

"Yes," I whisper. "But I don't care."

Matthew rakes his fingers through his hair, mussing it up. He does that a lot when he's overwhelmed or nervous about something. "You don't have to do this because you feel guilty, okay? I don't blame you for what you did. If it wasn't for you, I'd be dead, no chance to get home at all."

He's told me this multiple times since I told him the truth, mainly when I propose solutions for helping him escape that could also involve me receiving a Violation. He doesn't blame me for what happened to him, but I blame myself. It's more than that now, though. Now Haynes is more than certain of what I've done. Now the time we may have is limited. Now if I don't succeed, Matthew will be subjected to something worse than execution.

"You've done *enough*. I wish you'd just believe me. I don't expect you to put yourself in harm's way for me, especially considering what you've already done."

"I know you don't. I just..." The words die in my throat. Matthew is here for now, but he won't always be. He's alive and well, but for how long? The Federation will hurt him if I can't figure out where he belongs. "I'm not helping you because I feel obligated. I'm helping you because I *want* to."

He needs to know what they'll do to him if he can't leave in time—the horrible, awful ideas the Council created. "They aren't going to just kill you, Matthew. Doctor Perry told me the Council is going to take a vote if Reintegration fails. Depending on what they decide, they're either going to use you to find the rest of the Intolerants or continue to use you as a science experiment."

Shock flickers across Matthew's face. I wish I could be telling him I found out how to get him home. I'm not. I'm forced to tell him if he doesn't escape, the Council will hurt him even further than they already have. They'll prolong his misery all the more.

"As for whatever the pills are, Doctor Perry said it may

not work. He's not even done testing it yet." I hesitate. Matthew may not like what I'm about to suggest. "I think we should save it as a last resort. There's something else we can do, though. Haynes has a lot of files on her tablet. I can look through them to try—"

"Katherine." He seems to cram as much horror into saying my name as possible. "You just *stole* that medicine stuff. You aren't going to try stealing anything again. Especially not from *her*. You just said she's on to you. If you were caught..."

I pull the information storage device out of my pocket and hold it up. Matthew's voice trails off. I allow myself a confident grin, despite the circumstances. "I already did. Everything we should need, right here. I can look through the files to try to learn more about you. If I don't find anything, we'll consider using the stuff I took from Perry, okay? I just can't give it to you when there's other things we could try first. And if you decide it's not worth the risk giving this stuff to you, I understand. I'll let you decide."

"Got it. No more risky plans though, okay? Not without telling me first."

"Why? So you can just tell me 'no'?"

"Exactly." Matthew, too, grins. Then he grows serious again. "We're both involved in this, Katherine. If we're caught, we both face the consequences. We have to do things together. We make the decisions *together*. The two of us are partners now."

Partners. Matthew thinks of us as *partners*. Our lives have become intertwined in a way no one can ever unravel. Every single thing we do affects the other. Something also tells me we would sacrifice everything for the other. This isn't about my Final Test anymore. This is about finding Matthew freedom.

"'Partners' it is," I say in a whisper. "Katherine Holliday and Matthew Braddock, the two who dared to defy the Federation."

"And the two who are going to escape it."

"I don't know if anyone's ever escaped before. If someone has, I've never been told about it. Then again, why would the Federation tell us? Sometimes I wonder if the Wall was constructed to keep us in more than to keep you out."

"Maybe we'll be the first to make it."

Matthew keeps saying *we*. Does he really want me coming with him? Me, a member of the Federation. Me, a Regulator. Of course Matthew thinks of us as friends, same as I do. It's the rest of the Intolerants I worry about. Matthew grew up in a world so different from the Federation. How are things done in the Outlands? Would the other Intolerants accept me?

How can I tell Matthew I'm even more terrified of going to the Outlands with him than of what will happen to me if Haynes does prove what I've done?

Maybe Matthew is an outcast even among the Intolerants. How could the Federation have come up with a story like the one they teach us, if there isn't a shred of truth in it? What if some of the Intolerants are as violent as I've been taught, and Matthew is an anomaly of sorts?

What if I don't belong anywhere?

"Haynes is making it worse for us, though. She's limiting the time we're allowed to see each other. Mornings and evenings only. I don't know why she's doing this."

"Huh." Matthew frowns at the walkway, then smirks at me, amusement dancing in his eyes. "Can't bear to stand even a second away from me, can you? Which is it, my irresistible charm or my unbelievable good looks?"

I smother my smile. Why can't he be serious when he needs to be? Maybe his optimism is a good thing, since it's the only thing keeping me from losing my mind with worry.

"Could be a little of both, but if you keep bragging about how awesome you are, the effect might wear off." I match his teasing grin for a second, then clear my throat. "I was being serious, though. We need to be careful. Haynes is doing this for a reason. I don't know exactly what she's hoping we'll do. Maybe she's just trying to pressure me into making a mistake."

"Do you really think you'll be able to figure out where I'm from by what's in the files?"

"I hope so. I'm not a hundred percent sure what they'll contain, but maybe they'll have something we can use. If not..." I stick my hand in my pocket, fingering the edge of the plastic bag. I don't want to use it, but if Matthew agrees to it, we'll have no other choice. There isn't time for anything else.

"We'll figure things out when we get to them."

"I'm also hoping to learn what happened to Thompson. Maybe he can help us escape. Maybe he knows if anyone else has escaped before now and how they did it." Unless, of course, receiving a Violation will make him think twice before defying the Federation again. "He's been relocated, so I just need to find out where."

Matthew sighs. "I'm sorry I'm not more help. I'm still not remembering much, though. Not anything useful."

"It's not your fault. There's nothing you can do to remember everything."

He needs to remember something big soon. A place, a way

past the Wall, anything. The files may not have any useful information, and the stuff I stole from Doctor Perry...I want to avoid using it if possible. There's a chance both of my plans will fail.

What will we do then?

19

The cleaners came today.

The smell of cleaning supplies is stronger than usual. I open my closet. The basket filled with dirty clothes just this morning is now empty. I yank my jacket off the hanger and stuff the plastic bag with the pills in one of the pockets. Do the cleaners ever take my jacket to be washed? Next week, I'll make sure I remove the pills from my room before the cleaners come. I hang my jacket back in the closet, then close the door.

My normal routine involves showering before going to bed, but I can't wait any longer. I need to know what's on the files. I kick my shoes off and sit on the edge of my bed. Pulling the information storage device out of my pocket, I plug it into the side of my tablet. The screen lights up, displaying a box that reads "Download all files?" I tap "yes" and wait for the process to finish.

I prop my pillow up against the wall and lean against it. As

Reintegration

I set my tablet on my lap, another box pops up, informing me the files have been downloaded. I tap the messaging icon, but no one has tried to contact me. This shouldn't be a surprise. Thompson's gone, and Chelsea...who knows what's going on with her.

I initiate a search for any files with Matthew's last name. The list of files dwindles until only two are left. I select the first file. I'll see what the second one is later. The file I opened is a typical citizen's file.

Name: Braddock, Matthew
Current Status: Citizen (Temporary)
Citizen Number: 4591-334 (Temporary)
Violations: None

The file continues like this, giving details about Matthew's occupation, his place of residence, age, and basic appearance, like hair color and eye color. I already know this. A black-and-white picture of Matthew is included in the file. At the end is a lengthy summary of Matthew's capture, the Reintegration process, and his assignment to City 45.

No details about where he's from.

I read the file again. Did I miss something? No, nothing in the file provides the information I need. Too early to be discouraged, however. It's only one file. I probably have several dozen to look at. I open the second file. Another citizen file?

Name: Braddock, Andrew
Current Status: Intolerant
Citizen Number: N/A
Violations: None

Who is this? He has no citizen identification number, so he must be from the Outlands. He's an Intolerant but has no

Violations? Another sign he's from the Outlands, just like Matthew. I scroll through the file until I find the picture. I can't hold back my gasp.

He looks like Matthew, but several years older. The picture is black-and-white, but the resemblance is unmistakable. Same firm jaw, same permanent half-smile, same eyes. A shiver of excitement runs through me. Does Matthew know this person?

I continue scrolling through the file, then stop near the end when one paragraph catches me eye. Someone added a report, like the one at the end of Matthew's file. The report is dated fifteen years prior to now. Is that when the picture was taken, too? Council Member Josiah Whitley—the oldest member of the Council at the moment—wrote the report.

Yesterday our Regulators captured an Intolerant, the first we've found in years. He was caught attempting to break into City 47's communication center. After hours of interrogation, Regulator Johnson managed to learn some critical facts.

The captured Intolerant is named Andrew Braddock. He came from the Outlands, and is a member of the Underground. This news is very disturbing to the Council. The Underground hasn't made a move against the Federation in at least a decade.

What is the Underground? The context suggests the Underground is a movement or group of some sort. This Andrew Braddock person must be a part of it.

The Intolerant refused to give any more information about the Underground, but the Council has concluded he came here for an act of terrorism. He provided a different reason for his mission, but the Council agrees this reason is illogical and most likely an attempt to lessen punishment.

The Council votes that execution is the best sentence to carry out.

Reintegration

The report ends there. They killed Andrew Braddock? Maybe Matthew doesn't know him. Is the same last name a coincidence and nothing more? Another report follows the one I just read, this one dated one week after the first.

Regulator Johnson informed the Council that the Intolerant Andrew Braddock has escaped the Federation and into the Outlands. Nothing can be done except further increase security measures.

There are no more reports. Still no indication as to why this person has the same last name as Matthew. No indication of what the Underground is. No indication where in the Outlands Andrew Braddock came from.

I'll show Matthew this file tomorrow and see if he knows anything about it. I close the file and begin a new search, for anything about the Underground. One file comes up. I open it. Also dated around fifteen years ago, the file is a message sent to Haynes from one of the other Council Members.

In response to your questions about the Intolerant's disappearance and the Underground, Andrew Braddock clearly managed to escape City 1's prison through the use of violence. None of our Regulators were killed, but some suffered from minor injuries. I agree with Council Member Whitley that more security must be put into place. Our solution will be to give the Regulators throughout the Federation weapons—not to kill, of course.

The Underground is a group formed in the year 2025 by Intolerant Frederick Jules. The Underground's original purpose was to overthrow the Federation, and the members of this group settled in the Outlands, out of our reach. Our belief was that the members of the Underground had been scattered after Jules' death, but the arrival of Braddock proves otherwise.

We plan to vote on what measures to take at the end of the week.

The Underground. A group with the sole purpose of defeating the Federation. We aren't told any such thing exists—

maybe it doesn't. A lot of time has passed since Andrew Braddock escaped the Federation. But what if…what if the Underground does still exist? If this other Braddock was part of it, is Matthew part of it also?

Of course, it makes sense if Matthew is involved with the Underground in some way. Haynes seemed so horrified when I told her Matthew's name weeks ago. If she knows of the Underground and Andrew Braddock, no wonder Matthew's arrival shocked her.

I close the file. No information about Matthew's home. I do a third search using the word "Outlands", and several files display on the screen. I read through them all, but the only things discussed are the things I already know—information about the war that decimated the Outlands, how the Intolerants live there, and the reasons why the Wall was constructed.

I bite back a frustrated sigh. Why can't I find what I'm looking for? I need a break from searching for Matthew's home. Searching through all of Haynes's files could take hours. I wish there was someone else who could help me make sense of this mess. Matthew's even more clueless than I am since he can't remember anything. If only I knew where they relocated Thompson.

Will one of the files provide me with the information I need?

After typing Thompson's name into the search area, I wait for the process to complete. If I learn where he is and ask him for help, will he do it? My search has only one result. Thompson's citizen file. I select it.

Name: Thompson, Phillip
Current Status: Citizen
Citizen Number: 3377-008

Reintegration

Violations: Two

Two Violations? Haynes acted like Thompson has one Violation. But two? I listened to the recording of his argument with Haynes. He received one Violation for his defiance. What is the other Violation, though? I scroll through the file, until I reach a section describing what infraction was committed to result in a Violation.

Violation 1: Behavior suggesting insubordination
Violation 2: CLASSIFIED

Classified? What did Thompson do that was so horrible it can't even be mentioned? According to the Federation's laws, isn't breaking the Tolerance Act the worst crime a person can commit? Thompson never told me anything could be labeled "classified" on an official citizen file.

Why did Thompson have to be so cryptic about his past?

I read the rest of the file, but nothing tells me what this other Violation is. Thompson has, however, been relocated to City 1 where he now works as a normal Regulator. He's no longer a mentor.

Why have they treated him so strictly?

Have other citizens had similar punishments for receiving Violations? I search for all files with the subject of "Violations". There won't be very many, since only a couple of Violations occur every year, and none have happened in City 45 in five years.

Apparently not.

One-hundred-and-two files come up. One-hundred-and-two citizens have committed Violations in a period of three years, over three-fourths of them occurring in the past six months. I glance through the list of names, until one makes me stop.

Brian Coleman, the boy we were told died of illness.

I open his citizen file. He didn't get sick. He received his first two Violations for breaking the Tolerance Act, and the third for "behavior suggesting insubordination".

My hands shaking, I start going through the other files. I read through the first twenty files, the most recent ones. Twenty citizens who committed Violations in the past month, Thompson included.

What does this mean?

Why is the Council covering up Violations?

Why have we been lied to about the exponentially increasing Violations?

Did Thompson know about this? If he knew, he would have told me. With all he did to keep me from being caught, why would he hide this from me? I return to Brain Coleman's file.

A report is attached to the end of his file—a report similar to the one at the end of Matthew's file. Council Member Haynes wrote the report. As I read through it, a sense of dread creeps over me. This can't be true. How is this possible? The Council didn't simply have Brian Coleman executed.

He was the original Reintegration test subject.

Citizen Brian Coleman, age nineteen, committed three Violations in an alarmingly brief time period of two months. What attributed to this sudden change in behavior, we are uncertain. The news is disturbing, and for the peace of mind of the other citizens, I propose that the Council not reveal the news at this moment.

In addition to this, I propose a solution to solve the issue of citizens receiving Violations. Vincent Perry, City 1's medicinal specialist, has come up with a way to abolish the practice of executing citizens. He has created a procedure, which if successful, will erase the subject's memory and

Reintegration

enable us to return the subject back into the Federation. If this procedure works, Brian Coleman can be retaught his duties and role in society, and have his status be restored to citizen.

Doctor Perry calls this procedure "Reintegration". I propose that the Council give Doctor Perry permission to test the procedure on Brain Coleman, who will otherwise be executed.

Someone filed another report a week later, this one giving the specifics of the Reintegration process and what the expected results were. I read through the third and final report.

Brian Coleman showed signs of regaining memory thirteen days into the process. After analysis by Doctor Perry, it has been concluded that Reintegration is a failure. Brian Coleman will be executed tomorrow at 2:30 in the afternoon. A message will be sent to City 45 to inform the citizens there of Brian Coleman's unexpected death. The citizens do not need to know the specifics of this event.

The Council tested Reintegration on a citizen of the Federation. I always assumed it was tried on an Intolerant from the Outlands. But a citizen? The entire Council, not only Haynes, has secrets.

Why the sudden increase in Violations? Something happened in recent months to cause this. I've come to recognize the Federation's faults because of Matthew. Something must be happening to make other citizens break the Tolerance Act.

But what?

I try a combination of new searches, but nothing helps me know what is causing this. Or why the Council keeps secrets, even from the Regulators. Finally one search brings up a file, labeled *Project Endgame*.

Project Endgame? I tap on the file to open it, but a box pops up requesting a password. None of the other files required passwords to open them. This file is important. Even the name suggests something of significance. What could the password be? I type in *742*, the same password Doctor Perry used to access the medical cabinet. I wait a few seconds, but the numbers flash red and my tablet vibrates. It was worth a shot. What else can I try?

The one file I may need to open, and I can't.

I run a comb through my wet hair. What is the password to open that file? All through my shower, I tried to think of the file's possible contents. Something tells me it doesn't have anything to do Matthew or the Underground. The file name, *Project Endgame*, sounds more like a plan the Council recently put into effect or may soon put into effect.

After slipping the comb in one of the bathroom drawers, I walk back toward my bed. How late is it? I should go to sleep soon. The Federation can use my tablet to track my sleeping patterns based on how late I stay up using it. I disconnect the information storage device from my tablet.

I'm such an imbecile.

The Federation monitors my tablet usage. Won't they—whoever monitors our tablets—be able to see I looked at files I shouldn't have access to? They'll send a report to Haynes, who will question me, who will then have all she needs to give me a Violation, who will order Matthew's execution...

Deleting the files won't help me at all. I open the closet and shove the device in my jacket's pocket, with the medicine I stole from Perry. My palms sweat as I close my closet again.

There's nothing I can do. I learned nothing about where Matthew's from, but managed to bring us closer to trouble than ever. We may have no longer than one week to get out of here, because of one stupid mistake I made. More and more citizens are breaking laws and receiving Violations. A group of Intolerants formed an organization to stop the Federation. The first Reintegration attempt was performed on a citizen. I can't ask Thompson for help now, because if I do, he could be given a third Violation. I won't be the one to get him executed.

None of this helps me know how to get Matthew home.

My thoughts drift to the pills hidden in my closet. We have so little time to escape…what if the medicine is the only option we have? Matthew hasn't remembered anything useful so far. How long will it take him to remember anything more? Days? Weeks? Months? Why didn't the files contain anything I could use?

Nothing seems to work in my favor.

I look at the time on my tablet. How can I tell him now? With the security cameras in the hallways, someone will see I talked to him. Won't it look suspicious if I woke him up at this hour? The longer we can put off capture, the more time we have to try to escape. Besides, maybe with all the tablets the Federation has to monitor, they'll miss mine.

It's a petty argument, but it's all I have to reassure myself we'll actually be able to do it. Matthew and I will escape. Andrew Braddock, whoever he is, managed to escape the Federation's walls, all those years ago. Security is tighter now, but Matthew got in here, so there's some sort of loophole somewhere.

We can be free.

20

"So the amount of Violations is higher than expected?"

"Not just higher, Matthew. The amount of Violations received in the last six months alone is...ridiculous!" I shake my head as I walk with Matthew to his work. How can he understand everything I found last night, when I myself am still trying to make sense of what all this means? "Dozens of people are breaking the Tolerance Act. Twelve have been executed in recent months. I've always been taught only a few Violations happen every year."

"Okay." Matthew draws the word out, expression thoughtful. "Why? Why keep this a secret?"

"I don't know." And I don't. I wish I knew what was going on. Something's been off ever since Haynes told me the Council wanted to test Reintegration on Matthew. The procedure failed once before, so if they wanted to try it again, why let Matthew out into the world so quickly? If the Council is worried about Matthew being a terrorist, why have they allowed him to live among the citizens so early into the procedure—especially with all the recent Violations? Matthew's Reintegration fits into all this somehow, could even be the key to solving the puzzle.

"I think they want to hide the reason behind the Violations, not the Violations themselves," I say, more to myself than to Matthew. That's the answer, isn't it? The Council has never bothered to keep Violations a secret. On the contrary; they always made it clear to us what happens when we break the Tolerance Act.

Something happened to make others see the Federation isn't perfect. While I looked at the files, I noticed more and more instances of "behavior suggesting insubordination" rather than "breaking the Tolerance Act". These aren't cases of people accidentally saying a forbidden word. These are cases of people outright *defying* the Federation.

Like me.

People are questioning the Council's leadership.

"I didn't learn where you're from, though." Knowing about the increasing Violations provides no help in getting Matthew out of here. After I turn on my tablet, I pull up Andrew Braddock's file. I hand my tablet to Matthew. "I found this. He has your last name, and he's an Intolerant who lives in the Outlands. Do you recognize him?"

Matthew stares at the picture. I haven't told him of my blunder yet and of how little time we have. The last thing I want is to give Matthew Doctor Perry's pills. If Matthew agrees to use them, they could kill him. If he doesn't agree to it, he won't regain his memory. Why isn't there an easy path?

Whatever we do, there's going to be danger involved.

Matthew hands me my tablet back, smiling sheepishly. "I don't know. Seems familiar, but I can't place it. I'm sorry. I'm trying to remember, but it's all still fuzzy."

"That's fine." I look at the picture for another few seconds before slipping my tablet in my bag. Why do they have the same last name? "I don't know exactly what this person has to do with you, but I do think there's a connection. Figuring out what the connection is could help us a bit."

The breeze picks up, tousling Matthew's hair. He cocks his head. "Couldn't you ask your teacher? The guy who was given the Violation? It seems like he would know this kind of thing."

"I can't. He doesn't have one Violation, he has two. One more and they'll kill him. Technically, we're not allowed to have contact with each other. If anyone was to find out I went and talked to him..." I shudder, unable to finish the statement.

There it is, the *feeling* again. Thompson has his Violations because of me. He didn't have any before he stood up to Haynes on my behalf. I'm the reason Haynes had him relocated. I'm the one wanting to defy the Federation, but he's the one who's been punished.

How could I live with myself if anything more happened to him because of me?

"Okay, well, we'll think of something." Understanding lines Matthew's voice, maybe even a trace of discouragement. "We have a little time."

"No, we don't." Tears sting my eyes. How could I have been so stupid? "We don't have a couple of weeks anymore, Matthew. I messed up. By looking at the files on my tablet, I accidentally alerted the Federation that I stole them from Haynes. It's highly unlikely that they won't see I had access to files way above my clearance. You need to leave within the next couple of days."

"What do you think we should do?" Matthew's voice is quiet and subdued. We have so little time left to do so much. Not only does Matthew need to remember how he got inside the Federation, he needs to remember where in the Outlands he's from.

"I think our only option is to give you this." I reach into my pocket and pull out the plastic bag. "I don't want to give this to you. I promise. But right now…we don't have time to wait for you to remember things. The files told me nothing. I would say we could just leave the city and try to find the rest of the Intolerants, but I don't know how to get past the Wall."

Matthew glances over his shoulder at the towering barrier between us and success.

"I can understand if you don't want to. There's a lot of risk involved." What other options do we have? Is there something we can do that won't involve placing Matthew in too much danger? "I can go to the Regulation Center. They have a map of the city there. Maybe I can use it to find a way—"

"We'll go for it," Matthew blurts out. "We have no choice."

He can't be serious. There's so many ways this could go wrong, so many risks to Matthew's well-being. "But, Matthew, there's something else we can try first. I don't think we need to do this just yet. I'm sorry I brought it up. Just listen to me. There's other alternatives."

Matthew shakes his head with the stubbornness of a Primary School child. "How many 'other alternatives' are we going to try? We've waited for my memory to come back on its own, but it hasn't. You stole government records, but found nothing. You can look to try to find a way to escape, but if it doesn't work, we'll have lost more time."

"If this doesn't work, it could kill you." Doesn't he care about what could happen to him? Is he so desperate to regain his memory that he doesn't care? "At this point, all that matters is getting you out of the city."

"I know what it could do to me. But there's also a small chance it will work. You can't stay here either, Katherine. Once they see you stole those files, they'll know you've helped me. I doubt they'll go easy on you." Matthew looks away, but not before I see the look of genuine concern in his eyes. Does he care so much about what happens to *me*, even more than he cares about returning to the Outlands? "If there's a chance this could be what we need to leave, I'll take it."

He reaches for the bag, but I jerk it away. "Not now. You're already late for work. Later, when you get off of work. I don't know what this will do to you. What if it doesn't kill you but makes you pass out or something? Your tracking device will alert the medical workers. Last thing we need is for you to have to see Doctor Perry and have him figure out what happened."

"Shouldn't this be my decision?"

I wince.

"It is," I say softly. "But I don't understand why this has to be the only option."

"Because I need to know who I am! I want to go home, wherever home is. I want to sleep at night instead of lying awake trying to piece together the memories I do have. I want to know who I was before I came here. I want to know that I'm the kind of guy who could possibly deserve to maybe be more than friends with you someday." He takes a deep breath and his eyes meet mine.

Several seconds pass before I reply. "What are you saying?"

"I think I love you, Katherine."

No one has ever said those words to me before. Matthew loves me. Have I ever been able to fully comprehend the concept of love? The Federation always told me love is an emotion that comes and goes. Matthew told me love is more than that. He said you love someone when you're willing to do anything for someone else and all you want is to spend every moment with them.

He looks so nervous and so hopeful. What do I say? What do I *want* to say? I like him. I like him more than I've ever liked anyone. But I find myself shaking my head. "It could never work. I belong here, in the Federation, and you belong out there somewhere. You'll be leaving soon."

I'm being logical, but inside I just want to tell him that I think I love him too. I also think maybe we could be more than friends someday. He doesn't need to remember his past for me to know what kind of guy he is. I've already seen who he is.

"You could come with me, wherever I'll be going. You couldn't stay here after you helped me anyway. I mean, I understand if you don't feel the same way. I didn't want to tell you because I didn't want things to be, you know, *awkward*. I'm sorry."

All I have to do is tell him I *do* feel the same way. Then I can have the possibility of a future with him and a life outside the Federation. But I can't. I can't lose someone else close to me. I'll either lose him to a failure in my plan of helping him escape or to a failed relationship like all the others I've seen. He's different from the other guys I've known, but how can I know it would last? "*I'm* sorry, Matthew. I think you're a great friend and I will do anything I can to help you. I promise. But—"

"We'll always just be friends. I understand." The smile he gives me is strained and sad. He doesn't push, even though I almost want him to. Maybe I'll always regret not telling him the truth.

Silence falls over us until I break it. "You're late for work. You should go."

"Okay. See you later?"

"Of course."

It isn't until I turn around that I let the tears fall.

I've always found the Regulation Center's map of the city fascinating. In the Past, people would use a material called *paper* to make maps, but the paper was easily torn and soiled quickly. The Federation developed a new technique.

In the center of the map room is a large table that looks like the surface is made of glass. It actually functions like a bigger version of a tablet. You turn it on, and it displays an image of the city on the surface. You can zoom in or out by scrolling your hand across the screen. If you tap one of the buildings, it tells you what it is and what its purpose is.

Thompson showed me this when I was younger, but I was more interested in finding buildings I had visited than in learning about the city's layout. The train system runs beneath the city. The outermost edges of the city contain buildings for Regulators, doctors, government officials, and other things like that. Inside the outer edge is the industrial area, where the factories are. The dormitories lie in the city's center.

My main focus at the moment is the Wall. The map shows how the buildings are built up to the Wall's inside edge. The area outside the map is blank, in contrast to the colorful depictions of the buildings in the city. The Outlands. An area we know so little about; a place I'm still torn about going to.

I study the area around the Wall, looking for any inconsistency in the setup. The city's medical center, the communication center, the Regulation Center…nothing seems out of place. The Wall has no gate. There is no need for one, since the trains run below the ground from city to city.

Even as I look over the map, my last conversation with Matthew replays over and over in my mind. He loves me. He told me so. He wants me to come with him to the Outlands. Haven't I wanted him to tell me that? Then he finally did and I turned him down. I'm making the realistic decision, but I still feel like a fool.

My hand lingers over one building I don't recognize. It's on the opposite side of the city from the Regulation Center. I don't go there very often. I tap on the image, and a box pops up onto the screen. Where it should normally tell me what the building is for, the box is blank. I zoom in on the image. It's a normal-looking building, two stories, lots of windows, built of steel and glass.

One of the other Regulators enters the room, stopping when she sees me. My stomach flip-flops. Head Regulator Olson. I haven't talked to her since Thompson's arrest.

"Oh, hello, Trainee Holliday. I'm very sorry for what happened to your mentor. It must have come as a shock to you."

Judging by her attitude during Thompson's arrest, she too was stunned.

"It was." I knew Thompson did something Violation-worthy in defending me, but I never expected Haynes would give him more than one Violation and relocate him to the other side of the Federation. His second Violation…does it have anything to do with the crime they never caught him for? "I have a question for you."

"Hmm?" She glances at the map.

"This building here…" I tap on the building again, making the empty box return. "What is it?"

Head Regulator Olson blinks in surprise. "That is very unusual. Must be a glitch in the system."

Or the Council is hiding something. "Yes, but what is this building for?"

"I don't know for sure. I do believe the Federation closed it down several months ago, but I have no idea what it was used for. I'm sorry I can't be of more help to you, but I simply don't know."

"Thank you for your help, anyway."

Olson nods, walking over to a wall control panel. I glance once more at the building. More things I don't know the answer to. Even when I try to find answers, all I pull up is more questions. I may be overreacting. The building could be closed down like Olson said. Anytime I see something suspicious, however, my first thought is that the Federation has a secret.

The Federation is full of dark buried secrets the Council never wants to be brought to light.

After lunch, I head to the other side of the city. It's a long walk, but I don't mind. I've been trying to think of another solution besides giving Matthew the pills. How could everything else have gone downhill so quickly? Matthew's correct about one thing. The longer we wait thinking of other ideas could mean the difference between freedom and execution.

Still, the thought of what that stuff could do to Matthew...

I push the thought from my mind. Just thinking about it makes me feel sick inside. We've come so far. I can't imagine losing Matthew now. He's become more than just a friend, more than someone I can confide my secrets in. I trust him more than I've trusted anyone ever before.

I approach one of the buildings—the same unmarked building I saw on the map. Why is there no sign in front of it displaying the name? It can't be abandoned, like Olson suggested. The card scanner screen is lit up. Lights are on in the windows.

The building is in use, but why is there no indication as to what it's for?

"Katherine?"

I turn around. Chelsea? She walks toward the building, a look of astonishment on her face. She wears her white medical uniform and carries her trainee bag. Why is she on this side of the city, though?

Chelsea stops in front of me and plants her hands on her hips. "What are you doing here?"

"What am *I* doing here? I was just walking through the area. You work here, don't you?" I point over my shoulder at the building. "When they reassigned your occupation, this is where they reassigned you, isn't it?"

"Maybe." Chelsea shifts from one foot to the other, her expression neutral. Why is her behavior so...distant? Like the last time we spoke, it seems like she's acting this way because someone told her to. "The details of my reassignment are classified information. You of all people should understand how significant that is."

Oh, yes. There *is* something funny going on. Why has Chelsea been reassigned to a new occupation, and why does she have to be so secretive about it? How many secrets can the Council have?

"You can't be here, Katherine," Chelsea says, voice flat, but with a slight tremor beneath. "I'm sorry, but I can't tell you anymore. I-I need you to go."

She turns and walks toward the building, unclipping her identification card from her bag. I don't follow her, despite how much I want to. My body is numb. Chelsea's acting this way because of her new occupation, isn't she? Why would she end our friendship because of this?

Chelsea doesn't look back as she enters the building. What can I do but leave now? Walking back to the Regulation Center, I think less about Chelsea's behavior and more about Matthew's fate. As soon as Matthew gets off work, he'll want to use the stuff that will hopefully give him his memory back.

Will I be ready to give it to him?

Maybe the pills won't cause harm to Matthew—even though that is a possibility. He could remember everything with no side effects. But if it doesn't work...failure to bring Matthew's memory back will mean failure to leave the Federation.

The Federation has become a prison for me just as much as it is a prison for him.

21

I hate that I haven't found a way to help Matthew escape aside from giving him the pills.

His words from earlier echo in my mind, that he wants to regain his memory so he can know if he's good enough to be "more than friends" someday. How could he just blurt that out and change our friendship so suddenly? Things can't be the same, not with the knowledge that he feels the same way I do. Why didn't he think of that?

He wasn't expecting me to reject him.

I sigh and take a bite of my salad. What prompted him to tell me he's interested in taking our relationship further? Is it so obvious that I've developed feelings for him, too? I thought I'd hidden it well. Maybe not. I glance across the room at where Chelsea sits with a guy, giggling at everything he says. I chew slowly. Understanding the male mind must be much easier for her than it is for me.

"Hi."

Startled, I look up. Matthew stands next to his normal seat across from mine, holding his own food container. I swallow. "How was work?"

"Long." He slides into his chair.

The conversation that used to be so easy between us is now hindered by uncomfortable silence. Neither of us says a thing as he pulls the lid off of his container and starts eating something with pasta and meat. We both must know that at some point we have to address one of two important conversations: where our relationship is headed or if giving him the medicine I stole from Doctor Perry is the best option.

Matthew made both of those dilemmas related.

"Listen, Katherine…" He sets his fork down. "I can tell I've upset you and I'm sorry. I shouldn't have said anything. Earlier, I mean. I shouldn't have, y'know, put you on the spot. It wasn't the best circumstances and now I've made things weird."

He stammers through that, then resumes eating. He's concerned that he's upset me when I've done something worse. I've hurt him. I just want our friendship back. "You have to know we could never date. It just wouldn't work."

The look he gives me is one of confusion, but he doesn't say anything.

"Haven't you thought of all the ways this could go badly?" I lower my voice. I'm about to give Matthew an untested medicine that may or may not give him his memory back, and we're discussing why we could never have a more-than-friends relationship instead. "What we're trying to do is impossible. One or both of us could die or end up captured. There's no guarantee that both of us would make it."

"I have thought of that." Matthew's gaze is level with my own as he says it, then he looks down at his food. "I didn't mean that this moment we had to decide. I meant that maybe we could leave the option open for the future, but if you're not interested I'll respect your decision. Please know that I will."

I don't voice my final objection, my concern that he has a girlfriend in the Outlands. It's crazy to think that he doesn't, with his sweet smile and his sincerity. I've seen how the other girls act around him, although he is usually a bit oblivious to their flirting attempts. In fact, the only girl he's really payed much attention to…is me.

"Besides, you're leaving, Matthew. You have your own life in a world vastly different from mine. You'll return to your previous life once you get your memory back." Why can't I just stop talking about this?

"You sound like I'm going to start remembering things then forget about you. I guess I thought our plan was that you'd come with me."

"Do we even have a plan? You take the medicine that should give you your memory back, then we hope it works. That's all we have." I'm grateful I found a way to change the subject. "We're basing everything on *what-ifs*."

"We've made it this far." His tone is stubborn.

Have we ever argued before today? Excluding now at dinner and this morning, I don't recall a time Matthew and I have ever really argued. Maybe when he told me he disagrees with the Tolerance Act, but this feels…different.

I take the last bite of my food. The medicine could harm him in so many ways. I could lose the one person I have left, the one person I care about in a deeper, more complex way than I've ever cared about anyone in my life.

But I can't tell him how I really feel.

I love Matthew. I can never deny that. But there's too many risks. How can I get more attached to him than I already am when tomorrow I could lose him? I've already lost everyone else. The threat of heartbreak is too strong.

"I told you that when you got off of work I'd give you the medicine, and I'm going to." I grab my bag and stand.

"It's going to work." Matthew hasn't finished eating, but he, too, stands. "We have to do it."

I wait for him as he disposes of our containers, then together we go upstairs. It dawns on me that people probably assume Matthew and I are dating because we spend so much time together, however incorrect that assumption might be.

"One moment," I tell him in the hallway, then I enter my room. I look through my jacket pockets until I find the bag with the two blue pills. The bag quivers in my hand. How can I give it to him when his well-being could be put at risk? I take a deep breath to steady myself. Matthew's correct. We have to do this. I don't like it, but we have to do this.

I exit my room and Matthew still stands in the hall. I give him the bag, folding his hand around it so the security cameras won't be able to tell what it is. "This should fix your memory. Message me if you need anything."

"I will."

"As soon as you remember how you got here, you'll be free."

"We both will," he says, his tone soft.

I don't correct him that I could never go to the Outlands. "Good night."

"Good night."

I slip back into my room. It isn't quite bedtime yet, but

the more I'm around Matthew now the harder it is to keep from telling him the truth. The truth that I do often wonder about a future with him. The truth that I do want to leave with him, but I belong in the Federation.

His world will never be mine.

A steady *buzzing* noise yanks me out of sleep. I sigh and grope in the dark for my tablet. I pull the device off the shelf, then read the message displayed. Multiple messages, all from Matthew.

We need to talk.
It's important.
Sorry for waking you.
It really is important.

He sent each message about ten minutes a part. What time is it now? My alarm isn't set to go off for another half-hour. How long has he been up? I throw off the covers and slide out of bed. My irritation morphs into worry. Is he okay? Did something happen to him? I quickly change into my Regulator uniform, grab my card and tablet, and head across the hall.

I knock on his door. What if he isn't okay? If Haynes didn't find my meeting with her suspicious, someone at least will find my leaving my room at this hour odd. I yawn behind my hand, longing for the comfort of my bed.

Within seconds, Matthew opens the door. He looks...tired, but okay. He fixes me with a big grin. "Katherine, I'm remembering things."

"You did? Do you remember how to leave?"

He's already ready for work like I am. "No, not yet. But I remember a lot about home. Do you remember that file you showed me?"

"The one I showed you of the person who has the same last name as you?" I pull my tablet out from under my arm. Matthew nods. I find the file and open it, then hand the tablet to Matthew. He stares at the screen, recognition flickering across his face.

"Andrew Braddock." He draws the name out slowly, accentuating each syllable. Snorting a relieved-sounding laugh, Matthew points at the picture. "That's my dad. See? That's why we have the same last name."

"Your dad?" I haven't heard that word before.

"Yeah, my dad." When I don't reply, Matthew frowns and hands me my tablet back. "You know? My father?"

Father? Dad? Matthew's Intolerant vocabulary must be returning with his memory. He probably thinks I'm a moron, standing here stupidly. What is he talking about? "Oh, wait, you mean a parent?"

Matthew nods again, but watches me with a curious expression. "You've never heard the word 'dad' before?"

I shake my head. The way he says it, it sounds like a personal, endearing term. Not as vague and impersonal as "parent" or even "father". I tuck the word away in my mind so I'll remember it. I like it. "No. When the Federation came into power, one of the first laws they enforced was that parents could have no contact with their children. They reasoned that parents were the worst Intolerants, forcing their children to abide by their beliefs and altering the children's views of morality."

"So you don't know who your parents are?" Matthew's eyes widen. Did he notice for the first time I've never mentioned my parents before? I don't know who they are, so how could I have ever talked about them? Children aren't even told their parents' names. But Matthew knows? Matthew knows the identities of both his parents?

"You do? Your father and..." What is the word for a female parent? "Mother?"

"Yes. I know both my dad and my mom."

Mom. Is that the endearing term for a mother? I close the file on my tablet, a sense of jealousy creeping over me. When I was younger, I would ask my school teachers about parents. I wanted to know who they were and what they were like. Parents were mysterious figures, the people who brought me into existence but who the Federation forbid me from meeting. I caught on early in life mentioning parents was a line you didn't cross.

"I'm sorry," Matthew slips his hands in his pockets. "I didn't mean to upset you."

"It's not you." I'm suddenly aware that I haven't done anything with myself today and my hair must be a disaster like it always is when I wake up. "It just makes me sad what the Federation keeps from us. You sound happy to know who your parents are. I always wanted to know mine."

"Maybe you will someday, when this is all over."

Assuming the Council lets me live long enough for this to be over, if they catch me. "What else do you remember?"

"Mostly about my family and my best friend and my home." He grins again. "You're going to love it. It's different from here. A lot different, but I think you'll like it."

Again he's assuming that I could ever have a life there with him as...whatever friends who like each other but will always be just friends are. He *wants* me to have that. A small part of me wants that, too. I bite my tongue to keep from saying something I'll wish I hadn't later. "You remember a lot, then?"

"Mostly just people. A lot of people. I mean, big chunks are missing and it's kind of fuzzy, but..." He frowns. "I feel like there's things I *should* know, but I just can't grasp it yet. I'm remembering pretty recent things, I guess."

"About the Underground."

"Kind of."

"But you remember your family and friends?" Will he know the exact person I'm wondering if he remembers?

"Yes. I finally have something I know about, well, me."

"You believe me now that you must have come here for good reasons? Do you know why yet?"

"No, I don't know why yet, but..." He doesn't finish the thought, but winces.

"What's the matter?"

"Just have a headache or something. That's all." His expression changes back to one of relief. "But I know who I am now. I at least know *where* we're going, even if I don't know how we're going to get there."

"It'll take time, I guess." How much time though? How long do we have to wait before Matthew has to leave? Before Haynes figures out what I've done and can trap me with Violations?

"That's true."

Again, the unusual awkward silence falls over us. I'm dying to ask him. The questions that would be so easy to blurt out, but I keep swallowing down. *Does the old you have a girlfriend already? As you remember more, will you really want me to come with you? Now that you have your own people again, will you still care about me?* One question screams louder than the others.

Reintegration

If you remember everything, will you still love me?

But I don't ask. There's no point in thinking of what could be when I know it would never work. Matthew and I come from different worlds, and maybe the old Matthew is a little different from the one I know. He probably has dreams and goals I may never understand. Just like I have questions I'm too cowardly to ask him.

I look at my tablet as if I suddenly thought to check the time. "I should get ready for the day. I'll see you at breakfast, okay?"

"Okay."

I head back to my room and toss my tablet on my unmade bed. I hate always being the one to end our conversations, but I've lost my only remaining friend to this awful thing called love. If he hadn't told me he loves me, would I want to go to the Outlands with him? I go into the bathroom and grab my brush. Slowly, I work through the tangles.

If Matthew and I were still just friends, maybe I would feel differently. Or if I didn't feel the way I do around Matthew, maybe I could shrug off his confession that he would like to be more than friends and I'd go with him. But if I go to the Outlands now, it will be with the hope that I would actually have a future with Matthew.

I've lost too much.

It's better to accept now that Matthew and I can never be than watch that hope be shattered later.

22

"I'm glad you came by today, Trainee Holliday."

I follow Head Regulator Olson through the Regulation Center. It's strange coming here as usual, but not to train with Thompson. Haynes told me to let my life go back to how it was before Matthew's Reintegration. Resuming my Regulator duties is the only thing I can think of to make life feel normal again.

"Well, I don't have much else to do."

"It's good to get a head start before your Final Test is over. I'm very excited that you're going to be done with training soon so you can begin your full duties." Olson looks back and smiles at me. "I do have some tasks you can help with today."

"Great." I force a smile.

She takes me to the Weapon Storage Room and opens the

door. "I'll have you helping in here most of the morning. Regulator Wolfe usually does this assignment, but unfortunately, data processing takes priority."

Olson unplugs a device from the wall and leads me over to a shelf of stunners. Two or three dozen of them sit on the shelves, their silver coating gleaming in the brightness of the overhead lights.

"It's about time we check to make sure all of these are ready for use. Just use this—" She holds up the device and points it at one of the stunner's base. "—to scan each one. The device will tell you if the stunner needs to be refilled. Did Regulation Mentor Thompson show you how to reload these?"

"Yes, he did."

"Perfect. Go through each one until you've done them all. Come ask me if you need anything."

"I will."

Olson hands me the device and leaves. I set my bag on the floor. I would rather be with Matthew, but since Haynes is forbidding me from spending the day with him and I have no other escape theories, scanning stun weapons will have to do.

I better get used to it if I'm going to stay here.

I miss Thompson's advice. He at least provided me with someone to talk to, even when I performed mundane tasks like these. With Thompson I could talk about *real* things, not these superficial conversations I have with Head Regulator Olson.

Sighing, I scan the first stunner and read the device's screen.

This one is full.

I move on to the next one. Do I really even know anyone at the Regulations Center? I exchange greetings with Vail and

Weston on occasion, but that's about the extent of conversation I have with people. I don't want to have meaningless conversations about the weather or work duties. I want something deeper. Something like what I have with Matthew. We can talk about anything. I know him better than anyone else.

I want to have that again.

Shaking my head, I continue scanning the weapons. The fourth one needs to be refilled. I find the metal box that holds the refills, then pop open the bottom of the stunner and pull the empty cartridge out. The new cartridge slides in with a satisfying *click*.

I hate that all I can think about is Matthew.

Where is the old me, the girl who promised herself she would never fall in love? The girl who told herself over and over again to not get too attached to anyone? Where is she? Sometimes I want to be her again.

The fifth stunner also needs to be refilled. I go through the same process and withdraw the old cartridge. I try to shove the new cartridge in place, but it catches on something and won't go in all the way. Flipping the cartridge around, I try again. Still it doesn't go in. I put it back in the box find another new cartridge. That one goes in as it should.

I know too much now. I know about the Council's lies, the truth about love and parents, and who the Intolerants really are. If I was the girl I was before, I wouldn't know all that. I'd still believe the Federation is the safest place for me. Now I doubt that, and I will never view my life the same way again. I wish I could be happy again.

But was I? Was I ever really *happy?*

I set the device down on the shelf. Do I want this to still be my life? I look around the room. The security camera light blinks at me, reminding me that someone is recording my every move. Matthew tells me of a world filled with family he cares about and love and freedom. With people who want to bring truth back to the Federation.

He will return to that world.

I will stay here.

And be alone.

Until the day I die, this will be my life. Trapped in City 45's Walls, monitored by cameras, and stuck doing boring tasks like this. I'll try to forget Matthew, but I don't think I ever could, not after how deeply I've cared for him. I'll never care about someone the same way again.

Going to the Outlands with Matthew presents a certain amount of risk. There are too many unknowns, too many uncertainties. I want to stay here because it's the safe option I'm familiar with. I don't want Matthew to know how I feel because I might lose him later. I don't want to go with him because I'm afraid.

Even more terrifying is the thought of staying in the Federation.

Forever being alone again.

I wait outside Matthew's factory building, shifting from foot to foot. He should get off work for the day any moment now. I've rehearsed this over and over in my head, imagined the dozens of responses he could have. Saying what I need to say should be easy, since I practiced to myself so many times.

"Matthew!" I call his name as he exits the building.

He turns and sees me, and his eyes widen. "Is everything okay?"

"Yes, why?" My tone sounds sharp and defensive, even though I'm just trying to keep the nervous tremor away.

"Usually we meet at dinner. You don't usually come here."

"I know I don't. I just need to talk to you. I spent all day thinking about it and couldn't wait any longer."

"Okay."

I take a deep breath and finally blurt out what's been haunting me for days. "Do you really want to be more than friends with me? What about your girlfriend back in the Outlands?"

His expression is blank for a moment, then one side of his mouth quirks into a half-smile. "You want to know if I already have a girlfriend?"

"Yes. That's what I need to know."

"Well, to answer your questions, no, I don't."

"You're certain?"

"I've remembered a lot of stuff but nothing about a girlfriend. I would have told you if I thought I had one." Matthew is obviously fighting a smile and failing. "Why do you need to know?"

Another worker slips between us with a mumbled apology. I plant my hands on my hips. His sudden improvement of mood is disarming. "It's a legitimate question. Here guys like you aren't single for long periods of time, so I don't think it's crazy for me to wonder."

"Okay?"

I wasn't expecting for him to be so certain that he doesn't have a girlfriend already, and my previously-planned speech dissolves. What do I say now? Today I realized that I can't stay here. I want to go with him. Now I can admit how I really feel about him. Why won't the words come out?

Reintegration

He's the reason I learned the truth about the Federation. He's the reason I'm willing to defy everything I've ever been taught. Matthew is, as always, strong and determined, unlike me. He's the only thing that's held me together through the chaos and confusion of the past few weeks.

And I'm a fool if I don't tell him so.

"Matthew, I…" I fumble for the words to say. "You told me you care about me in a more than friends way, and saw a potential future with me. I told you it could never work. But the truth is, I care about you a lot, too. More than I've ever cared about anyone. I wasn't expecting you to be, well, you. I thought I'd hate having to spend time with you, but then you were the opposite of everything I expected you to be. You were a better friend to me than anyone else has been. I knew I had to help you. I would help you leave so you could return to your home. Then this crazy thing happened. I didn't like the idea of you leaving."

While fidgeting with my identification card clasp, I avoid his gaze. I already turned him down. I understand completely if he doesn't accept my pathetic attempt of trying to fix things. Even if he won't, I have to say it.

"You told me you love me, and I told you we couldn't be more than friends. Because I'm scared. I can't stand the thought of losing you. So many things could fail in our plan to escape. We might not make it out of the Federation without being captured or killed. I'm terrified of having to say goodbye to you, either because we fail to escape or because when we leave I may not be important to you anymore. I've seen relationships fall apart so many times, that I'm just terrified you'll stop loving me once you remember everything."

Matthew isn't smiling anymore. I've offended him, by telling him I'm scared to love him. He isn't like all the other guys I've known, and I don't think he'd ever break my heart intentionally. But there's so many things that could change our circumstances.

"I can't let you leave without telling you that I think I love you too. If you're still willing to love me after all of this, then I want to be more than friends with you. And I'm sorry I've been too cowardly to tell you."

Without saying a thing, Matthew kisses me.

It's a brief, light, innocent kiss, nothing like the kisses I've seen other people have. But it's pure. It's perfect. It's *ours*. My very first kiss, shared with the most amazing boy I've ever met. The boy I love in a way I didn't know existed until I met him. Matthew's eyes lock with mine. My Final Test became the only boy I've ever loved, the only boy I ever *want* to love.

"You'll always be important to me, Katherine. I promise."

"Do you still want me to come to the Outlands with you?"

"Of course." Matthew pulls me close, and for a moment I let myself stop thinking about Haynes and the files and the Wall. For a moment it's just Matthew and I, and the growing hope that I have a brighter future than the Federation could ever offer me.

I'm going to the Outlands with him.

After dinner, Matthew and I walk down the hallway, hand-in-hand. I like the way this feels, walking beside him with my fingers interlaced with his. If only we didn't need to discuss how to escape. If only the threat of our crimes being discovered wasn't looming over us. If only all we had to think about was where our relationship is headed. Matthew's hand is warm to the touch. He tightens his fingers around mine—until he jerks his hand away, out of my grasp. What is he doing? I turn around to look at him. My confusion changes into horror.

    He looks ill. Is he going to throw up? Matthew leans against the wall, like he can't stand on his own. Fear grips my heart. What's happening? Is it the pills? He's not even looking at me, but focusing on some unknown point in the distance. Matthew slowly sinks to the floor, one hand pressed to his forehead.

    "Matthew?" I stammer and kneel down next to him. A look of pain flashes across his face. I lay a hand on his cheek, which burns like he has a fever. "Don't do this…"

    He can't be dying. He *can't*.

23

I brush his sweat-dampened hair away from his forehead. How did this happen in such a short amount of time? Matthew moans, a pained sound. I lay a hand on his cheek. Why is he so warm? Whatever happened can't be good. What did Thompson teach me to do in emergencies? Stay calm and find help?

How can I stay calm when Matthew could be dying? Where do I go to find help? Once I take Matthew to a medical center, they'll know Reintegration failed. He may live, but he'll still be a prisoner.

Every passing second feels like an hour. I murmur his name over and over again, but he doesn't respond to me. Matthew curls up on the floor, a shudder running through his body. I grab his wrist, feeling for a pulse. Where do doctors find it, anyway? I can't—there. His heartbeat seems fast and erratic.

"Don't do this," I whisper, sitting next to him, holding his hand in both of mine. What can I do? How can I help him?

Am I only waiting for him to die? I choke back the sob threatening to escape. He'll be gone, and it'll be all my fault. I gave him the pills. I should have talked him out of it. I should have tried harder to find another option.

He would be okay if only I had done more.

After a few seconds, Matthew's body relaxes and his hand goes limp in mine. What? He can't...couldn't have...no. I release his hand and roll him onto his back. His head lolls to one side.

"No, no, no, no...." I can't say anything else, but stare at Matthew's still form. Tears slip down my cheeks, one after another, but I don't wipe them away. I slowly, cautiously lean forward and touch his face. He's so still. The pain in my heart is *so strong*. Dealing with Thompson's relocation was nothing like this. Thompson's alive and well, in a place where I can't drag him into any more trouble.

But Matthew?

I reach for Matthew's wrist, feeling again for a pulse. A glimmer of hope creeps through the numb emptiness inside me. He's alive. He's breathing. I let go of his wrist and lay my hand on his chest. Yes, he still has a heartbeat. Slower, steadier than it was before. Is this a more normal rate?

His pulse continues to grow steadier. I don't dare to breathe until Matthew stirs with a low groan. He's okay. He's going to be okay, isn't he? Matthew's eyelids flutter and then he opens his eyes. He stares up at the ceiling, then his gaze meets mine.

"What happened?" Matthew murmurs, voice groggy. He presses his hand to his forehead again, like he has a really bad headache.

"I thought you..." A hiccupped sob prevents me from

continuing. I thought Matthew died. I thought I lost him. He sits all the way up and I throw my arms around his neck, pulling him into a hug. "I don't know what happened. Do you think it was the medicine?"

Matthew shakes his head and doesn't say a word. I pull away and search his eyes, making sure he's still *here*. His eyes are bright and alert. Is he fine now? Will he be okay? Wiping my nose on my sleeve, I hop to my feet. What happened to him? I grab his hand and help him up. "Can you stand?"

He nods, then manages a smile. "My head just hurts. That's all."

This makes me giggle, despite the horror we both just went through. My optimistic, carefree Matthew is here, smile and all. I don't want to go through anything like that ever again. I've never seen Matthew look so afflicted before, so pained, like he was a few moments ago. I shiver when I think of what the Council will do to him if we fail to escape.

"You should rest," I whisper, as two chattering trainee girls step off the elevator. "We can talk more in the morning."

Matthew nods, reaching for his identification card. Then he stops. "I remember more."

"You do?"

"Just more details about home, but it's starting to come back now. Maybe by morning I'll know more." Matthew squeezes my hand, then uses his card to open his door. "Good night. I guess I can tell you that I love you now, too."

"I love you, too, Matthew."

And I really do.

Another morning complete with the sun shining through

my bedroom window.

Another day Matthew and I have to avoid capture.

What am I going to do today while Matthew's working? Yesterday I searched for a way to leave the city. Today? I'm stuck waiting for Matthew's memory to return. The longer we stay in City 45 the more likely it is for someone to learn what we've done. Communication workers could read the files I opened on my tablet. Someone could see the security footage and realize I stole the pills from Doctor Perry. Haynes, who knows more than she'll admit, could decide at any moment to reveal my infractions against the Federation.

Why hasn't she arrested me for them yet?

Council Member Haynes frightens me the most. How much *does* she know? What proof does she have? Is that why she hasn't arrested me—she has no proof of what I've done? During my last meeting with her, I decided she more than suspects me of committing a crime. Does she have evidence, or is she basing everything on intuition?

I exit my bedroom, waiting by the door until it closes. Maybe today will be the day Matthew remembers something substantial, something we can use to escape. This thought is the one keeping my fears from consuming me. Someone can learn what we did, but they can't punish us if we're outside City 45's walls. Unfortunately for us, we have to know *how* to escape before we can take that step.

I cross to the other side of the hallway and knock on Matthew's door. Two trainees brush past me while I wait for Matthew to open the door. He doesn't. After waiting about thirty seconds, I knock again. No Matthew.

Panic settles over me. What if he died in the middle of the night? What if his tracking device noticed something was wrong with him and he was arrested? I unzip my bag, shaking my head. Maybe he overslept. Unlikely. Matthew is *always* ready by the time I am. I'll send him a message, but if he doesn't respond...

Before I finish pulling my tablet out of my bag, the door slides open and Matthew—finally—exits his bedroom. I zip my bag closed. "You had me worried for a second." I laugh, annoyed with myself for panicking over something so trivial. After tugging the zipper closed, I glance up at Matthew.

He looks terrible.

Did he sleep at all last night? He's still in his sleeping clothes, his hair mussed like he just now got out of bed. Matthew yawns and leans against the doorframe, staring at the wall behind me like he didn't hear a word I said.

"What's the matter with you?" I take a step closer toward him, my attempt at a quiet whisper sounding more like a frantic hiss.

At last he meets my gaze, looking more exhausted than I've ever seen him. "It happened again."

How much can he take? Whatever happened to him last night occurred again. It hasn't even been one day since I gave him the pills, and already he looks like he needs to be in a medical center.

"I'm sorry. How long ago was it?"

He can't go to work like this. But what can we do? The only way he can have the day off is if he's physically unable to work. Matthew keeps passing out—but if he reports in sick, regulations require he also goes to a medical center for examination. If I take him to a medical center, they'll learn that he's regaining his memory.

"Few hours ago, I guess. Just now fell back asleep." He

rakes his fingers through his hair, making it even messier than it already is.

"Was it better than last time or worse?" If it's worse this time, will his condition continue to decline until he dies? What if the only way to save Matthew's life is to take him to a medical center and risk our plan for escape?

"'Bout the same, I'd say." Matthew shrugs.

"How do you feel?"

"I feel fine. I'm just really tired. I remembered more stuff, though."

If Matthew remembers how to escape City 45, all my worrying will have been for nothing. "Like what?"

"I'll show you. Wait here." Matthew slips back inside his room.

What could he possibly *show* me? Can't he tell me what he remembers? I stand in the hallway, glancing at the elevator. If this doesn't take very long, we may have time to eat breakfast before the cafeteria closes for the morning.

Matthew returns about a minute later wearing his uniform. Even when he steps into the hallway, he's still in the process of pulling on one of his shoes. He looks like he could pass out or throw up at any second, but even so, he shoots me a relieved grin. Sometimes he's like a young child with how quickly his mood changes.

"What do you remember?"

Matthew doesn't answer. Instead he kisses my cheek and starts walking down the hallway. I run for a few paces to catch up to him. "You aren't being very helpful."

"I'm not one-hundred-percent sure what I remember. I don't know how or why I came here, but I think I'm getting close." Matthew's eager grin changes into a wry grimace. "I remember getting captured."

He pushes the button for the elevator, waits a few seconds, and then pushes it again. I run my hand over my stunner. Does it hurt? I used a stunner while training with Thompson, but training involved aiming for inanimate targets, not people. The Regulators must have used their weapons when they captured Matthew—and maybe even again when he tried to escape.

"So what are you showing me?" Before he answers, the elevator doors open. A brown-clad trainee steps off, slipping between Matthew and me. I follow Matthew onto the elevator. "If you don't remember how you got into the city, where are we going?"

"Be patient." He winks.

So says the one who pushes every button twice if it doesn't work fast enough for him.

We reach the ground level floor of the dormitory and I follow Matthew down the hallway. He passes by the clamor of the cafeteria but walks outside. My stomach growls. No breakfast this morning?

"Do you know where you're going, or is this what you need to find out?" I reach for Matthew's hand as we walk side-by-side past the buildings. The sun is warm this morning, a nice change from the biting wind of the past few days. Not a cloud in the sky above. We should be trying to figure out what to do since Matthew isn't going to work. If Matthew's plan is to stop pretending he's a compliant citizen and start trying to escape, now isn't the time. Where does he think we can hide until he remembers everything? Even if there was a good hiding spot, we both have tracking devices.

Reintegration

No matter where we go, the Regulators will find us.

"I think I know where I'm going. We'll figure things out."

He thinks he knows? This'll be an interesting morning.

"You're certainly chipper today."

"We're going to do it, Katherine." Matthew stares at the Wall, giving my hand a small squeeze. "You and I...we're going to escape the Federation. I just know it."

Are we?

We have no plan, no idea how to get past the Wall, no clue how to avoid arrest. Matthew believes we're going to make it. I can't be so certain. Waiting for Matthew's memory to return might take too long. If Haynes knows what I've done, if Matthew's tracking device records his health, if our activities were caught on security footage...waiting is the last thing we should do. But if we act now, if we choose now to abandon any and all precautions, aren't we shortening the time we have even more? What if no matter what we do, we'll be caught?

What if we never had a chance of succeeding?

24

"What are you doing?"

I place my hands on my hips, watching Matthew as he kneels on the ground. A Regulator could walk by at any second and ask the same question. Anyone who sees Matthew will find his behavior suspicious.

Matthew reaches behind a thick bush growing by the Wall. He stretches a little further, grunting as he does so. Why won't he answer me? I look over my shoulder, not for the first time. Matthew still hasn't told me why we're here or what he remembers. Does he remember how to get past the Wall? Does he remember why he came to the Federation in the first place? I can only speculate until he talks to me.

"Got it," Matthew mutters, jerking something out from behind the bush. He sits in the middle of a narrow alley space located between two buildings. Flashing me a confident grin, Matthew tosses something between us.

Reintegration

It's a bag of some sort, made of a faded, dirty material. Matthew brushes dirt off of it, then starts undoing the zipper. I crouch down beside Matthew, running my hand over the bag. The material is thick and course. "What is this?"

"It's the stuff I brought with me when I came here." Matthew undoes the zipper all the way and pulls something out of the bag. He looks at the object, then sets it down next to him. I pick it up, then shake it. Some sort of liquid sloshes around inside. It's a cylindrical metal object, hollow and filled with liquid. Used for transporting water? I turn the object upside down. The letters "MB" have been stamped on the bottom. No, not stamped. *Written.* Someone wrote the letters with pre-Federation writing utensils. Now everything is done electronically. No one writes letters in the way of the Past. I set the water container on the ground.

Next Matthew pulls out a white bottle. A Federation-style pill bottle? I saw some just like it when Doctor Perry did his inventory. Matthew turns the bottle around, looking at the label. After he stares at the bottle for several seconds, a look of realization passes over his face.

"I remember I broke into one of the hospitals here. It was late at night and everyone had gone. I took this. They nabbed me the next morning before I could leave." Matthew sets the pill bottle down next to the water container.

If Haynes were here, she could see Matthew came for non-violent reasons. "Why did you take it?"

"That's what I don't know." He shrugs and pulls something else out of the bag. It's a small electronic device with a thin chord sticking out one side. "I have no idea what this is."

And so he places it with the other objects. I pick up the device, turning it over in my hands. It's bulky and made of a rag-tag assortment of pieces—not a Federation device. What is it? How does one operate it? The device has a screen and a few buttons. What do the buttons do? I set the device aside.

The next thing Matthew grabs is obviously an assortment of trash—pieces of plastic and what looks like foil. Did they contain food at one point? He doesn't bother to analyze the pieces for more than a couple of seconds before stuffing them back in the bag.

Matthew unzips another pocket, this one bigger than the other. Out comes a rectangular object about an inch thick. Matthew sets it in his lap, and then he opens it. My eyes widen. It looks flat, but it actually consists of many ultra-thin sections. Matthew looks at the first few section, then sets the rectangular object aside.

Someone passes by but doesn't bother looking in the alley. I wrap my hand around my stunner. "Am I allowed to see that?"

"Sure," Matthew picks it up again and hands it to me. The object is heavy, the top, bottom, and one side covered in a thick, rough material I don't know the name of. The top has the words "HOLY BIBLE" printed on it in gold letters. What do those words mean? The letters aren't written, but seem to be imprinted on the top.

I open the object to the first section. This one is filled with words, not pictures. Non-written words. These sections are very thin, the letters very small. I open the object at about halfway, scanning the sections. The sets of words are numbered. Why? Sometimes the sentences are underlined. Are they important? I read the underlined portions before flipping to the other sections.

Reintegration

The sentences are about people, mainly. Are they real people? Does Matthew know them? Some sections contain stories, others brief little sayings about what to do and not to do. Some sections are about not being afraid. I like those sections the most, since it seems as if the words are written just for me. I've been so terrified lately that we're going to get caught before we escape. The verses say to trust the Lord. What is that? I close the object and lay it on top of the other.

"Matthew?" I wait for his answer.

"Yeah?" He starts stuffing everything back inside. When he grabs the pill bottle, he doesn't put it back right away. Matthew stares at the label. Is he even listening to me? Even if he isn't, I might as well ask.

"What is 'the Lord'?"

He looks up from the pill bottle. "Oh, you know, God."

"God?" There are so many things I don't understand. Words I've never heard before, objects I've never seen before...what else will I learn from Matthew? I always knew the Outlands are different from the Federation, but all this tells me the Outlands are *very* different. If we escape, how will I ever belong?

"God is...God." Now Matthew seems confused. "I don't...I don't know how to explain it to you. I—"

He doesn't finish, but grimaces as if in pain. I hold my breath. Is *it* happening again? Matthew runs both hands through his hair, a pained look on his face. It's impossible to tell if he will or won't pass out.

"Matthew?" I whisper, starting to get to my feet.

"What are you doing?"

I freeze at the confused, suspicious voice behind me. Matthew's face is an unhealthy pale. If we're captured, he won't be able to escape, not in his current state. He leans back against the wall of one of the buildings, his hands shaking.

I turn around. A Regulator stands in the entrance of the alleyway, arms folded across his chest. He watches me, then his gaze shifts to the bag on the ground, then to Matthew curled up in a ball in the corner. I've seen the man around the Regulation Center before—a big bulky man with a permanent scowl. He's tall, even taller than Matthew. Does he recognize me? Does he know who I am?

"Don't move," he orders, taking a step forward.

I can't waste any more time. The Regulator reaches for my arm at the same time I reach for the stunner clipped to my belt. I hold the weapon out in front of me, aiming it at the Regulator's chest. His jaw drops and he lowers his arm. I bet he's never had a stun weapon pointed at him before. I don't want to do this, but I have to. He can't possibly know what we're doing, but he knows something's up. I can't risk him telling anyone about us and our questionable behavior.

Before he has time to speak, I push the button on the stun weapon. Stunners work differently from the weapons of the Past. No noise. No permanent wounds. No blood. No sign the victim was injured at all.

The Regulator staggers, then lays a hand on the wall to steady himself. I take a step back as he collapses to the ground and doesn't move again. I bend down and feel his wrist. He's still breathing, still alive. Grabbing his arms, I pull him further into the alley. He's extremely heavy, so it takes several tugs before I'm able to get him out of sight of any passers-by. I glance at the walkway. No one else is around, thank goodness.

After clipping my weapon back onto my belt, I kneel down next to Matthew, who is unconscious. These attacks don't last long, but will the pain prove to be too much for him one of these times? He's regaining his memory, but at a high price. This attack doesn't seem as severe as the last one. I brush Matthew's hair away from his face, staying by his side, hoping he wakes up soon.

My heart doesn't stop pounding until he opens his eyes and sits up. How long until Matthew's tracking device alerts someone he had three unusual changes in health in the past twenty-four hours? I turn and look at the Regulator's still form. How long until *his* tracking device alerts someone he was knocked unconscious?

Matthew blinks several times. He glances around, then his eyes rest on the Regulator. He starts to stand, but I push him down. "Wait. You need to rest for a minute, okay?"

He doesn't look away from the Regulator. "What happened?"

"This man saw us. I had to knock him out." I bend down next to the Regulator. How long until he wakes up? I roll the man onto his side, exposing his stunner. I unclip the weapon from his belt. "We don't have much time before someone comes to look for him."

"Okay. We'll find somewhere else to hide all this and then I'll get to work before—"

"There's no point. I'd say they find him within the hour. He'll tell them he saw us. I don't know if he recognized me. If he did, it's only a matter of time before they'll have other Regulators after us in no time." Kneeling in front of Matthew, I shove the weapon into his hands. "Keep this with you."

"How does it work?"

I adjust the way he's holding the weapon, so he can push the button. "This button fires it. It's used to stun, not to kill. It shoots out little darts filled with a serum powerful enough to knock someone unconscious. Each weapon holds ten darts. The only way to get more is at the Regulation Center. I don't know what all we'll need to escape, but we'll have to make do with what we have."

Matthew fumbles to clip the weapon onto his belt. He leans back against the wall, glancing up at the sky. "I still don't know how to escape, Katherine. I can remember a lot of stuff after I got inside the city, but not before. If I don't remember soon—"

"Everything's going to turn out just fine." *Am I trying to convince myself or Matthew? We couldn't be in a worse situation. Matthew doesn't remember how to leave the city but the time we have keeps getting shorter.* "We'll just have to stay quiet for a while. You seem to be remembering things quickly."

I push myself up so I'm standing again. Grabbing Matthew's hand, I help him to his feet. Matthew hoists his bag over his shoulder. "Where do we go from here? We can't stay here forever, like you said."

"I don't know."

The Regulator on the ground stirs, letting out a low moan. I grab my weapon again, shooting the man in the back. He goes still again. *The effect from the stunners doesn't last very long. We shouldn't stay here any longer. More Regulators could be here soon. They'll find him through his tracking device.*

Is that how he found us? Through our tracking devices? Maybe Council Member Haynes pieced everything together and sent this Regulator to arrest us. She had to know sending one Regulator wouldn't do any good. She could have sent more. We need to leave, now, before any more Regulators arrive—too many for us to fend off.

Reintegration

Where can we go? We need somewhere safe, where no one will find us until Matthew can remember something useful. The tracking devices pose a problem. I roll up my sleeve so I can look at the scar. How do you remove a tracking device? Can they even be removed?

"You're sure you don't remember anything else?" The walkway is empty. Even so, I keep my hand close to my stunner. How long until more Regulators arrive? If the one I stunned didn't come here to arrest us but was simply curious about what we were doing, there's still the risk of Haynes figuring things out. Matthew's work supervisor will notice Matthew's absence and report him. And there's always the issues of our tracking devices, the security footage, the files on my tablet...

We need to move as soon as we can.

"I don't think so. But..." Matthew's voice trails off. After a few seconds, he sets the bag down and unzips it, pulling out the pill bottle again. Then he looks back at me. "I remember why I came here, Katherine."

"You do?" He remembers, but he doesn't seem happy about it, judging by the look in his eyes. He had the same look when I interrogated him weeks ago, although it feels like months have passed.

Worry.

Desperation.

Fear of failure.

Matthew came here for something—to help someone he loves—and he's terrified he won't succeed. He knows the same thing I do. If we don't escape, if we're captured before we can leave City 45, then he came here for nothing.

I don't have the heart to remind him.

"Yes." Matthew nods and runs his fingers through his hair. Is he trying to fill in the details? "I came here to find this 'cause Lydia's sick."

The last part hits me hard. Lydia. A girl's name. What if my first assumption was right, and there is a girl in the Outlands Matthew loves? My thoughts drift to our kiss. What if we should never have had it? What if the only reason he loves *me* is because he doesn't remember *her*?

"We didn't have the right medicine back home, so I left to find some."

I'm not really listening to him anymore. How can I go with him to the Outlands if he loves someone else? Yes, I want to know the freedom offered in the Outlands, but I also want to go because Matthew's going. If I can't be with him...what's the point? How could I be happy, watching Matthew with some other girl?

"She's dying, Katherine," Matthew whispers, pulling me back to what he's telling me. Something underlies his voice, a tremor that reminds me of the nameless emotion which plagues me sometimes. "I came here to help her, but it might be too late now."

Should I say something? What *can* I say?

Matthew shoves the pill bottle back in the bag. A not-so-nice part of me wishes he'd never remembered anything, not this other girl who he was willing to get himself killed for. If he didn't remember this, he would still be *my* Matthew.

"I'm sure everything's going to be fine," I say, the words sounding hollow even to me. "At the moment, we need to leave. The Regulators could be here at any minute to see what happened to this one."

I glance at the stunned Regulator's motionless form. How

long until he wakes up for a second time? Matthew tosses his bag over his shoulder again, nodding grimly. "I guess we gotta find somewhere to hide for now. Maybe I'll remember enough so we can leave this horrible place for good." He frowns for a second. "I know where I hid while I was trying to figure out how to get into the hospital."

Matthew lets out an exhausted sigh. He needs to remember, but how much more of these frequent assaults to his body can he undergo? Matthew forces a smile. Is he trying to appear brave, even with everything going wrong around us? How can I voice the fear that refuses to become more than a thought in my mind? It's so…*petty* at a time like now.

Does Matthew really love someone else?

Matthew walks down the walkway, and I fall in step next to him. Silence settles over us, such an unusual thing. Where are we going? My hand never strays far from my weapon. I look over my shoulder, expecting a group of Regulators to show up at any second. None do, but I can't relax.

"When we stop, there's something I need to show you, okay?" Matthew sounds excited about whatever it is.

"Okay." I can't bring myself to match his enthusiasm.

"Have I said something?" Matthew shoots me a confused glance. He can't possibly comprehend how selfish I am. We're so close to capture, but I'm worrying about whether or not Matthew has another girlfriend. Shouldn't I be focused on trying to escape? The fear that I'll lose the last person I have left clings to me like a foul stench.

How long can I avoid the issue? I need to know. I might as well learn the truth. "Who's Lydia?"

I try to sound like I don't care, like it's nothing more than a casual question. A hint of bitterness creeps into my voice, despite my best attempts to mask it. Matthew blinks in surprise, then an amused smile tugs at his lips.

"Oh, Lydia's my little sister."

"Your what?"

"My sister." Matthew stares straight ahead while he walks. "A sister is a sibling. I guess you don't know what that means either, do you? Siblings are children who have the same parents. That's what makes a family. A mom, a dad, and the kids. There's three kids in my family. There's me, Lydia, and Sarah."

Family. A group composed of parents and their children? The longing in my heart to know this world of Matthew's grows. My jealousy abates, but the awareness of my selfishness doesn't. If Matthew does love someone else, if there is another girl in the Outlands…shouldn't I be willing to let him go?

What's the matter with me?

25

Matthew pulls me into another alleyway, this one between the communication center and the medical center. Matthew sets his bag down, unzipping one of the pockets. After pulling out the mysterious device, Matthew walks toward a door on the side of the communication center. Does he remember what the device is used for and how to operate it?

This plan of his needs to work. I look around, clutching the strap of my bag with both hands. When will more Regulators arrive to arrest us? Matthew left his Federation bag with the unconscious Regulator. In our haste, neither of us remembered to grab it. Now he has no tablet and no identification card.

Too late to go back now.

Matthew holds up the device and unwinds the cord sticking out one side. What does he intend to do with it? He plugs the end of the cord into a port on the card scanner, then pushes one of the buttons. The card scanner light flashes green and the door slides open.

He gestures at the open door, a relieved grin lighting up his face. "Ladies first."

"Where did you get that?" I ask, entering the communication center. We enter a storage room, the shelves lined with various electronic devices. I push the button on the wall that turns on the lights.

"I don't know." Matthew sets his bag next to the door, then shoves the device back in the pocket. "But we can wait in here. I hid here last time and no one ever came in this room."

At least we can have a brief respite before we have to move again. I look down at the scar on my arm. My tracking device. I always believed it was for my protection. Now it could be the cause of my demise.

Matthew sits cross-legged on the ground. Will he remember how he got inside City 45 soon? We can move and hide for a while, but it won't be long until the Regulators find us from our tracking devices. I sit next to him. How can I relax when we're so close to failure? Matthew, too, seems tense, but is his discontent the result of worrying about his sister, not of our imminent capture?

I scoot closer to him, wanting him to hold me again. My fears are always present, always in the back of my mind. Matthew is the one thing I can cling to for comfort. He wraps his arm around my waist and pulls me close.

"We're gonna be okay, Katherine." Matthew kisses my forehead. "I know I'm close to remembering how I got here. I just need a little more time."

Time. How do we know if we have enough? Matthew's returns in memory don't seem to follow a pattern of any kind.

Reintegration

We can't be certain he'll remember how to escape before we're captured.

We can't be certain he'll remember how to escape at all.

Why can't I be strong like he is? Why can't I assure myself we're going to make it out of this alive?

I want to fall asleep and forget about all our problems, but my thoughts refuse to drift from our fates. Images pop into my mind. Matthew, being used further as the Council's science experiment. Me, facing execution. I shake my head. We have to succeed. Matthew and I have to escape the Federation.

Matthew adjusts his posture and reaches for his bag. After unzipping the biggest pocket, Matthew pulls out one of his objects, the rectangular one with words.

The words that seemed meant just for me.

I sit up straight as he sets the object on his lap. Excitement dances in Matthew's eyes. "I want to show you something, okay? It's probably the biggest thing the Federation keeps from everybody. It's also the biggest reason we're Intolerants."

Now my curiosity is piqued. What could be bigger than families and love and freedom? He opens the object, scanning one of the sections. Before he says anything, I point at the object. "What is this?"

"It's a book. In the Past, people would write stories on paper and then distribute them for everyone to read. The stories were usually fake, but sometimes they were real." Matthew smiles. "This one is real. It's history, Katherine. A history the Federation doesn't talk about."

All the history stories I've ever heard are the ones about the start of the Federation and the origin of the Tolerance Act.

"I've never really had to explain this to anyone, but I'll do my best." Matthew snorts a laugh, then grows serious again.

He shifts the book in his lap, clearing his throat. "Well, earlier you asked about God. God is the One who created the world. He's all-powerful and knows everything. He created the first people. These people lived in a place that was perfect, until they broke the only rule God told them to follow. That's when they became aware of right and wrong."

Right and wrong. The Federation tells us those things don't really exist, but I've learned they do. I've felt it inside. "What exactly does that mean, they became aware of right and wrong?"

"God has laws He put into place for us to follow. It's not 'cause He's strict, but He puts the laws in place so everyone can be happy and safe. Well, we all have what's called a conscience. It's inside of us and lets us know when we've messed up. We feel guilty when we do."

"Guilty?" Another word I've never heard.

"Guilt is the feeling you get when you know you've done something wrong. It makes you feel sick, because you know you've broken one of God's laws."

So that's what I've been feeling every time I lie or feel jealous? Guilt? The sound of the word fits the horribleness of the feeling. The Federation doesn't teach us about guilt. How could they, if the basis of our society is that there is no right or wrong? Morals are always right and wrong, no matter what. Is that why I felt guilty when I lied to Matthew and when I lied to Haynes? Because lying is *always* wrong?

"What happened next?" This is an interesting story.

"Because of what the first people did, they brought sin—disobeying God—into the world. We all sin, every single one of us. Because of this, we're separated from God, temporally and eternally. When we die, only our bodies die. Our souls don't die. Because of our sin, we're doomed to spend the afterlife in a place called hell, a place of eternal pain."

"Why?" A chill runs through me. Why would people have to go there?

"Because God is perfect, and we aren't. It's hard to understand, but God punishes evil because He's good. He wants us to love Him and serve Him, but our sin keeps us from doing that."

"So there's no hope?" We all have to go to this place called hell?

"Wait, I'm not done yet. God does love us and wants us to spend eternity with Him, in a place called heaven. He doesn't force us to love Him, because He wants us to *choose* to love Him. Our sin, like I said, keeps us from that.

"God wanted to give us hope, so He sent His Son to come live with us, here on earth. His Son was killed, because the people didn't believe what the Son told them. But the Son's death was part of God's plan. His Son lived a perfect life, and so was able to save mankind from having to be doomed to hell. When the Son died, He paid the ultimate price for man's sin. He died in the place of all of us, so we could be free.

"But He didn't stay dead. Three days after He died, He came back to life and went back to heaven so He could live with His Father again. Because of what He did, we all have the opportunity to go to heaven and be with Him. All we have to do is believe that He died for us and repent."

Why can't Matthew use words I understand? "Repent?"

"Oh. Repenting is acknowledging you've done wrong and promising to try your best to follow God's laws. When you're truly repentant, you'll *want* to please Him. You won't want to sin anymore."

After that, Matthew shows me different sections—which he calls *pages*—and groups of numbered words, called *verses*. The verses he shows me are all the things God deems wrong for us to do. So many of them are things the Federation encourages us to do. Some of them I haven't done, but many of them I have. I've done all these things to displease God?

I lie, all the time.

I've been selfish and bitter and jealous.

I don't want to live this way anymore. I mess up, all the time. Even worse, I do the same things over and over again. I want to be different. I want to know this peace and freedom Matthew talks about. Can God really love me, with all I've done for the Federation? Matthew forgave me for what I did to him, but I've done so much more against God. Will He forgive me?

I want to be forgiven and loved by God.

"I want to believe," I whisper, and I start to cry, but I'm not so sure it's from my guilt anymore. "I do believe, and I do want to please God."

The second I say those words, the overpowering burden of everything is gone—the knowledge that I helped with Reintegration, that I'm the reason Thompson has his Violations, that I've lied to everyone, and that I've been so, so selfish.

I feel lighter.

I feel a sense of freedom I've never felt before.

We sit there for another half-of-an-hour, while Matthew shows me verses about God's love and how He's always with us. There's a verse about how God's plans for us are always good, even if we don't know it. Another verse says God will never stop loving us, no matter what we do.

These verses affect me the same way the ones I read earlier

did, except this time I know how to explain it, maybe because I understand who God is now. These verses tell me God is always with me.

I don't need to be afraid anymore.

"Why doesn't the Federation teach us this? Why would they not want everyone to know about God?" I run my finger over one of the pages, this one about how God created the world just by saying the words. He created oceans and animals and stars. It sounds bizarre, but at the same time, I *know* it's true.

When I was younger, before beginning my Regulator training, I took basic science classes with the other children. The teacher explained how the world formed itself by accident. Now as Matthew explains a different story to me, the first doesn't make sense. What about the human body, which I learned about in Primary School? How could something be so complex if someone didn't make it?

Matthew sets the book aside. "'Cause of the Tolerance Act. Even before the Federation came into power, people chose to disobey God, because they wanted to please themselves, rather than Him. Well, part of what we're told to do is tell the other people of the world about God and what Jesus—His Son—did for us. Problem is, we can't tell people they need to repent without telling them they're wrong.

"When the Tolerance Act was passed, people expected no one would say they were wrong again. The people who believe in God, called Christians, were more determined than ever to help people see they needed God. Because of the Tolerance Act, though, that was now a crime. Some Christians kept quiet, but others continued to defy the Tolerance Act. They became the first Intolerants."

God created the world. He also established laws we have to follow and gave us *consciences* so we know when we're following those laws. "The Federation doesn't want us to know this because it proves that there's right and wrong."

"Yes."

I jump to my feet. "Then people need to know, Matthew. I'm sure there's lots of people like me, who have seen the irony of the Tolerance Act but don't know there's something better than the Federation. We need to tell all of them!"

Of the thousands upon thousands of people in the Federation, only Matthew and I know about all this. Everyone else is in the dark. Thompson. Chelsea. They need to know the truth, too. Would they believe like I have? Would they believe God is real and understand they need to repent? I want them to, so they can know the freedom I've found—a freedom I've discovered while still living within the Federation's walls.

Pure excitement surges through me. I've kept a lot of secrets lately, but this is something I can't just keep inside forever. People need to know this. I reach for Matthew's book. I want everyone to know the truth it contains.

Matthew, too, stands. Maybe it's from the momentary period of rest, but he doesn't look as pale or exhausted. I glance around the storage room, and then an idea forms in my mind. All my other plans were haphazard, but this one…this plan just might work.

I allow myself a smile. "I know just how we can do it, too."

26

"They use this building to monitor messages sent to and from tablets. The communication workers here also have another important duty." I hand Matthew my tablet. "Sometimes City 1 needs to send out important messages to City 45. The officials are in charge of making sure the messages get sent to every tablet in the city. It's a rare occurrence, though. I think it's happened only once in my life. They had changed the date of when we were to take our Occupation Placement Tests."

Matthew looks at my tablet, then at me. "What do you want me to do with this?"

I take it from him and open the messaging system on the screen. "Write out what you just told me, about God and hope and why the Federation keeps it from us. We can access their equipment and send it out to the people of the cities."

I don't bother hiding the happiness in my voice. People need a nudge, a push to make them see the Federation is wrong to keep things like hope and love from us. There is a way better than the Federation.

Matthew sits on the ground again, setting my tablet on his lap. He hasn't had another attack in a while. Will Matthew's memory return on its own now, without causing him pain? Or will his health continue to decline? I watch him as he writes, a look of concentration and determination on his face. Every few seconds, he pauses, like he's trying to think of the correct words to use.

I squat down next to his bag and pull out the strange device he brought with him. "This can be used to bypass the card scanners?"

"Yeah." Matthew looks up for a moment, then goes back to what he's doing. "I still don't remember where I got it, but I do know how to use it now."

"Great. We can use it to access whatever we need."

"How do you know this'll work?" Matthew reaches for his book that I set back on the ground a few minutes ago. He turns to one of the pages, reads part of it, then continues writing.

What are other books like?

"Thompson brought me here when I was younger. The people who work here have jobs close to Regulation, since they have to monitor people's messages and report suspicious ones. Thompson figured it was important for me to know how the system works, see what the first steps in arresting a citizen were. He showed me where they do this." I glance away. The reason we're able to do all this is because of Thompson. He didn't even know it, but he showed me so much that I'm now able to use to defy the Council.

"They let him show you? I'm starting to pick up on the strict rules about learning here. You only learn what you need to. Everything else is off-limits. I guess they do that to make sure no one person knows too much about how the system works. They can keep people in the dark."

Still Matthew doesn't look up, but keeps writing.

"Thompson was...confusing. Most people saw him as the kind of man who never broke the Tolerance Act and always performed his duties. With me, though, he tended to show a more lenient, rebellious side. I guess most people never saw that side of him. Only me." I shrug my shoulders.

Maybe Thompson wasn't so much an enigma as he was a paradox. If they assigned him a new student, would he have been the same way? Or did he just want one person to know how he really felt about the Federation, and for some unknown reason he chose *me*? Thompson's words and actions inspired me to rebel, just as much as Matthew's. Does Thompson know what I've done? Would he be proud of me if he did?

I've been forgiven, but something gnaws at me inside. Is it guilt or something else? Thompson's in trouble because of me. He wouldn't have any Violations if I hadn't pulled him into my scheme. I wish I could find him and apologize, tell him how sorry I am for what happened to him. I can't, though, because someone will find out I talked to him.

Several minutes later, Matthew looks up from my tablet. "Done."

"Good." I manage a smile. I'm defying the Federation—again—but not to save myself and Matthew this time. I'm going to help the citizens of City 45 see what is missing from their lives. They can finally know the truth.

I take my tablet from him, then grab the device Matthew brought with him. I check the time on my tablet. "Most of the communication workers will be at lunch now. We need to go upstairs. That's where the room we need is."

Matthew nods and grabs his bag. Did the time we have to rest help him recover, at least a little? He stands without looking like he's going to collapse at any second. Will he be okay? Will he make it through this?

I open the storage room door—the door leading into the building, not outside of it—and stick my head out. It opens into a long hallway. Not a person in sight. I step into the hallway, Matthew following behind. The door slides closed behind us. To the left is the elevator, to the right is the building entrance. Matthew and I walk toward the elevator.

"Do you remember anything else?"

He shifts his bag from one shoulder to the other. "No. I remember a lot of what I did after I got here, but not how I got in. Crazy, huh? The one thing I *need* to remember, but it's completely eluded me."

"It'll come." I push the button that opens the elevator doors. "Matthew?"

"Yeah?"

We step into the elevator. Which floor do we need? I select the button for the top floor. Isn't that where Thompson took me last year?

"How does God know when we need help?" Maybe it's a stupid question.

"Well, He's all-powerful, so He already knows. But we can pray, too." Matthew must see my confused expression, because he adds, "Praying is when you talk to God. You can tell Him when you need help and thank Him for when He's helped you in the past. Praying is part of how we can maintain a personal relationship with Him."

"And He always helps?"

"If it's best for us. Sometimes what we want or think we need isn't what He has planned for us."

The elevator doors slide open and I walk out onto the top floor of the communication room. "So if He believes it's best for us to escape the Federation, then we will? He'll help you remember?"

"If that's His will, then yes."

I really, really hope God's will is for us to escape.

While we walk down the hallway, I look at the devices by the door displaying the room's purpose. Floor 2 Storage. Tablet Monitoring System. Training Room One. A faint hissing noise from behind us makes me reach for my stunner. A door opening? I turn around. A middle-aged communication worker exits one of the rooms. His jaw drops when he sees us.

"Excuse me?" He strides over, eyeing our uniforms. "You don't have clearance to be here. How did you get in, anyway?"

Matthew, standing next to me, balls his hand into a fist. I finger the clip attaching my stunner to my belt. Is there an excuse I can come up with, or will I have to knock the man out? He'll report us if we don't have a reason for being in the communication center.

"You didn't answer my question. Neither of you work here. You shouldn't have been allowed in the building. I'll have to contact your supervisors." Exasperation creeps into the worker's voice. He pulls his tablet out from under his arm, casting a suspicious look at the name and number on Matthew's uniform shirt. The worker starts typing, muttering to himself. "Braddock. Four-five-nine—"

I withdraw my stunner and point it at the worker. Before he has time to look up, I push the button on the stunner. There is no sound from the weapon. The communication worker staggers, his tablet slipping from his grasp. The device hits the floor with a loud *crash*. I wince. Are there any other people on this floor? Could they have heard the noise? A few seconds later, the man collapses.

I bend down and grab his tablet, which is still intact despite the impact from hitting the tile flooring. He never finished sending his report. No one, except whoever monitors our tracking devices, knows we're here. "We need to move fast. He won't be unconscious very long."

"Close, huh?" Matthew smiles a nervous yet relieved grin.

"Too close," I stand up straight. "Let's find the room we need."

Matthew and I continue down the hallway, but I keep my stunner in hand. Next time, I won't hesitate to knock someone out. The workers won't hesitate to turn us in. They know Matthew and I aren't allowed to be here.

I stop in front of the door to the Message Distribution Center. Using his device, Matthew opens the door. Where did Matthew find the device? Did he make it, or did someone else? I don't have time to inquire about Outlands technology, however. We have work to do. I enter the room, holding my stunner in front of me with both hands. Matthew smacks the button on the wall to turn on the lights.

No one is in the room. I breathe a sigh of relief, clipping my stunner back onto my belt. Most of the communication workers are on their lunch break at the moment. On the far wall is a control panel. I turn my tablet on again and pull up the message Matthew wrote.

"So do you know how to do this?" Matthew sets his bag on the floor. He jumps a little as the door slides closed.

"I think so. How hard can it be?" I tap on a small screen

in the center of the control panel. The screen hums to life. A long gray cord dangles from one of the control panel's ports. I examine the end of the cord. It's like the cord I use to charge my tablet. Is this what I need?

I plug the end of the cord into my tablet, then set the tablet on a shelf on the wall. Within seconds, a list of files displays on the control panel screen—all the files on my tablet. I select the one Matthew just created, and then a box pops up asking me what I want to do with the file. I choose to "send to all tablets in City 45". It then asks me if I'm sure this is what I want to do. Why would I go through the hassle of selecting a file and preparing to send it if it's not what I want to do?

Before I can tap "yes", the door to the room slides open.

Matthew and I both turn around as five Regulators enter the room. I swallow. It was only a matter of time before they found us. One Regulator takes a step toward Matthew, reaching for his arm. Matthew pulls away, then actually *punches* the man in the face. The Regulator takes a step backward, blood dripping from his nose.

I toss Matthew my weapon, then tap the blinking icon labeled "yes" on the screen. A bar slowly fills up, preparing the file to be sent. Will everything go through before the Regulators can halt the process?

Five percent complete.

Matthew glances down at my weapon, adjusting his grip on it. Where is the stunner I gave him? My gaze lands on Matthew's bag. Did he put it in there? If he did, the Regulators are in my way to grab it. What can I do to help?

Fifteen percent complete.

The Regulator Matthew punched holds up his weapon, aiming it at Matthew's chest. Matthew lunges forward, tackling the man to the ground. The stunner slips free of the Regulator's grasp and skitters across the floor. I bend down and grab it, whirling around to stun a female Regulator.

We're trained how to use stunners but not how to fight in any other way. Matthew, however, knows how to defend himself. The Regulator shoves Matthew off of him, but the effort is pointless. Matthew hits the man once, dazing him, then stuns him with the weapon in his hand.

One of the other Regulators approaches me, staring over my shoulder at the control panel. Do they know I'm sending the message? How long do I need to hold them off for?

Thirty-seven percent complete.

The one Regulator grabs my wrist in a firm grip, dragging me away from the control panel. He yanks the stunner out of my hand, then pushes me aside, into one of the other Regulators. The first looks at the control panel for a moment. Is he trying to shut it off? The other Regulator wraps an arm around my waist and pulls me to the door. I reach out, groping for anything to hold onto as he drags me away. The walls are smooth. I claw at the Regulator's arm, risking a glance at the control panel.

Fifty-nine percent.

Matthew rises to his feet, then stiffens, a far-away look filling his eyes. Not now. Why now? Of all the horrible times for this to happen to him...I try to wrench myself free of the Regulator who holds me back. With his free hand, he reaches for the metal cuffs clipped to his belt. Some Regulators carry handcuffs, even though most don't. Once he binds my hands, once Matthew passes out, once they figure out how to stop the message from going through...all this will have been for nothing.

The third of the still-conscious Regulators, a bearded man, glances down at one of his fallen comrades. He knows Matthew's an Intolerant, a rebel, a fighter. Matthew could take him down before he has time to reach for his stunner. Except Matthew sinks to his knees, agony marring his face.

Sixty-four percent.

"Matthew!" I want to help him. I want to hold his hand and make sure he's going to be fine. He looks so worn. The Regulator holding me shoves me against the wall, forcing my hands behind my back. The next few moments go by in a blur. He tightens the cuffs around my wrists, the cool metal digging into my skin. He jerks me away from the wall.

Seventy-eight percent.

The Regulator by the control panel unplugs the cord from my tablet, but the numbers keep counting. The file has already been downloaded into the system—I just need to buy enough time so it'll get sent.

Ninety-one percent.

We can't fail, not now. Not when we are so close to success. Matthew crumples to the ground, his body shaking. The bearded Regulator stands over Matthew, pointing his stunner at Matthew's back. He must have pushed the button, for one last shudder runs through Matthew's body and he doesn't move after that.

Ninety-seven percent.

They still don't know how to stop the message from being sent. The Regulator by the control panel glances at the others and shakes his head, a look of pure confusion on his face. I hold on to that, the small glimmer of hope surging through me. Even if we fail, the people of City 45 will be able to see the truth.

The door opens again and in steps the last person I want to see. "You really didn't think you could get away with this, did you?" There's no mistaking the cool, smooth voice and perfectly enunciated words.

Council Member Haynes.

27

Why is *she* here?

Haynes walks to the center of the room, hands on her hips. One of the fallen Regulators stirs with a low groan. The Council Member shakes her head, murmuring something about "why things need to change". What does she mean? The Regulator sits up, wiping blood off his face with his sleeve.

Did the message send? The number is still frozen at ninety-seven percent complete. I need to distract Haynes and keep her from deleting the message. We may be captured, but I won't let everything we've done unravel.

"We haven't—" I start to say, but the Regulator tightens his grip on my arm to the point that it hurts.

"They did something with the messaging system," The Regulator holding me says. "We don't know how to stop it."

Haynes' gaze flickers away from the fallen Regulators and toward the control panel. I, too, look at the panel. Ninety-nine percent now. Horror passes over the Council Member's face. She strides over to the control panel. "What did you do?"

"We're showing people the truth," I say, holding my head high. They can capture me and plan to execute me, but I've done the right thing. Even if only a few people actually believe the message, at least some will see the truth. Some will see the Council's lies.

Haynes doesn't reply. She pulls her identification card out of her pocket and holds it under a card scanner by the control panel. She then pushes a button below the card scanner. One hundred-percent! The numbers flash blue on the screen a split second before all the lights go off in the building. The control panel dims, and the room and hallway outside are plunged into darkness.

Everything goes quiet. The Regulator holding me takes in deep, exhausted breaths, the only sound in the room. About thirty seconds later, all the lights turn back on. Haynes watches the control panel screen, fingering the edge of her identification card. She's nervous isn't she? She's worried that the message went through.

She reads something that pops onto the screen, then looks at her tablet. I can't see her face because her back is turned to me. Haynes types out a message to someone before turning off her tablet. When she turns back around, her expression is unreadable. Did we succeed? Was the message sent?

Or did we fail?

Haynes' tablet beeps, so she looks at it again, reading whatever message comes in. Once she finishes, she gestures at Matthew and me with a dismissal wave of her hand. "Cuff him, then follow Regulation 57-D and Regulation 57-K so both can be processed."

Regulation 57? Regulation 57 contains rules for giving Violations in abnormal circumstances. They must be following nonstandard procedures because Matthew is an Intolerant.

The bearded Regulator bends down next to Matthew, slipping the cuffs over Matthew's wrists and tightening them. Haynes exits the room, typing something on her tablet. Who is she contacting? The Regulator holding me drags me into the hallway. Matthew hasn't woken up yet. Will he be okay?

Even if the message went through, we failed to escape.

Regulation 57 involves taking us to a medical center, not the Regulation Center.

I'm in a special room, not the typical examination room citizens go to for checkups. This one is windowless with security cameras in all four corners. The door can only be opened by entering a password into a keypad by the door. The Regulators removed the cuffs from my wrists, leaving me in this white, sterile-smelling, horrible room.

How long have I been here? Two hours? Maybe three? They didn't let me see Matthew before locking me in here. I sit on the edge of the cot. There's no way to escape from this room. I can't open the door. Nothing I can use as a weapon, either. The only furniture is the cot and a counter built into the wall. I'm not tall enough to reach the security cameras. What would I do with them if I could?

I hold a small wad of cloth over a spot on my arm. Little dots of red mar the perfect white color. A kind-looking medical assistant came in about five minutes ago to draw blood and assured me this is for my own good. What are they doing? Why are they keeping me here instead of giving me Violations?

What have they done with Matthew?

"Is it Your will for us both to die?" I whisper. Can God hear me? Does He listen to me, or are there other people He needs to help first?

I would cry, but that's all I've done for the past few hours or however long I've been here. I don't have any tears left. They're going to do terrible things to Matthew, if they haven't done so already.

The door slides open and two white-clad medical workers enter. The assistant with the kind eyes and Doctor Perry. Why is he here? They whisper to each other in hushed tones, giving me the occasional analyzing glance. I set the blood-stained cloth wad next to me. Are they going to execute me now? Why wouldn't they do it in the execution room in the Regulation Center?

Doctor Perry walks over to me. "Hello, Katherine. How are you feeling?"

His voice is pleasant, soothing almost. The same tone he used while telling Matthew of his "amnesia". I grip the edge of the cot with both hands. Something's off here. "I'm fine, thank you, other than the fact that no one will tell me why I'm here or what's going on or what happened to Matthew…"

My voice shakes and my eyes burn with tears I didn't know I had left. I won't cry in front of them. I won't let them see my confusion and worry. Death doesn't hold the same sense of dread as it did before, but my worry for Matthew's safety is stronger than ever.

"You've been through a traumatic experience." Doctor Perry continues in that calm tone of his. He leans against the side of the counter, looking at his tablet. "No one's going to hurt you. We just want to talk to you."

"About what?"

"About why you helped the Intolerant." Perry reaches into his pocket and withdraws a small device that fits in the palm of his hand. He pushes a button on the side of the device then sets it down next to the syringe. A recording device. He's recording our conversation. My heart pounds a little faster now.

"What's there to talk about?"

Perry whispers something to the assistant and she leaves. The door closes, leaving me alone with Doctor Perry, who knows more about what's going on than I do. "There's no need to be defensive, Katherine. I want to help you. I need you to cooperate and *let* me help you. I understand there's a good chance you may not be to blame for the events of the past couple of weeks. This may not be your fault."

What is he saying?

"Your case is unusual. You committed at least six Violation-worthy acts in a two-week time period. I don't think anyone's done that in the history of the Federation, especially not someone like you." When I don't reply, the doctor shrugs his slim shoulders. "You're the perfect citizen, Katherine. You obey the laws, you respect authority, and you understand why our system operates the way it does. Considering the circumstances, I think there may be a logical explanation for your recent actions."

"You mean other than the fact I learned the Federation is wrong?" Where is he going with this? What is he trying to get me to say?

"'Wrong' is relative, Katherine." Doctor Perry blinks, the only glitch in his otherwise neutral expression. "You know that. You see? The behavior you're exhibiting at this very moment suggests you aren't yourself."

"I don't understand." And I don't.

"I guess there's no easy way to explain this to you. Due to the complexity and irregularity of your situation, I don't think you're the offender. I think you're the victim." He pauses. "The Intolerants have exiled themselves, but their use of technology and medicine is far from primitive. We think that perhaps there is a chance Matthew Braddock may have drugged you once he figured out about Reintegration, and then manipulated you into helping him escape?"

He poses this as a question and waits for me to answer. How can he think Matthew would do such a thing? Doctor Perry thinks Matthew *drugged* me, altered my mind in some way to make me help him? "No, that's not true."

Before he can say anything in response, the assistant returns with a hand-held device. She hands the device to Doctor Perry, who reads whatever is on the screen. The doctor frowns, glancing up at me. "Well, we performed some tests on your blood sample, and we found no indication that you have been drugged in any way."

He seems genuinely confused and disappointed. If I performed six Violations, shouldn't he *want* me executed? I'm now considered a threat to the Federation. He could care less about Matthew's fate. Why does he care so much about mine? Why does he want to prove me innocent of my crimes of treason?

"Is this the normal procedure when people receive three Violations?" I've never heard of any kind of procedure like this.

"No, your case is unique because of your first-hand dealings with the Intolerant. Council Member Haynes is curious as to why you assisted him. She asked me to help with this because of my familiarity with the situation." Doctor Perry hands the device back to his assistant. "Did Matthew Braddock threaten you into helping him?"

So Haynes still has no clue as to why I betrayed the Federation. I resist the urge to tell the doctor the only reason Haynes asked for his help is to limit the number of the people who know about the increasing Violations. Doctor Perry is one of few who knows of the Council's predicament. He created Reintegration *because* he knows. Why would Haynes risk another doctor knowing how fragile the system is?

"Why would Matthew threatening me change anything?" I still broke the Tolerance Act and countless regulations.

"It wouldn't be your fault, Katherine. If the Intolerant forced you to help him, then you didn't choose to betray the Federation. Your Violations wouldn't be the result of a desire to rebel against our society. The need to live is one of the strongest motivators a person can have. If the Intolerant threatened your life, it would only be natural for you to give in for the purpose of preserving your personal safety."

My teachers taught me this in Primary School. Every living thing wants to survive, and it will base its actions on that want to survive. The Federation created a world based on surviving. The citizens are safe, live long lives, and think they are happy. But isn't there a difference between surviving and living?

"If you were threatened into helping the Intolerant, a case could be made that you do not deserve your Violations."

I could avoid my Violations. I could avoid execution. All I'd have to do is tell Doctor Perry that Matthew threatened me into stealing the pills for him. For a brief second, I consider this proposal.

How could I do that? How could I deny everything I've seen and learned? How could I deny my love for Matthew and my love for God? If I told Perry what he wants to hear, wouldn't I be a selfish coward? I would only be trying to save myself and turning my back on the truth. I would be the person, like Doctor Perry talks about, whose sole goal in life is to survive.

Isn't love, not the need to survive, the greatest motivator of all?

"I helped Matthew of my own free will."

Doctor Perry straightens his posture, staring at me with a dumbfounded look in his eyes. I'm defying everything he knows, aren't I? I'm defying everything the Tolerance Act talks about—everything the Federation stands for. He wanted me to say I didn't freely choose to betray the Federation. If I did, I would have chosen the logical choice. Saying what he wanted me to say would prove everything we're taught since childhood.

I didn't, and now I've made it clear I no longer believe in the Tolerance Act.

The doctor nods at his assistant, who types five numbers into the keypad by the door. What are the numbers? She types too fast for me to see. The assistant sticks her head out the door and whispers something to someone outside. Two Regulators enter the room. I stand and ball my hand into a fist, like I've seen Matthew do.

One Regulator reaches for the cuffs attached to his belt. I take a step forward, but before I have time to do anything else, the second Regulator grabs his stunner and points it at me. Pain flashes through my shoulder. My legs give out beneath me and I hit the floor. "Please…" I whisper, the only part of a prayer

I manage to let out. My body won't respond to anything I tell it to do.

I need to get up.

I need to fight.

I need to find Matthew so we can escape.

What's happening? Everything is so fuzzy now. Someone bends down next to me, grabbing one of my arms. The pain in my shoulder subsides, replaced by a dull numbness. Then everything fades into blackness.

I sit on the cell's cot, hugging my knees to my chest. I've been here about an hour, waiting to know my fate—and Matthew's. What are they doing to him? What if they're sending him to City 1 at this very moment, while I'm helpless to do anything? No one's told me what the Council decided to do with Matthew. Neither option will be pleasant for him.

My shoulder throbs, the only reminder that I ever was stunned. I've never seen Regulators act so impulsively. The Regulators who stunned me at the medical center…they didn't act like normal Regulators. It's like they expected me to fight back. They were ready to use force. The Regulators who captured Matthew and me anticipated us to resist, but they weren't as prepared to subdue us. We most likely wouldn't have been captured if Matthew hadn't passed out when he did.

What's different about the Regulators who stunned me?

The cell door slides open, and two Regulators shove Matthew inside. He's here. They haven't sent him to City 1 yet. The door closes, leaving us alone. He's okay. We can try to plan our escape, figure something out so we can leave the Federation for good. Matthew doesn't say anything. I stand. They removed the cuffs before leaving me here, but Matthew's hands are bound in front of him.

The Regulators know Matthew is the more dangerous of the two of us.

"I'm sorry," he whispers, avoiding my gaze. "This is my fault. If I hadn't—"

"Shh, it's okay. You can't control when this happens to you." I reach out to grab his hand, wishing the cuffs were gone. How can he blame himself for our capture? He couldn't stop himself from passing out.

"I remember now. I remember how to get home, but what good does it do us now?"

A renewed since of hope is kindled inside me. Matthew remembers. Isn't there a chance we can still make it out of here and finally be free? Matthew is right, though. He may remember how to leave the Federation, but it doesn't mean we'll escape.

"They took me to the stupid medical place. Doctor Perry did some tests and stuff. He used a lot of scientific garbage to explain what's going on with me. I didn't understand most of it, but he did say I'll live. He gave me something to counteract it or whatever." Matthew sighs, exhausted. He's going to live? The pills won't kill him? Matthew frowns at me. "Are you all right?"

"Yes, I'm fine." I don't tell him about Doctor Perry's probing questions or the throbbing pain in my shoulder. Matthew has enough to worry about. I sit on the edge of the cot again, tugging on Matthew's sleeve. He sits next to me, running both hands through his hair. Of the two of us, Matthew's had the worst of it.

Reintegration

"We failed to escape, Katherine. I don't know what they're going to do to me, but you...they're going to execute you. We both know that after everything you've done, you've committed more than three Violations. They're going to kill you."

"It's okay. There's something better after this, remember?" I manage a smile, quoting Matthew's words from weeks ago, before we Reintegrated him. As soon as the words are out of my mouth, I know deep inside they're true. After I die, I'll see God. For a moment, confidence replaces my own fear of death.

But not my fear of what will happen to Matthew.

Matthew stares at the floor between his shoes. "I'm sorry I dragged you into this."

"I'm not. Meeting you is the best thing that ever happened to me. You taught me things to help me see the Federation isn't what it claims to be. You showed me how to be free, even without ever leaving the city's walls." I grab his hand. "No matter what happens to me, I don't regret meeting you, defying the Federation, or believing in God."

Matthew stares at the blank, gray wall in front of him. "I don't regret any of it either."

Does he mean that? Does he mean that he doesn't regret coming to City 45 or being captured or having his memory erased? "I love you, Matthew. No matter what happens, I'll always love you."

"I love you too, Katherine." I wish he could hold me close, like he's done in the past. He does, however, lean in and kiss me.

A kiss that ends when the cell door slides open and a Regulator enters.

No, not a Regulator. This man wears a green uniform and

boots instead of standard shoes. His weapon, bigger and bulkier than the standard stun weapon, is clipped to his belt, as is his identification card and silver handcuffs. The name "Smithson" is stitched into his uniform. He's young, about nineteen or twenty-years-old. His expression is void of emotion, but even so, it doesn't take long for me to recognize him.

He was the Regulator who stunned me at the medical center.

He was also one of the Regulators who arrested Thompson.

"Council Member Haynes would like to speak with you."

Matthew and I both stand, but the man holds up a hand. "Just her."

"Why?" Matthew manages to get the word out a split second before I can. "What does the Council Member want with Katherine?"

"I'm not permitted to tell *you*."

Smithson spits the last word out. He keeps his hand on his weapon at all times, like he's ready and waiting for us to attack him. Most Regulators will try to reason with an unruly citizen before stunning them, but this one won't hesitate to use force. He's tall and muscular—not the kind of opponent who's easily defeated.

Have they taught him how to fight?

"It's okay. I'll talk to her," I say, more to Matthew than to Smithson. Besides, it's unlikely I even have the right to refuse. Playing along may enable me to postpone my execution long enough to figure out a way to escape. What does Haynes want to tell me? The green-clad Regulator grabs my arm and pulls me out of the cell. He pushes the button on the wall, and the door slides closed.

Reintegration

Two more people wearing green uniforms stand by the elevator. I won't be able to escape at the moment, even with my hands free. I might manage to escape from the man holding my arm, but I wouldn't get far. Who are these people? As if able to read my thoughts, the man unclips the handcuffs from his belt and pushes me against the wall, rougher than the Regulator at the communication center.

"Don't try to escape." He pulls my arms behind my back, tightening the cuffs around my wrists. "If you do, we will kill you."

I'm already scheduled to die, so does he think threatening me with execution is going to make me change my mind? Unless, of course, he means they'll kill me on the spot. Impossible. Stun weapons aren't used to kill. He knows how to fight, but does he know how to kill with his bare hands?

I shiver.

Smithson places a hand on my back and steers me toward the elevator, where the other two green-uniformed people stand. One, also a young man, taps the button on the wall to open the elevator doors. The other one...

Chelsea?

My best friend, the girl I've known since Primary School, is one of the people holding me hostage. She too carries a weapon and handcuffs. So this is what they trained her to be? Not that I know what these people even are.

"What's going on?" I study her face. She won't meet my gaze and she doesn't say anything.

How can she do this to me, after all the years we've been friends?

The man shoves me into the elevator, keeping one hand on his weapon. Why won't Chelsea help me? The elevator doors close and the elevator descends down, taking me further from Matthew and closer to Haynes. She wants me for something. What could she possibly have to say to me, the girl who committed six Violations and isn't ashamed of it?

Four more people wearing green uniforms are in the hallway on the bottom floor—two by the elevator, two by the interrogation room door. I keep my head high. I refuse to show any sign of fear.

I wait in the middle of the corridor. One of the people opens the interrogation room door using her identification card. Haynes rises from her chair and approaches the open doorway.

"Sit down. We have a lot to talk about."

28

"I'm very disappointed in you, Katherine."

The Council Member returns to her seat, gesturing at the chair opposite her own. Between them is a silver table. I don't sit. I won't be interrogated like a criminal. I haven't done anything wrong, regardless of what the Tolerance Act says.

Smithson doesn't respect my act of defiance. When I don't sit, he grabs my arm again and drags me over to the chair. I slide into the chair. Without a word, the man exits the interrogation room.

What a jerk.

"Who are these people?" I watch the door slide closed.

"Mediators." Haynes types something on her tablet. Am I supposed to know what a Mediator is? Or why they've taken over the Regulation Center? I haven't seen a normal Regulator since Matthew and I's arrest. Haynes stares at her tablet screen. "As of today, we are replacing the Regulators with a new set of peacekeepers. *Effective* peacekeepers, something the Regulators will never be."

"Because of the increasing Violations."

"Yes." Haynes sighs. "The Intolerants have, for several years now, found ways to sneak into our cities. They break into our communication centers and circulate their propaganda. Because of this, the people of the Federation are doubting the Council's leadership. We need to establish new security measures."

"So you knew Matthew wasn't a terrorist. Even if you didn't know what he came here for, you suspected it had nothing to do with an act of violence. And yet you lied to me, tried to convince me Matthew was dangerous." Indignation sweeps over me.

She wanted me to see Matthew as a violent criminal, because that's what we're all taught to believe. Haynes lied to me from the start. From the day we met the Council Member has done nothing but deceive me.

"Matthew Braddock *is* still dangerous, and the Intolerants are growing bolder with each day that passes. They've taught him violence, as I've seen in the security footage. The Intolerants are biding their time, waiting for a moment when the Federation is vulnerable. The Council will not give them the chance."

"You haven't seen Matthew like I have." Haynes hasn't seen the selfless boy who risked his life to help someone he loves. She hasn't seen his innocence, his loyalty, his humility. Who is she to say Matthew would commit an act of terrorism?

"You see what you want to see. My first assumption was correct. You've become smitten with a young man who is an enemy of the Federation. You see a handsome boy and nothing else. I didn't think to review any of the security footage until this morning."

Haynes pushes her tablet toward me. I watch the screen and heat rushes into my cheeks. She's showing me a security footage clip. The black-and-white video displays Matthew and I walking down the dormitory hallway, holding hands. This isn't fair. Is every moment of my life recorded and documented? Can I not do anything without the Federation knowing every detail of it? Either Haynes turned her tablet's volume off, or the security camera doesn't pick up sound.

Why is she so stuck on trying to prove my actions were based on teenage infatuation? Is it the only explanation she can think of? Maybe so. Doctor Perry must have told her how his interrogation of me went. She knows I rejected the idea that Matthew threatened me into helping him. What else can she think of, other than that I helped Matthew because of silly feelings? Council Member Haynes has no choice but to think of me as a shallow girl who can't see past Matthew's good looks.

The only other option is to question the validity of the Tolerance Act, something she will never do.

"No, I chose to betray the Federation for other reasons. I do love Matthew, but it is so much deeper than the love I've been taught about. I've seen things to prove how wrong our society is. Safety isn't everything. Right and wrong do exist. Children should know their parents. Matthew told me about God, too."

Haynes laughs, a sound more mocking than amused. "I never realized you were so gullible, Katherine. And to think we considered—"

The Council Member clamps her mouth shut. *Who* considered *what*? What was she going to say? What can't I know?

I'm going to die, so why keep secrets from me? I'll have no one to tell. "Considered...?"

"Haven't you ever wondered why we chose you for this assignment in the first place? Why we let you make such an important decision, determining whether or not to Reintegrate the Intolerant?"

"I have." A lot. The question of "why me" has stayed in my mind since Haynes gave me my Final Test. There's hundreds, thousands, of trainees in the Federation. Why not choose one of them? Why let a trainee handle the issue at all? The Council usually makes the important decisions. Besides, they wanted Reintegration kept a secret. Why tell me about it?

"The Mediators are different from the Regulators. We selected young citizens to re-train based not only on their Final Tests, but on every report we ever received about them. We need Mediators who are loyal and who care about the overall safety of the Federation, but there are...other qualities we look for. The ability to make quick decisions and also to make *hard* decisions. The Mediators can't be hindered by any adherence to their personal beliefs."

Why is she telling me all this? I know the Mediators are colder, more indifferent than any Regulators. The Regulators served as peacekeepers, yes, but they also were less willing to use force.

"Before we made the Mediator's existence public, we needed a leader for them. We needed someone who exhibited all these qualities and then some. This person would need to be tested in a way that we could be sure they would be able to carry out their duties."

What? She can't be saying what I think she's saying.

"We let you choose between Reintegration and execution

not to test you as a Regulator, but as a potential Mediator. The Council and I needed to see that you could make decisions based on an ability to see past the present moment. If you chose execution, we would have realized you were only making a decision based on what had been done before.

"If you chose Reintegration—which you did—it would show us your ability to make a decision that could involve risks. But choosing Reintegration wasn't all we could use. We needed to see how you handled being so close with an Intolerant. If Reintegration failed, and you turned Matthew Braddock in, we would see you could make a difficult choice."

No, no. They wanted to make me a *Mediator*? I could never be one of those cold, violent people. Could I?

"I never expected you to become so involved with the Intolerant. You've never had a lot of friends, never became attached to any one person. You never dated. The last thing the Council ever expected was for you to fall in love with Matthew Braddock, or for the relationship to last quite this long." Haynes taps her finger on the table.

They know *everything* about me. They know I've never dated before and that Chelsea is my only friend. Did they know how close I became with Thompson? Was no aspect of my life private?

"So you chose me because I don't allow myself to get close to anyone?"

"We took that aspect into consideration, but it was more than that. Katherine, you were *the* perfect citizen. The Council chose you because we believed you were strong enough to do what was best for the Federation."

Most trainees would be ecstatic to learn of the Council taking such an interest in them. Weeks ago, maybe I would have been, too. I was the girl who always followed orders and always cared about preserving the Federation more than anything else. The perfect citizen. They chose me because they believed I could be a Mediator.

The urge to vomit rests in my stomach.

The Council needs the Mediators to deal with citizens who commit Violations. The Tolerance Act isn't working, so they need a more drastic method of maintaining order. The Mediators are more willing to use force than the Regulators. If the Mediators are needed to bring the Federation back to a state of peace and perfection...

"Are creating the Mediators part of Project Endgame?" Not that I know what Project Endgame even is.

Haynes opens her mouth then stops. Color drains from her cheeks. "How do you...? Oh, yes, the files you stole from me."

She knows I stole the files from her?

"Don't act so surprised, Katherine. I knew you stole those files minutes after you left my office. I didn't tell the Council, but decided to wait and see what you would do. We spent so much time planning for you to be Head Mediator. I didn't want to cast you aside so easily. I hoped you would see the files and come to the same conclusion I did. I hoped you would realize the Intolerants pose a real threat to the Federation. Creating the Mediators is not a step in Project Endgame, but they will play a part in it. Assuming the Council agrees with me that Project Endgame is necessary."

"What *is* Project Endgame?"

If the Mediators are a part of Project Endgame...what could it be? Nothing good. Haynes glances at the door, a tight-lipped expression on her face. Is she contemplating telling me?

Reintegration

Or deciding to have me taken back to my cell?

"Endgame," she says at last, "is a battle strategy."

A battle strategy? Isn't a battle a skirmish in a war? The reason for the formation of the Federation was to eliminate violence. Now the Council wants to start a battle? With who? Why? "If there's going to be a war, then the Mediators will be...?"

"Soldiers."

An archaic word. The Federation has always had peace-keepers, not soldiers. The original Council needed a group to enforce the Tolerance Act, not to start a war with the Intolerants. Yes, the Tolerance Act is wrong. Yes, the Regulators execute citizens for wanting something *more*. Yes, the founders of the Federation created a corrupt, prison-like world.

But this is an entirely different level of tyranny.

"We need a way to eliminate the Intolerants, once and for all," Haynes continues. "The Council believes taking additional security measures will be enough. But capturing an Intolerant every time they enter our cities won't fix anything. I've spent months trying to convince the Council of this. Neither execution nor Reintegration will permanently solve our problems."

They didn't want me to be a peacekeeper, but a soldier. The *head* soldier. If the Mediators are soldiers, then they know how to kill. They know how to do violent things. If I hadn't met Matthew, would I have been willing to do those things? Would I have known it was wrong, but stifled that knowledge because the Council gave me orders?

Haynes wants the Mediators to attack the Underground. Is Matthew's family there? If the Mediators do attack, will his family survive? This is why Haynes wants to find the Underground so badly, why she wants to glean any information out of Matthew before they kill him. She needs him to find the others.

So the Mediators can kill the people Matthew loves.

Once Matthew's family dies, once the Underground is destroyed...there will be no one left to defy the Federation. No one will sneak into cities and tell the people of the Federation the truth. No one will stop the Council and the Mediators from violently enforcing laws. The Council will win.

If Reintegration worked, would Endgame not be an option? Haynes said Reintegration and execution aren't long-term solutions, so the Intolerants have to be destroyed. The only way the Council can prevent chaos in the cities is by eliminating the threat altogether. Council Member Haynes has been trying to convince the Council of this...

Wait.

"You've spent *months* trying to push Project Endgame because you knew Reintegration wasn't a solution? You advocated for Matthew's Reintegration just a few weeks ago."

Why would she want me to choose Reintegration if she knew the effort was pointless? I can understand the other Council Members wanting Reintegration to work, but Haynes? If Endgame is her idea, if she's the one who wants the Underground destroyed, why did she want me to choose Reintegration so badly?

"I didn't say 'months'," Haynes says, but the way she clenches her hands belies her words. Besides, I'm not deaf. She did say she's spent months trying to convince the Council to enforce Project Endgame. Matthew was Reintegrated a few weeks ago. Why the discrepancy? What am I missing here?

Reintegrating and executing Intolerants won't solve the problem of the Violations.

The only way to stop the increasing Violations is destroying the Underground.

Haynes needs the Council to agree to Project Endgame.

These facts don't help me in any way. They don't explain why Haynes wanted me to choose Reintegration. Or do they? A cold, unsettling feeling washes over me and icy pinpricks shoot up and down my spine.

That's impossible, isn't it? She wouldn't...couldn't...no. I'm only guessing. But the facts line up. All the pieces I haven't been able to find fit into place. Why she never turned me in. Why she was so certain I lied to her. Why she tried so hard to catch me making a mistake.

"You wanted Reintegration to fail. You wanted to force the Council to agree to Project Endgame. You altered the procedure, didn't you? Somehow, you made it where Matthew's memory would return."

The Council Member doesn't flinch at my accusations, but her dark eyes flash. "I did. I had to."

How did she do it? Doctor Perry never seemed to realize Reintegration was doomed to fail, so she left him in the dark, too. Haynes isn't trained in the scientific field, so how could she have sabotaged Perry's work?

She would have had access to the files from the first Reintegration attempt.

What if Haynes switched something around, made it where Doctor Perry essentially repeated whatever went wrong when they tried to Reintegrate Brian Coleman years ago? In doing so, she could guarantee Matthew's memory would return.

"So you see, Katherine? You say you helped the Intolerant because you realized right and wrong do exist, but don't you see how silly that is? Matthew Braddock didn't retain his 'conscience', as the Intolerants call it. Reintegration failed, and that is why he held to his Intolerant beliefs."

Haynes altered the Reintegration procedure so Matthew would regain his memory. Does that mean my initial assumption was incorrect, when I wondered if right and wrong are absolutes? I decided everyone has a sense of right and wrong they can either choose to follow or ignore. I made my decision based on Matthew's actions after Doctor Perry erased his memory. What if Reintegration failed to erase all of his memory to begin with?

What if Matthew really did *remember* his Intolerant values?

But he didn't remember anything about his past. Whenever anyone told Matthew he was from the Federation, he always responded with a complacent smile and obedient nod. A week or two passed before he showed any sign of remembering anything, and even then, nothing to make him doubt what we told him. No, there was something other than a memory telling Matthew when something was morally wrong.

What about all the people breaking the Tolerance Act? They weren't raised to believe in the same values as the Intolerants, so why would they break the Federation's core law? Why did they rebel, if not because *something* told them their lives were wrong?

If our values are shaped solely by what we're taught in childhood, why are citizens of the Federation believing the messages circulated by the Intolerants? Why did it not work the other way around? Even if Matthew did remember some about his past from the very beginning, but not enough to know he wasn't from the Federation, why didn't he act like a normal citizen? Why didn't he adopt a casual view of dating?

Reintegration

Why didn't he smile and nod when I explained the Tolerance Act to him, considering that's how he responded to anything else I told him?

People from the Federation, with their memories perfectly intact, have chosen to believe in God. Matthew, a naïve, brainwashed teenager, refused to believe in the Tolerance Act. Doesn't that prove the human conscience *must* exist? Doesn't that prove there is no evidence for the Tolerance Act?

Besides, I've felt it myself.

I've felt the urge to do the right thing, felt the nauseating sensation when I know I'm doing something wrong. I've felt the horrible, overpowering emotion called guilt. I felt it, long before I ever met Matthew.

I meet the Council Member's smug, confident eyes. She thinks she proved my reasoning incorrect. But she's the one who's incorrect. Haynes can hold to the Tolerance Act all she wants, but in the end, the Tolerance Act doesn't stand up to the truth of God.

"I've felt that right and wrong are real. Haven't you? Every time you lie to the Council or you have someone executed just for standing up for what they believe in, don't you *feel* it?" None of this—the Mediators, Project Endgame, the destruction of the Underground—will happen if Haynes can see the lie found in the Tolerance Act.

"I'm doing what is best for the Federation." There isn't a trace of remorse in her voice. "Any good citizen would do the same."

Is there no changing her mind?

Me, Matthew, even Doctor Perry...we were all pawns in Haynes's plan to destroy the Underground and kill the Intolerants. She used us to make the Council agree to whatever she wants. The other Council Members won't know she deceived me into believing Reintegration was a viable option. They won't know she ruined Doctor Perry's work. They won't know she pretended to offer Matthew a second chance, when all she wants from him is the location of the Underground.

She couldn't give me a Violation unless she caught me in the middle of doing something illegal. Otherwise the Council would demand to know how she was so sure I broke the law. She couldn't blame me for anything without revealing what she herself did. The only reason I avoided capture this long is because she needed definite proof.

Was this all a cruel, sick game—a game Matthew and I could never win?

"Due to the number of your Violations, your status has been changed. You are now an Intolerant and your execution is scheduled for tomorrow morning." Haynes stands and grabs her tablet.

My execution.

Tomorrow.

I'm going to die.

They're going to kill me for what I've done. I'm going to die for doing the right thing. The Council is punishing me because I dared to question, but I've done nothing wrong. I'm not afraid of dying, but I'm afraid of what they'll do to Matthew. I'm afraid of what the Council will tell everyone. Will they be open about why I died, or will they try to cover it up like they've been doing for years? Will they tell everyone Matthew was a terrorist? Will they continue to deceive the people?

"Wait," I say. "If I'm going to die tomorrow, can I at least talk to Thompson one last time?"

"No, Katherine. You aren't allowed to have any contact

with your mentor." Haynes purses her lips into a tight line, then walks toward the door. Without looking back at me, she pushes the button on the wall and opens the door.

"Yes, but—"

"I'm finished," Haynes snaps to Smithson, who waits in the hallway. Why can't I talk to Thompson? Why did the Council Member act so disgusted when I suggested it? "You may take her back to her cell. I must return to City 1 so the Council and I can determine what will be done with Matthew Braddock."

Haynes will try to convince the Council to allow her to learn whatever she can from Matthew. What will she—or the Mediators—do to him? Thompson told me once about *torture*, something people did in the Past. Will Haynes torture Matthew to get what she wants?

"You can let him go. Let him return to the Outlands. Please. You've already taken so much away from him." I stand. What are the chances of her listening to what I have to say? The Mediator enters the room, but I don't stop talking. "Can't you see he's not what you think he is? He's not what you want him to be? I—"

"He's an Intolerant, an enemy of our society." Haynes lingers in the doorway. "And so are you."

I curl up on the cot, burying my face in the thin pillow. Fresh tears sting my eyes. They shoved me into a different cell, so I'm alone. Why didn't they let me see Matthew again? Will they let me tell him good-bye tomorrow, before they kill me and they send him to City 1 and do terrible things to him?

I've accepted my fate. Tomorrow the Mediators will execute me, and I'll be free of the Federation. I'm not afraid of what they'll do to me, since there's a better life after this one. All I want is for Matthew to be free. He deserves to go back to the Outlands, the place where he belongs. Now he'll be subjected to who-knows-what. He won't see his family ever again. He can't take the medicine to his sister.

If I can't escape, how can I make sure Matthew will?

Haynes told me everything. What if I found a way to contact the other Council Members and explain to them they've been duped? No, even if I could contact them, they would never believe me. They would assume I was making up a story in hopes of avoiding execution.

"Okay, God," I whisper. "I don't understand what Your plan is."

Did our message even go through? If I'm going to die, I at least want the other people in the city to know the truth. They deserve to know what the Council doesn't tell them about. Everything we're taught is a lie. If Haynes would have let me talk to Thompson one last time, I could have told him the truth. He showed me so many things that need to change in the Federation. I want to reciprocate in kind.

If the Council approves of Project Endgame and if Haynes learns of the Underground's location, there won't be anyone left to defy the Federation. No one will be able to tell the people the truth. Haynes always had the upper hand. Once she convinces the Council to go through with Endgame…

What happens next?

29

Two Mediators lead me down the corridor, past all the other cells. I try to twist my hands free of the cuffs, but the metal only tightens around my wrists. If I can't escape, then my chance of saving Matthew will be lost.

Every step toward the elevator grows heavier than the last. Once they take me to the execution room, I will die and Matthew will be subjected to whatever cruel fate the Council decides for him. Have they voted yet? What *will* they do to him? Haynes will try as hard as she can to convince the other Council Members to accept her plan.

Another Mediator stands by the elevator and pushes the button on the wall. Mediator Smithson tightens his grip on my left arm and pain shoots through my shoulder. The woman holding my right arm is a little gentler, although not much. Neither of them shows any sign of caring that they're taking me to my execution. Will they be the ones to kill me? Or will other

Mediators do it?

They pull me into the elevator and I do my best to steady the churning panic in my stomach. Every second slipping by is another second lost in trying to escape. I need to get away from the Mediators so I can rescue Matthew. If only they would let me talk to him one last time. I hope even if I fail to save him, Matthew can at least find a way to escape on his own.

I hope he can get back to the Outlands, where he belongs.

The elevator doors hiss closed and we drop down, closer toward my fate. I need more time. I need more time to figure this out. My stomach refuses to settle and nausea threatens to overtake me.

"Please help us find some way out of this," I murmur. I can't tell if God ever listens to me.

Smithson tightens his grip on my arm even further. "Shut up."

I'm going to be executed within minutes. I never thought I would die before completing my Final Test. Then again, I never thought about defying the Federation until these last few weeks. I've committed crimes against the only world I've ever known and now I'm going to face the consequences of my actions. I don't care what they do to me.

How can I save Matthew's life?

The elevator doors open and the Mediators shove me into the hallway. A third man stands by the execution room door. This is it. They'll take me in there, strap me down, inject me with a lethal drug...

And they won't care.

If I passed my Final Test and became one of these Mediators, would I be so cold and unsympathetic? Could I take someone to his or her execution, unable to show any sign of pity? The Council believed I could. They thought I was loyal enough that I would do anything they wanted. How loyal to the Federation was I?

Would I have cared about how *wrong* all this is?

The man by the door unclips his identification card from his belt and holds it under the card scanner. Where is Chelsea? I haven't seen her here today. Does she know what they're doing to me? Does my best friend know I'm going to die? Tears sting my eyes. Am I all alone?

Chelsea's a Mediator.

Thompson was relocated.

Matthew will be sent to City 1 soon.

If I fail, all the work Matthew and I did will have been for nothing. We came so far, tried so hard to escape. What happens now? God is with me. At least, I want to believe He is. I'm not afraid of dying. But what about Matthew? Will God let Matthew suffer unmentionable things because of my stupid mistake?

The third man enters the execution room first, tapping the button on the wall to turn on the lights. The execution room reminds me of medical rooms. White walls, white tile floor, bright lights. One wall is lined with drawers and cabinets. The opposite wall has a sink and a trash container. There is a bed pushed against the wall opposite the door. It too looks like one of the beds in the hospital—except for the straps used to hold the victims down. The Mediators holding me drag me into the room, the soles of their clean boots squeaking against the shiny white floor. After several seconds, the door closes. I stare at the bed, taking in the sight of the leather straps. Has anyone ever escaped? I risk a glance toward the cabinet containing the poison vials. Does it hurt when they inject the stuff into you?

How many people have they executed in this very room?

"Let's get this over with," Smithson mutters, releasing my arm. Will they remove the handcuffs? They'll have to, if they're going to strap me down. As soon as they free my hands, I'll try to escape. Three of them. One of me. All of them carry weapons. I have nothing to assist me. I may not have much of a chance, but I have to try.

For Matthew.

The Mediator named Hoff—his last name is stitched in black lettering on his uniform—grabs a device off of the counter. What is that? "Once we're done taking care of her, we're to contact the Council."

Smithson grunts in response. Well. Haynes will be happy to know I'm gone, won't she? I can't cause any more problems if I'm dead. She told me everything—how she altered the Reintegration procedure, what Project Endgame is, and how she's deceived the Council. I can't divulge this information once I'm nothing but an execution statistic.

Why aren't they undoing the handcuffs? I won't be able to do anything with my hands forced behind my back. The Mediators make no move to strap me down or open the cabinet. Hoff taps the screen of the device he holds. The woman maintains a tight grip on my arm. Smithson frees his weapon from his belt and examines it. What are they doing?

Hoff holds up the device and nods at the other two. "Ready when you are."

The woman kicks at the back of my legs and I sink to my knees. My eyes start to water from the throbbing pain in my right leg. The female Mediator keeps her hand on my shoulder, keeping me from getting up. Smithson holds up his weapon and walks behind me. The already fast beating of my heart speeds up even more and my thoughts become jumbled. What *are* these people doing to me?

"Three, two, one..." Hoff taps the device's screen. "Go."

"This," Smithson says from behind me, "is Katherine Holliday, a citizen of City 45. She—"

A shrill beep rings through the air. The woman releases my shoulder and pulls a hand-held device from her pocket. Hoff lowers the device he holds. The woman shakes her head, reading her hand-held one.

"An unauthorized person has entered the building." A hint of incredulousness lines her words. Someone forced their way into the Regulation Center? Who could it be—and why? Whoever they are, the Mediators will subdue them within minutes.

"Go take care of it," Smithson barks in his deep, gruff voice. "We'll finish this here and join you when we're done."

"Be quick about it." The woman grabs her weapon and exits the room.

Hoff watches her leave. After the door closes again, he holds up his device. "I guess you'll have to start over."

"This is Katherine Holliday, a citizen of City 45. She committed three Violations against the Federation. The Council will not stand by for such insubordinate behavior. Katherine Holliday determined her fate when she willingly chose to break the Tolerance Act and betray everyone in the Federation.

"It is because of people like her, people who threaten harm against the Federation, that the Mediators have been created. This rebellion in the cities cannot continue. For years, the Council hoped those of you who choose treasonous behavior would see the turmoil your actions cause."

Are they *recording* his words? Is that what the device is for?

Why would Smithson need to say all this? Why aren't they executing me? I again try to twist my hands free of the cuffs but they only seem to tighten.

"Where are You?" I whisper.

"The Council hoped those who broke the Tolerance Act would change their ways, but no. These same people continued to rebel, and are now the reason why we, the Mediators, are necessary. Katherine Holliday is one of these rebels." Smithson presses the end of his weapon against the side of my head. "This is a demonstration, to remind those who are thinking of committing treason of what happens when they dare to betray the Federation."

They *are* executing me. All this is my execution, and they're recording it. The Mediators carry weapons to kill, not to stun. Why didn't I realize sooner? Haynes said the Mediators need to be more effective than the Regulators. They're replacing the people *and* the weapons they carry.

Judging by Smithson's words, they're going to show the recording to the people. The Mediators will show everyone my death, but why? To frighten people out of breaking the Tolerance Act?

"Katherine Holliday is hereby sentenced to—"

The door behind Hoff slides open. He starts to turn around, but then his body stiffens. The recording device slips from his hand and hits the floor, but it doesn't break. Smithson pulls the weapon away from my head, shoving me aside. Hoff collapses to the ground and someone enters the execution room. I glance up to see who my rescuer is and my heart skips a beat.

Thompson.

"Don't come any closer," Smithson snarls, pointing his

weapon at Thompson. "You aren't authorized to be here."

If my mentor does anything stupid...I shudder. The Mediator will kill him. Even if Smithson spares Thompson's life now, this will be his third Violation. No matter what, they'll execute him. Why did he come? Thompson doesn't lower his stunner, but glares at the younger man. Something very protective lurks in my mentor's eyes, a look I've never seen there before. "Just let her go and we can make this easy."

"I have my orders from the Council. She is to be executed for her crimes against the Federation." Impatience breaks through the Mediator's bland, indifferent voice. Smithson takes a step toward my mentor, leveling the weapon at Thompson's chest. I can't be the reason Thompson dies. I can't.

I kick at Smithson's leg. A loud *bang* cuts through the room and one of the cabinet doors shatters. Fragments of glass rain down, covering the floor in tiny crystal pieces. My mentor raises his stunner again. Smithson staggers, dropping his weapon. Then he, too, falls to the ground.

Thompson bends down and grabs my arm, helping me to my feet. "Are you okay?"

I nod, staring at Smithson's prone form. He won't wake up for several minutes, but even so, I don't like being in the same room with the man who tried to kill me. I nudge his weapon away with my foot. Thompson bends down next to Smithson and rummages through his pockets.

"What are you doing here?" I whisper. Thompson came to save me. Doesn't he realize what this means? If the Council learns what he's done, they'll give him a third Violation. They'll execute him. Thompson will die, and it will be all my fault.

"Haynes was kind enough to inform me of your execution." He pulls the handcuff's key out of Smithson's pocket. I frown. Why would Haynes want to tell Thompson of my imminent execution? Thompson straightens up, crunching bits of glass beneath his shoes.

The screen of Hoff's recording device flickers. "What *were* they doing?"

"The Council sent out a message to all the tablets this morning." Thompson grabs one of my wrists. "Apparently, the Mediators aren't new. The Council created them years ago, but kept their existence secret, just like the Violations. Many of the Mediators were placed in Regulation positions, and are the ones who carried out most of the executions. The Council didn't want to 'alarm anyone'. But now, they realized keeping the Violations secret wasn't solving the problem. Haynes told me the Council believes reminding the citizens of what happens when they break the Tolerance Act will stop the problem."

"The Council intends to frighten everyone?" I pull my hands free of the cuffs as soon as Thompson unlocks them. "So that means…?"

"They were recording your execution to send to all the tablets in City 45."

I pull in a breath of air. Haynes didn't only want me killed. She wanted to use me as an example. If the Mediators showed my execution to everyone in City 45, people would think twice before disobeying any regulations.

"Why did you come?" I'm grateful for what he's done, but how many rules has he broken in doing this? The last thing I want is for Thompson to face execution for helping me. How could I forgive myself if he died because of me?

Thompson steps over Smithson's body and opens one of the drawers. "Ask me again later. We don't have much time.

Reintegration

We need to rescue the boy and remove your tracking devices. Do you have a plan for escape?"

"Not really."

"Oh, well. Removing your tracking devices will at least help buy you time." Thompson shakes his head, then pulls a surgical knife and a wad of bandages out of the drawer. "First, let's go find your friend. It won't be long before these two wake up. I stole the identification cards from the ones I stunned earlier, so they won't make it very far in trying to find us."

He fixes me with one of his wry grins, then pushes the button on the wall to open the door.

"Let's go find Matthew." I follow Thompson out of the execution room.

"He's in this cell." I point at the wall screen next to one of the cell doors. Thompson tosses me his identification card, then bends down next to one of the Mediators he stunned. I hold my mentor's card under the scanner. Why is he here? I've caused him nothing but trouble, yet here he is, saving my life.

The cell door slides open. All we have to do now is free Matthew and leave the Regulation Center. Thompson will help us remove our tracking devices so the Federation can never find us again.

Matthew's asleep on the cot, one arm dangling over the side. Did he pass out again? Even in his sleep, his face looks pale. I shake his shoulder. How long until the unconscious Mediators wake up? I glance behind me. Thompson pulls one of the Mediators' arms behind his back, then slips the cuffs over the man's wrists.

"Katherine?" Matthew murmurs, yawning. He reaches up

to brush his hair out of his face.

"We're going to escape now, Matthew. Thompson's helping us. We're going to do it." I grab Matthew's hand and help him to his feet. Matthew and I may have planned our escape for days, but I can't believe that we're going to do it now.

The Federation won't be my prison anymore.

30

I stare at the bandage wrapped around my arm which hides the spot where Thompson cut out my tracking device. Rolling down my sleeve, I try to block out the dull, throbbing pain. The Federation won't be able to find me. Once we all leave the city, we'll be *free*.

The Federation can't control me anymore.

Behind me, Matthew inhales sharply. I glance over my shoulder. Thompson wraps a bandage around Matthew's arm, then nods at me. "You're both ready to go."

"What about you? We'll need to remove your device also." I won't leave my mentor here. Thompson has to come with us to the Outlands. If he stays in the Federation, the Mediators will execute him. I thought I lost him once before. I won't lose him again.

A shrill beep cuts through the air. Thompson reaches into his pocket, withdrawing a handheld device, which he took from one of the Mediators he stunned. All the Mediators carry the small, tablet-like objects. My mentor reads the screen, then mutters something under his breath. "More of them are coming. We need to leave the Regulation Center as soon as we can."

I frown at the cell where Thompson and I locked up the Mediators we knocked out. "So they can't escape?"

"No, they can't," Thompson says. He hands Matthew his identification card. "Go grab your things. Last door at the end of this hallway. There should be some food rations in there, too. The stuff they feed the prisoners. It's the only food I think you'll be able to take."

I crinkly my nose. The Mediators gave me one of the ration bars for dinner last night. They're disgusting. But we'll need something to eat on the trip.

"Yes, sir." Matthew jogs to the end of the corridor, stopping in front of one door.

I watch Matthew, an uneasy feeling sitting in my stomach. We can't be caught again. Not only will Matthew be sent to City 1 so the Council can do who-knows-what to him. Not only will I face execution. Now Thompson faces punishment for my actions as well. I point at Thompson's arm. "We need to remove your tracking device."

"Of course." My mentor rolls up his sleeve and holds out his arm. With his other hand, he gives me the knife, which he cleaned earlier. This may not be what an actual doctor would do, but it's our only option. "You caused quite a panic with the message you sent out."

"So it went through?" With shaking hands, I press the tip of the knife into Thompson's skin. A thin trail of blood slides down Thompson's arm and I resist the urge to vomit. I should have had Matthew do this.

"It took them about five minutes to wipe the message from the tablets. Not much time, I know, but still enough time for people to read it, I think. Not many, but some. It's a start." He doesn't use that tone often. If there's one thing my mentor hides more than anything else, it's when he's proud of me.

I avoid his gaze and focus instead on removing his tracking device. Using the tip of the knife, I drag the tiny chip out of Thompson's arm. I'm the reason behind his two current Violations, and the reason he'll most likely be given a third if we fail to escape. Despite this, Thompson is pleased with what I've done. I swallow. I don't deserve that pride, not after what I've done to him.

"They haven't given me a new tablet yet, so I still receive messages from City 45. I saw what he wrote," Thompson says quietly. I let the tracking device fall to the floor, then wrap a bandage over the bleeding cut. "Before they managed to delete it. Makes a lot more sense than what the Federation tells us, doesn't it?"

"You believe it?" My eyes widen. "You believe in God and His Son who died?"

"Yes." That's all he says, but it's enough to satisfy me. He sounds confident, like he doesn't need to explain why he believes it. After a few seconds, Thompson clears his throat. "I'm guessing other people will believe it too."

What's taking Matthew so long? I turn around, staring at the doorway Matthew disappeared into. What if he passed out again? What if he can't find his things? I take a step forward, but Thompson grabs my arm.

"Katherine, there's something I need to tell you."

"Yes?"

"A few minutes ago, you asked me why I came here to help you. I think you deserve to know the truth, Katherine." Something passes over Thompson's face, a mix of fear, nervousness, and uncertainty. "I've done something the Federation couldn't let go unpunished. I don't regret what I did, even though I was given a Violation for it."

Thompson's second Violation?

"I've kept this hidden from the Federation for years, but Haynes finally pieced things together. I—"

Behind us, the elevator door hisses open. Thompson stares over my shoulder, a look of horror filling his eyes. I start to turn around, to see what he sees, but my mentor shoves me aside. I hit the ground, falling to my hands and knees. Three loud, ear-drum piercing *bangs* cut through the air.

What was that?

I lean back against the wall. My heart pounds so hard my sides ache. A Mediator stands in the hallway, arm extended, weapon in his hand. Thompson pushed me aside. The Mediator fired his weapon. My brain struggles to link those two events together. Only one thing could have happened. One horrible, impossible thing.

A pained gasp escapes Thompson's lips. A look of agony contorts his face. His body stiffens. The Mediator strides forward, weapon pointed at me. I'm next. He's going to kill me now. Thompson's legs buckle, and he hits the ground, hard. A scream rises in my throat, but it comes out as a strangled sob. I should stand and see if he's okay, but my legs refuse to move.

The Mediator lowers his weapon so it's aimed at my head. He shot Thompson. Now he'll shoot me. Thompson's stunner is clipped to his belt. I won't be able to grab it before the Mediator kills me.

I don't have to.

The Mediator stumbles, dropping his weapon, then collapses to the ground. I glance over my shoulder. Matthew stands behind me, a stunner gripped in one hand. He sets his bag on the ground and kneels next to me.

"Are you okay?"

Words won't form. I stare at my mentor, horror creeping over me. Blood oozes from three holes in his chest. Red stains the front of his uniform. What do I do? His chest heaves and his breathing sounds pained and raspy. I sit next to Thompson, wishing there is something I can do to help him.

"Katherine?" Thompson murmurs after a few seconds, like it takes him a while to recognize me.

"Y-you're going to be okay," I stammer, tears stinging my eyes. But he won't be okay. I'm not a doctor, but I do know his condition isn't good.

He pushed me out of the way. Thompson saved my life, again. The first time he risked receiving a Violation. This time...he gave away his life to save mine. Why did he do it? He's done so much to help me, but all I've brought him is trouble.

"I'm sorry, Katherine." Matthew's quiet, solemn tone only reassures I'm losing Thompson. "I don't think there's anything we can do at this point."

"But—"

"Katherine?" Thompson says again, more strained this time. I grab his hand, so he knows I'm there. Tears slip down my cheeks. He can't be dying. Not because of me. "Katherine, there's something I need to tell you."

Matthew gives my hand a squeeze and then releases it. He straightens up, walking toward the unconscious Mediator. I watch Matthew as he bends down next to the man and cuffs his hands behind his back.

"You shouldn't have done this. You didn't have to. I'm so, so sorry." I blurt the words out. His life is slipping away, all because he was trying to help me. The Federation killed him. Peace doesn't matter anymore. The Federation is now going to maintain control by fear and violence. Tolerance doesn't really exist in the Federation either, does it?

And it never did.

Thompson makes no reply. Is he…? No, he's still breathing. But for how long? What did he want to tell me? He's dying, and talking must cause him a lot of pain. Matthew drags the Mediator's body into one of the cells.

"Just stay with me, okay?" I whisper, tears streaming down my cheeks faster than I can swipe them away.

Thompson manages a faint, pained smile. He tightens his grip on my hand, like he wants to make sure I'm there. "The little girl I never got to hold, all grown up now."

What is he saying?

"That's my Violation, Katherine. I didn't know for sure until after I trained you a few months. I suspected. I wondered because you looked just like her, and…" His voice trails off and he coughs. I can't breathe, even though my heart pounds so hard it might explode. Her? By *her*, does he mean my mother?

"I knew I shouldn't have…but I needed to know. I couldn't stop thinking about the possibility that maybe what I thought was true. So I—" Another raspy cough. Blood trickles out one side of his mouth. "I looked through the files your Primary School teachers sent me. You were the correct age. I had to search very hard, but I finally found what I was looking

Reintegration

for. The names of your parents. I was correct. I should have reported it, but I couldn't. I couldn't let you go."

So this is why Thompson tried to protect me? Why he would never allow himself to show when he was proud of me? My head spins. If this is true, then Thompson isn't only my mentor, but something much, much more.

He's my *father*?

No wonder the Council tried to cover up his second Violation. Thompson did the unthinkable. He found me and chose to have a relationship with me. The Council couldn't risk any other parents doing the same. Is this why Haynes told Thompson of my execution? To hurt him?

"You can be free now, Katherine," Thompson whispers, reaching up and brushing his fingers against my cheek. A shudder runs through his body and he lowers his hand. I learned who my father is. Now I'm going to lose him. He was there, all along, but I never saw it.

I want to take him to the Outlands with us, so he can be free too. We can have a family, at least part of one. Thompson was my mentor, my father, my friend. How much has he given up for me? I should be the one bleeding to death on the floor, but I'm not. He is, even though he doesn't deserve to be.

"Thank you for everything. I-I'm proud to be your..." What is the word? "Your *daughter*."

The Federation makes errors sometimes. The Council accidentally assigned Thompson, my own father, to train me. They didn't realize the mistake for years. The Council doesn't do everything perfectly.

The Federation can fall.

Each painful breath Thompson takes stabs me like a knife, straight through my heart. I wrap both of my hands around his, hoping this is nothing but a nightmare. But I can't wake up from this. Ever.

Thompson's hand goes limp in mine.

"No!" I scream, feeling his wrist for a pulse. He's not breathing. His head lolls to one side. He can't be dead. He'll wake up any second. Thompson will open his eyes and come with us to the Outlands. I just need to wait.

But Matthew wraps an arm around my waist and pulls me to my feet. "We need to go now. I'm sorry, Katherine, but we have to go."

I pry at his arm. We can't leave now. I can't leave Thompson behind. I struggle against Matthew's grasp, but he holds me back. More Mediators could arrive at any second, killing us both. Matthew's right. We can't stay here. A sob rises in my throat, and I let Matthew lead me toward the elevator, but I glance one more time over my shoulder.

I look back at my mentor, who taught me everything I know.

I look back at my father, who risked everything to help me be free.

31

Thompson can't be gone.

I tap an icon on the elevator's control panel, then clench my fists at my sides so Matthew won't see my shaking hands. The elevator hums as it climbs to the ground level floor. Everything inside me screams to go back. Maybe he's okay now. Maybe I felt his pulse incorrectly. Maybe…

Thompson is gone, and I can't do anything to bring him back.

Fresh tears slip down my already-wet cheeks. I lay my head on Matthew's shoulder, although what I really want to do is go back to my apartment, crawl into bed, and cry until I have no tears left inside.

"I'm sorry," Matthew says, breaking the suffocating silence. "I'm so sorry I couldn't save him, too."

If Matthew stunned the Mediator even a minute earlier, Thompson might still be alive. My mentor—my father—could be coming with us to the Outlands. But it's not Matthew's fault. It's the Mediator's. And what if it's also my fault, because Thompson died saving me? "It's okay." I haven't spoken since Thompson took his last breath, and those two words sound shaky and uncertain.

Matthew slides something into my hand. I look down and wrap my fingers around what he gave me. A stunner. We aren't free yet. The Regulation Center lobby could be filled with armed Mediators. I tighten my grip around the weapon as the elevator doors *hiss* open.

The closer we get to the lobby, the more certain I become that we're going to do it. No Mediators in the hallway. We're going to do it. Matthew remembers where we need to go. The Federation can't find us without our tracking devices. Once we're out of the Regulation Center, we're free.

I freeze when we round the corner and enter the lobby. One Mediator stands between us and freedom. One young woman with red hair pulled into a high ponytail, standing in front of the main entrance, weapon aimed at us.

Chelsea.

The weapon shakes in her hand, but she keeps it level at my chest. My best friend since childhood, and she's going to shoot me? After everything we've been through, will she be able to *kill* me? I don't think she could, not Chelsea. Not my best friend.

Maybe I'm wrong. I've been wrong about a lot of things.

"Don't do this," I say, but I'm not sure if I said it loud enough for her to hear. My voice is quiet and hoarse.

Matthew pulls me behind him. Chelsea still has the weapon pointed at us, her eyes determined but conflicted at the same time. "I have my orders to take you in." She draws out each word. "Or kill you if you don't comply."

I swallow and shake my head. "I'm your best friend. Even after all this, we're still friends. Please, don't do this. Let us go."

"I've been given orders. You're an enemy to the Federation, Katherine. Both of you. Just give yourself up so I don't have to do this." Chelsea's voice shakes, a sign that maybe there's hope she won't be able to kill us.

"This isn't you, Chelsea. What they want you to do, it isn't *right*."

"Shut up," she snaps.

"They've trained you to kill people. Doesn't that go against everything the Federation seems to stand for?" The image of Thompson bleeding to death pops into my mind. I fight the tears as best I can. "If our world is based on peace, why are they training people to kill and force citizens to submit using violence?"

Chelsea adjust her grip on the weapon's handle. Her eyes bore into mine as she takes one step forward. Matthew tightens his grip on my hand. She's going to do it, isn't she? I duck my head. How will it feel, bleeding to death on the floor, each breath growing more laborious than the last…?

I stiffen as the loud *bang* resonates through the room. Matthew's muscles tense, then he relaxes. Neither of us are harmed. I risk a glance at Chelsea. The weapon is still gripped in her hand, but she's now aimed it high above our heads.

"Go," she says, lowering the weapon—and her gaze. Chelsea won't meet my eyes. Without another word, she turns and exits the building. I pull away from Matthew and run after her.

She can come with us. We can remove her tracking device, and she can come with us to the Outlands. Chelsea is my best friend, no matter what they've trained her to do. What will they do to her if they find out she's failed? By the time I make it outside the building, she's nowhere in sight. I look both directions, but no sign of Chelsea.

Matthew comes to stand next to me. I look around. "Where could she have gone?"

We don't have any time to wait. Another loud *bang* rings through the air and the glass door behind us cracks and shatters. I look over my shoulder to see a Mediator walking through the lobby, weapon raised to take another shot.

Matthew and I run for our lives, hopefully for the last time.

I don't stop running until we're several blocks away and no Mediators are in sight. I duck between two buildings, gasping for air. I haven't had to run like that before. "I know we need to keep going, but I need to rest for a moment," I say. "I'm sorry."

"It's okay. We can take a break." Matthew holds my hand, looking at the bandage wrapped around my arm. Sympathy lines his voice. "They can't find us anymore. We're as good as gone, now."

I brush my fingers against a fresh bruise on his right cheek. I close my eyes and take a deep breath. How close I came to losing Matthew, too. "I love you, Matthew. I don't know what I would have done if you'd been killed, just like..."

Suddenly, I can't hold in my sobs anymore. I don't try to blink back the tears filling my eyes. All the emotion brewing inside me spills out, a wave of grief I can't contain. Next thing I know, Matthew pulls me close. I bury my face in his chest and cry, loud, painful sobs that make my sides hurt. I don't care. It feels so good to cry.

I cry because Thompson's gone and I'll never see him again.

I cry because I've finally learned who my father is, only to have him snatched away from me.

I cry because of the gruesome, painful way he had to die.

Matthew whispers "it's going to be all right" over and over again in my ear, holding me tight. I run through verses I can remember in my mind, drawing some comfort from them. My sobs abate, until I'm left sniffling and hiccupping.

"Please help me," I pray in a nearly-silent whisper. "I don't know what to do."

Still Matthew doesn't let me go. I'm grateful he's here to hold and comfort me. Tears slip down my cheeks, and I close my eyes to try to control them. A shiver runs through me as I think again about how Thompson died.

"I'm sorry, Katherine. I know how important he was to you, and couldn't help but overhear, when he told you he was your dad. I'm so sorry he's gone."

"I don't mean to be so upset." I've never cried like this before.

"It's completely understandable. Don't apologize. It's normal to grieve when you lose someone you care about." Matthew kisses my cheek. "I was so worried for you, 'cause I knew they were going to execute you today. But we're going to do it, Katherine. We're going to escape. *Finally.*"

"Will the pain inside ever go away?" I pull away from him and look into his eyes. My heart hurts as much as the rest of me does. It's like my body also knows something is now missing from my life.

"It'll get better in time. I promise. Doesn't mean you won't ever miss him, but you'll slowly start to heal." Matthew frowns.

"What's the matter?"

"I just…hope I'm not too late," Matthew says, pulling the pill bottle out of his pocket. "It's been two weeks, maybe two-and-a-half since I left."

"I'm sure your sister will be okay." I give his hand a squeeze. Maybe I'm giving him false hope, but Matthew needs me for comfort like I need him.

Matthew manages a smile. "We'd better get going."

We arrive at the other end of the city, near the medical center after a half-hour's walk. A stressful walk, as I constantly looked over my shoulder, expecting a Mediator to appear at any second. Matthew slips into an alley, and I follow him. He pulls a metal grate, built into the concrete, off the ground. A grate is built into each alleyway for water drainage. When it rains, the water dumps into an underground system. Where does the water go after it drains under the city?

Matthew lifts the grate and pushes it aside. He looks down. It's pitch black inside the hole. Before I can say anything, Matthew shoves his bag through the hole and into the darkness below. Seconds later, he too, disappears into the inky blackness.

I linger at the edge. What's down there? I crinkle my nose. Something smells foul. After several seconds, I start to panic. What if we get lost and never make it out?

"C'mon, Katherine," Matthew calls, his voice echoing. "There's a ladder leading down. It's perfectly safe. Some of the

Reintegration

rungs are a little wet, but it's not a very long way down. I'll be right here."

My legs shake as I lower myself down. One of my feet touches the rung, so I set it there and move the other foot to set it on the rung, too. I lower myself further so I can grab the ladder with both hands. The metal is cold, and like Matthew said, wet. "I'm coming down."

"I'll be at the bottom, I promise." Matthew's voice sounds closer now.

I slowly and carefully lower one foot to the next ladder rung, than the other. I don't go too fast. I don't want to fall. What is at the bottom? How far is it from here? My fingers are going numb from how cold the metal ladder is. I reach the ground, my feet hitting the concrete with a light splash. I landed in a small puddle when I fell.

I can barely see, the only light coming from above. Matthew climbs back up the ladder and pulls the grate in place. The air is crisp and bitter down here and I wish I had a jacket.

Matthew climbs down again and picks up his bag. "Not too far," he promises. He grabs my hand and pulls me deeper into the darkness.

"Is it safe? The Outlands?" I whisper. "Wasn't everything decimated by the war?"

Matthew stops walking, and I almost run into him. "There was no war, Katherine. The early government leaders made that up to make sure the citizens stayed within the Federation's walls. They wanted to keep the citizens within the Federation even more than they wanted to keep the Intolerants out of it. It's a world without boundaries, without security systems, without tracking devices...but it's a world that offers freedom."

I follow as he continues walking. Another lie of the Federation's. Matthew was right when he said all those weeks ago I was a prisoner just like he was. The Federation *is* a prison that controls every aspect of our lives. We have to accept the lies because we don't know anything better. We believe the Federation helps us have the perfect society, but it's really just a frantic effort to maintain control. Everyone in the Federation is a pawn, and none of us know just how much we are being used.

Matthew turns around the corner, and I hold back a gasp. Light, up ahead, promising an end to the darkness. For the first time, I'm going to see the world beyond the Federation. I'm going to see the world Matthew grew up in, a world that allows people to believe in what they want to believe.

Pure excitement races through me as we come closer to the end of the tunnel and the light becomes brighter. Matthew climbs out first, hopping to the ground. I linger at the edge, taking it all in. Then I follow after Matthew.

32

Council Member Amelia Haynes steps into the Council meeting chamber, her irritation growing. Even with the new Mediators, two prisoners managed to escape from City 45. Two prisoners: a girl who was supposed to be executed and a boy who would provide a swift end to this conflict.

Both gone from the city's walls, without a trace.

Haynes takes her seat, avoiding the disappointed looks of the other Council Members. She promised them answers that would end the Intolerants' resistance. Then their one chance of finding the Underground *escaped*.

"The report received this morning was not what we expected," Council Member Josiah Whitley, the oldest and most respected member of the Council, says. "We managed to capture not only an Intolerant, but a member of the Underground. The report this morning indicates that this same Intolerant fled into the Outlands and can no longer be traced."

Whitley types a message on his tablet, then pushes the device aside. "I think we can all conclude the root of our problem is the Intolerants. They must end their excursions into our cities. Each time they come, the Violations in the cities increase."

"City 45 has been one of the more...problematic cities," Council Member Kyle Molina says. "The tablet message sent throughout City 45 will make things worse. Now City 5 and City 1 are the only two locations the Intolerants haven't managed to break in to."

"I suggest we have officials scour City 45 to find out how the Intolerant managed to sneak into our city." Council Member Zane Crowley speaks for the first time. "I also suggest we increase security again."

"Increase security? We can increase security all we want, but the truth is, the only way we keep the Federation intact is by finding the root of the problem." Haynes taps one finger on her desk. "And the root of our problem, as Council Member Whitley just said, is the Intolerants."

"Who live in the Outlands, out of our reach, especially now that the one we captured managed to escape." Crowley scowls at Haynes.

"Katherine Holliday and Matthew Braddock escaped not an hour ago. If the entry point is found soon, I'm certain it's not too late to still find the Underground." Haynes needs the Council to see what she's been saying for months. "I propose that we reexamine Project Endgame."

Crowley shakes his head. "We abandoned the idea of Project Endgame months ago."

"Because we didn't have the proper resource then. Now we do, if we take advantage of them. How long will we let the Intolerants make the first move? They pose an imminent threat to the stability of the Federation. *We* have to be the ones to cease the conflict." Haynes pulls up the file outlining Project Endgame on her tablet, reading it over. "Once the Underground is defeated, we can lessen security again."

Victoria Rush, the youngest member of the Council, looks at something on her own tablet. "I don't know. We've all seen the footage. I wasn't the only one who saw how Regulator Phillip Thompson died. Is violence really the answer?"

"Endgame will ensure that what happened on the footage won't occur in the Federation ever again. I suggest that we hold a vote on what to do with this matter." Once the Underground is destroyed, the bloodshed will no longer be necessary. Things can return to how they were.

Whitley nods. "I think given the circumstances, we should. I for one believe Project Endgame should be reexamined."

"I agree," Council Member Molina says. "We've wasted too much time scrambling to fix issues after they occur. It's time we make the first move."

"Are we really ready to begin Project Endgame?" Crowley clearly isn't convinced.

"Yes. With the Mediators and the other recent decisions we made, Project Endgame is all but ready to be initiated." Haynes tries not to be too annoyed. Endgame is a big undertaking. There will be consequences if the plan fails.

"The Mediators are now without a leader, since Trainee Holliday fled into the Outlands. We were waiting to publicly announce the formation of the Mediators until her Final Test was complete. Now our new peacekeepers are without a leader." Crowley shakes his head. "What do you propose we do now? We *need* a Head Mediator before we carry through with Project Endgame."

"We establish the other candidate. We knew there was a chance Katherine Holliday would fail her Final Test, so we needed more than one candidate for Head Mediator." Haynes glares at Crowley. Can he not see that Endgame is the only logical solution?

"Is the other candidate ready?" Rush opens a file on her tablet.

"The second candidate was tested, although not as thoroughly as Trainee Holliday." Whitley, too, looks at a file on his tablet. "However…we need a Head Mediator. I say we prepare the second candidate and begin Project Endgame as soon as possible."

"If the second candidate is ready for this responsibility and we have a Head Mediator, then I see no other reason to delay Project Endgame." Crowley sighs.

"Then the vote is complete. The majority is in favor of beginning Project Endgame." Whitley stands. "This meeting is adjourned until the Head Mediator is put into place. Then we will further discuss how we are to proceed."

Victoria Rush frowns. She never voted did she? Haynes pushes the thought aside. No matter. Her vote wouldn't have made a difference. The Council will put Endgame into action. Haynes smiles. "Now, if you'll excuse me, I will inform the new Head Mediator of the duties that will need to be fulfilled."

The Mediators can enforce the Tolerance Act in ways the Regulators never could.

Project Endgame will be enacted.

The Underground will fall.

33

I've taken the last step in leaving my life in the Federation behind.

My feet hit the ground, which is reddish-brown sand instead of concrete. My shoes sink into the sand a little. I look down and watch the breeze blow the little granules over the tops of my shoes. Little sprigs of brownish colored grass stick out of the ground and fist-sized rocks cover the sandy surface. Some are pretty and little silver specks glisten when the sun hits them just right, while others are dull brown in color. I haven't seen anything like them before. I pick up one of the shiny ones, turning it over in my hand. It's warm to the touch, having soaked up the sun's warmth all day.

Surveying the landscape around me, I take in the details of the way the land rises and falls and the deep reddish-brown hills stand against the rich blue of the sky. The sun shines brightly overhead in a nearly cloudless sky. Deep ruts cut through the ground in the distance, and they'll be bigger once we get closer to them. I've never been able to see so far in my life. Way off in the distance, something sticks up against the sky. Is it another Wall? The top is jagged and varying in height. What is it? It's beautiful.

"They're mountains," Matthew says, as if reading my mind. "We won't be going that far, but we will get closer. They're amazing up close."

They're amazing *now*.

"Why would anyone not want to see this every day?" I shake my head. This is all so much to take in. The Outlands is so different from the Federation, without the streets and buildings and trains. There is something dangerous about the rugged terrain of the Outlands, a journey into the unknown. The Federation may offer safety and perfection, but the Outlands offers so much more.

"'Cause it makes you wonder, doesn't it?" Matthew says quietly. "It makes you wonder how something as beautiful as this could have happened by accident."

I nod. Just like how by looking at the way the human body works gives reason to question what the Federation teaches, the landscape here makes me wonder about how God made something so beautiful. How could anyone look at this and still believe the world came about by random chance?

Matthew and I stand in silence. My brain can't process everything fast enough. Matthew, too, looks like he's in awe, even though he's most likely seen a sight like this hundreds of times. Maybe he still doesn't remember everything and this *is* new for him. Maybe he's savoring what he's feeling, because he's finally going to get back where he belongs.

"We did it, Katherine." Matthew grins, excitement dancing in his eyes. I survey the landscape, which is so very different from the cities of the Federation. He's right. We did it, together. Matthew and I made it out of this alive. A girlish, giddy laugh escapes me, because we're free now.

He'll get to his family again, his parents and his sisters. Matthew has a home waiting for him out here somewhere, with people who love him and a place he can belong. Will I be able to call that place home, too? The Intolerants may not accept me. Maybe I'll always be just a girl from the Federation. God will help me adjust. I have to remember that.

"Thank You," I whisper, the breeze whipping my hair around my face. We only made it out because God helped us do it.

I've changed from when I was given my Final Test two weeks ago. I've changed, in more ways than one. The old Katherine was a perfect citizen, always following the Federation's rules and never daring to question the orders she was given. She was surviving, not really living. Now I know I *should* have questioned. The world I thought was perfect is far from it. The Federation is a suffocating, dark place, but somehow we all trudge through it and call it life.

I don't think I'm the same girl anymore.

Matthew and I have endured so much, but now we're *here*. We've made it to the place where the Federation can't control us. They won't even be able to find us, because we're out of their reach. I can make a new life for myself here and leave the emptiness of my last one behind me. I can have a new life with Matthew, where I can do and say and believe what I want. The Federation can't keep lies from me anymore. I know the truth. I know there is right and wrong and there is a power higher than the Council. I hope the people who read Matthew's message will know that, too.

Some people have already seen it. There are some in the Federation who have been able to see through the lies and hypocrisy. They're rebelling.

Things are going to change in the Federation. The Council can't maintain control if the current system is kept alive. That's all this has become—a fight for power. Maybe long ago, the people of the Federation really believed in a lie called tolerance. Now they are starting to see just what kind of system they've created and everything the Federation keeps hidden. I hope another change will come about soon, one that enables the citizens to find the truth of God in this mess of lies.

What about Chelsea? I should have told her what I've learned. What will they do to her if they learn she let us escape? How lenient are the Mediators with someone who fails? If only she could have come with us.

She's not the only one I wish could have joined us.

Tears well up in my eyes as I think of Thompson again. How long will it take me to recover from losing him? I will heal. I murmur a quick prayer to God, asking Him to help me with my grief. Thompson saved my life more than once. I'm thankful God was able to use him to help Matthew and I find freedom—even though it meant Thompson's death.

Thompson's more than my mentor—a fact that is strange and wonderful at the same time. I found my father. He is one of many who lost his life defying the Federation. Countless others have been executed, although maybe not in the brutal way he was. I'll always be thankful for everything he did to help me. I won't let him be forgotten as just someone else who committed three Violations. He did so much more.

Reintegration

My mother is out there somewhere, too, a woman whose name I don't know. Does she live in City 45? Have I met her before, but never realized who she was? Does she ever think about me, the daughter she didn't get to raise? Does she ever wish things were different so she could have known me?

Someday, I'll return to the Federation and try to find her.

"We're going home," Matthew says, his words filled with awe, like the reality of this hasn't fully sunk in with him yet.

He kisses me, once, then twice, both quick and brief. Matthew pulls me close and holds me tight. Neither of us says anything, because neither of us needs to. We're free, at last. I want to stand here forever, with the breeze blowing through my hair and the sun warm on my back, Matthew right by my side.

I look over his shoulder, at the Wall that cuts through the landscape. The Wall that served as a barrier between me and *this*. I once thought it was there to keep me safe. Now that I'm beyond the Federation's borders, I don't ever want to go back to being trapped behind them.

I was safe there, yes, with the security cameras and the Regulators and the Tolerance Act.

I was a prisoner, every move I made monitored and pre-chosen for me.

I was dead inside, not knowing what it feels like to have hope and understand that Someone bigger than all of this is watching out for me.

I turn away from what once was and kiss Matthew's cheek, unable to put my gratitude into words. Two weeks ago, I was less than thrilled that my Final Test was making sure Matthew believed every lie the Federation fed him. But what would my life be like without him? He's shown me so much, so many things the Federation doesn't tell us about. I pull away from him and take in every detail of the Outlands. I interlace my fingers with his and cling to his hand. We still have a long way to go, but no matter what happens, God will be with us. A shiver runs through me, not the cold kind, but a shiver of excitement.

I've never been so uncertain of what lies ahead.

I've never been so free before—free from the Federation's control and free from my own wrongdoings.

I've never been so *alive*.

COMING SOON….

UNDERGROUND
BOOK 2 OF THE REINTEGRATION TRILOGY

ACKNOWLEDGEMENTS

Writing and preparing this book to publish has been a several-year journey. A worth-while journey, for certain, but not one I took alone. So many people made the book you're holding in your hands possible, and they will forever have my gratitude.

My Creator and Redeemer, Jesus Christ, deserves all the thanks I can offer for His unfailing love toward me. Writing would have no purpose without Him.

My super-duper awesome mom and dad. You guys rock! Thank you for reading countless drafts (even the awful ones), giving feedback, letting me babble incessantly about the writing process, driving me to conferences, and believing in me and my writing even when I didn't. Sometimes I wanted to give up, but you always pushed me to make my dream happen. You are the best cheerleaders I could ever have.

Authors Kim and Kayla Woodhouse, Darcie Gudger, Tim Shoemaker, Chris Richards, Shantelle Hannu, Allison Tebo, C.J. Darlington, C.B. Cook. Whether you took the time to help me with editing, signed my books, or answered lengthy emails with publishing questions, I'm grateful.

Dave Fessenden—thanks for taking a chance on a seventeen-year-old with nothing but a manuscript and a dream. And for patiently answering my endless questions (even the really, really obvious ones).

Gabrielle, my "long-distance bestie"—I'm so grateful we met at that writer's conference. You've been a fantastic friend and sister-in-Christ. Thank you for the encouragement, prayers, and of course, all of the book recommendations.

Thank you to my writer friend Melinda, for letting me bounce ideas off of you and giving feedback on my opening chapters. I always look forward to your e-mails!

Magpie Designs—thank you for that phenomenal cover. Wow. You captured the feel of *Reintegration* so well, and I can't wait to see what the next cover looks like.

There isn't enough room to mention you all by name, but I want to thank all of the friends and family who waited very patiently to read this. You cheered me on through this whole process.

I also want to give a big shout-out to my cover reveal and blog tour teams, who were so supportive when they learned I would be publishing my first novel. Your excitement was contagious and made me even more eager to share my writing with you. You made sure the world knew my book was coming, and I'm so grateful to you all.

And, last but certainly not least, thank you to the reader. I had a lot of fun writing *Reintegration,* and I hope you enjoyed reading it.

God bless,
Ashley Bogner

ABOUT THE AUTHOR

When she was in third grade, Ashley Bogner decided she would be a published author. In high school, she became serious about seeking publication of her work. She attended writer's conferences and learned everything she could about growing as a writer. *Reintegration* is her second completed novel (well, third if the forty-page talking cat story she wrote in fifth grade counts) and also her first published work. Ashley is a homeschool graduate and has lived in seven different states. When not writing, she can be found baking, posting book reviews on her blog, and watching her favorite movies over and over to the point of memorization.

You can connect with her on her blog:
www.ashleybogner.com

Made in the USA
Middletown, DE
26 December 2017